I0574571

Resilient

Kari Lee Harmon

OLIVER HEBER BOOKS

Published by Oliver-Heber Books

0 9 8 7 6 5 4 3 2 1

This book is dedicated to one of my dear friends, Liz Lipperman, who helped me with the original version of this book. She's an original BC Babe and makes me laugh every time I'm around her. Thank you for brainstorming whenever I needed it and for being a fresh pair of eyes in a pinch. You are one of the most talented authors and classiest ladies I know, and I love having you in my life.

Thank you to my best friends, Danielle LaBue and Barbara Witek, who are also BC Original Babes and the best critique partners ever. There is nothing more special than having you both to lean on. I can vent, laugh, cry and everything in between and know you won't judge me or laugh at me or criticize me. You'll simply be there for me, to listen and hug and offer advice and pick up the pieces, no matter what. I love that we talk every day and get together often. You're my soul sisters, and you'll be in my life until the day that I die. I have to go first, because I can't live without either one of you.

A very special thank you to my editor, Alaina Crosby. Once again you have an amazing eye. Thank you so much for helping me bring this story up to date and make it so much better. I can't wait to write the rest of the stories in the series. You're a rock star!

Chapter One

re·sil·ient

ADJECTIVE

    (of a person or animal) able to withstand or recover quickly from difficult conditions.

"I must be having a mental breakdown. Why else would I have swiped right?" I said into my cell phone with shaking hands as I headed down the hall away from the dining room.

I had been married for a long time to my high school sweetheart. Our love life had been sweet and innocent at the beginning, and then more like a routine scheduled appointment at the end. I had no clue what I was doing, and had certainly never done anything quite so adventurous before. Now that the moment of truth had arrived, I wasn't at all sure I could go through with tonight.

"Zoe, you don't have to go through with this," one of my best friends, Tiffany, said from the other end of the phone line. "It's not too late. You can just leave. Men do it all the time."

"No, no. I need this." I took a deep breath. "We all know the mayor will never choose me as the party planner for the Labor Day bash over my rival Bitsy if I don't loosen up. It's time." I'd worked my way into such a frenzy I'd barely tasted the succulent lobster dripping melted butter all over my plate at the quaint little seafood restaurant on the shores of Cape Cod.

My hand rested on the doorknob to my room at Hilda's Bed and Breakfast, and a slight frown tipped down the corners of my mouth. Max. The last time I'd visited the Cape was when Max had surprised me on our fifteenth wedding anniversary. I ordered lobster then, too, and vividly remembered the tender meat falling apart in my mouth, seasonings oozing over my tongue, and Max's finger reaching out to swipe a drop of butter from my lip.

My frown turned to an outright scowl. Now that I knew what a deadbeat husband and father Max had turned out to be, the lobster sat in my stomach like a lump of angry crustacean trying to claw its way out. I couldn't blame it, really. It was a shame to eat lobster and not enjoy it.

"Well, if you insist on going through with this, you know we're here for you, doll. You'll be fine. You always are." Tiffany's encouraging voice brought me out of my lunchtime lamentation and back to my nighttime nightmare.

Twisting the doorknob, I pushed it open and felt my stomach cramp as the lobster pitched and rolled down Nervous Highway, heading north towards Esophagus Drive. I pressed my lips together, hoping I wouldn't throw up, but when it decided to take a sharp detour south onto Large Intestine Avenue, my eyes sprang wide.

"Fine, my foot. Hang on a sec." I tossed my phone on the bed and bolted into the bathroom just in time.

After twenty years of marriage, the thought of sharing my bed with another man terrified me, but I needed to move on. I needed to know I *could* move on. That I was still a desirable woman. Except, now I was petrified even a gallon of Pepto-Bismol wouldn't be enough to get me through this evening.

Groaning, I stepped out of the bathroom, when I realized I hadn't locked the door to my room earlier. Good Lord, now I'd become a complete scatterbrain, which was quite unlike me. Then again, so was going on a date with a man I'd never met. I liked what I saw in his profile, and that I would never have to see him again.

I was only looking for one night.

A whiff of the sea floated by, and I took a breath. I loved the sea: the salty crispness, the untamed beauty, the wild unpredictable nature. One minute calm and tranquil, while the next, stormy and raging. I could relate, though today was not a day to lose control. If I could just breathe, maybe I would survive tonight.

I dropped my purse on the lighthouse comforter draped over the king-sized bed and sighed as I picked up my cell phone. I'd almost forgotten Tiffany was still on the other end of the line. "Can't say I'm better than ever, but I'm back, anyway."

"Are you okay?" Her voice rang with concern. I loved my best friends. It was nice to know they were always there for me, no matter what.

"Oh, I'm fine. Just having trouble digesting the enormous lunch I stuffed myself with this afternoon."

"Now why would you go and eat a big lunch when you knew you were going out to dinner?"

"For that very reason. There's no way I'll be able to eat in front of a man I don't even know."

"You're so funny, but hey, whatever works for you, doll."

"Room service would work wonders for me instead of a public restaurant with the way my stomach's acting up. I hate the whole dating scene. It's so awkward. I just want one night to relieve my stress. It's been way too long. I want to win this party-planning job over Bitsy, whatever it takes."

"There are other ways to relieve your stress than a man, you know. It might even become your new best friend."

"Good lord, I wouldn't have a clue where to begin. I got married so young, I never needed *other ways*, and I have you girls as best friends. I don't need any more." I laughed as I fanned my face, feeling warm all of a sudden. "Goodness, it's hotter than heck in here."

"You need to relax."

"I did. Thank you for the massage you scheduled for me. It was wonderful." Maybe housekeeping had turned up the heat. I walked over to check the thermostat. Sixty-eight. I should be freezing. I felt my forehead. "I think I have a fever. Maybe I shouldn't go to dinner. I don't want to make the poor guy sick."

"You don't have a fever. You're just having a panic attack. Like I said, it's not too late to back out," she added with an understanding tone to her voice.

My stomach pitched again. Not a good sign. I started to pace to take my mind off it. "No, I've come too far. It's been two years. I need to break my celibacy streak, and I can't do that with anyone I know. Our town is too small. The gossip mongers would have a field day. They already gossip over my divorce. I don't need any more rumors started."

"You've got a point. Mount Saint Zoe is long overdue for an eruption after lying dormant for the past two years. Max doesn't deserve to take anything more away from you. And who knows. Maybe you'll like this guy."

"Don't even go there. I just need to control—"

"See, now, that's your problem," she said gently. "Since Max left, you've become a control freak."

"I have not become a control freak," I said, then thought, *Have I?*

"Please don't take this the wrong way. I'm just pointing out how the girls and I feel. You never do anything spontaneous anymore. If you don't know the outcome, then you won't take a chance of something going wrong."

"That's not completely accurate. I don't know how tonight is going to turn out, but I'm here, aren't I?"

"Very true. You shocked us all with your spontaneous night out of town with a man you've never met. That's why we're worried about you. What if this guy is a creep?"

"That's why I chose Hilda's Hideaway. A public place where help will come running if I scream."

"You're not going to back out of this, are you?"

"No."

"Just, please be careful, okay?"

"I will, I promise." I rubbed my chest, which had begun to ache. "You know, I haven't had a panic attack in over a year, and now I can't breathe." I wedged my phone in the crook of my neck and yanked open the window. Inhaling the frigid air, I listened to the sounds of the waves lapping against the shore, the peace and tranquility of the ocean soothing my nerves as I strove to stay calm.

"Breathe slow and deep to the count of ten and go into the yoga pose I showed you last week. That should help."

"Already in it." I lied.

Tiffany's body might be able to go into pretzel mode, but mine hadn't gone there since the halftime show during our high school homecoming game. I chose the saner route: focusing on the soft snowflakes falling to the ground and sparkling through the moon's reflection off the water.

I thought of the shaken snow globe my children bought me for Christmas last year and smiled, feeling my breathing return to a resemblance of normal. Then I remembered this was my birthday, not Christmas, and I was about to receive a gift I wasn't at all sure I was ready for. I shut the window with a resounding clunk.

"Better?" Tiffany asked.

"Always, with you girls by my side. I seriously don't know how I could have gotten through my divorce without you all. And I definitely couldn't make it through tonight without you talking me off the ledge."

"You know we're here for you, doll. Same as you are for us."

Tiffany, Harmony, Morticia and I had met back in high school when we all made the cheerleading squad, and we'd been cheering each other on ever since. For years, all I'd had to worry about was taking care of my kids and my husband, making sure everyone was happy, even if it meant I had to put my needs last. It had been worth every second. Then, after Max up and decided he didn't want to be married anymore, my whole world spun out of control. It had taken me two years to get my life back on track, but I still didn't feel like I could breathe again.

I might not be able to breathe easy yet, but I was on the upswing, darn it.

I had opened my own business and finally felt like I had something to contribute. I had learned to cope with raising four kids alone, which quite frankly, warranted a medal. Heck, I had even started remodeling my ancient colonial house, though Max used to kid I wouldn't be able to tell the difference between a pencil and a pair of pliers, even if they jumped up and pinched me on the fanny. Well, they *did* pinch me, and I *could* tell the difference. Okay, so they pinched me with the help of my younger son's devilish hand, but I still knew the difference between the tools. Better yet, how to use them. I nodded to myself, feeling accomplished. Shows how much Max really knew about me: not a heck of a lot.

But life was good again, now. Well, sort of, anyway.

Tiffany rambled on through the phone, giving me more

encouraging words, but I didn't hear half of what she said because of my nerves. Kicking off my boots, I glanced around the room. Well, I had to give Hilda's staff credit. They must have finished unpacking for me to the state of perfection while I was at lunch. I liked perfection. The neat, orderly room calmed me more than anything Tiffany could say. I sucked in a few more deep breaths for good measure and slid my trousers down over my hips.

"Zoe, you'll be fine. It sounds like this Chaz guy will be a perfect choice. And he's a doctor. What more could you ask for?"

Just hearing the name Chaz made my stomach turn over. Was I really going to go through with this? I swallowed hard. My old friend Panic Attack had paid me a visit earlier, and judging by my pulse, didn't intend to leave anytime soon. At least the Pepto had kicked in, and my stomach cramps had stopped, thank God. But with my luck, they'd return in full force later, roaring down the highway as they attempted to exit off Large Intestine Avenue and blast their way straight through Panty Parking Lot.

Darn Metamucil.

I filled my lungs one more time and answered her question. "What more could I ask for? To have met him, for one." As I stepped out of the beige cotton material surrounding my ankles, I unbuttoned my mauve sweater. "God, this makes me look so desperate."

"You're not desperate, doll, you're forty and fabulous. You just need to be reminded of that. Max was an ass, but not all men are. If this is what you need, then the girls and I stand behind you. You've got this, Zoe. It's time you got back in the game." Her voice became peppy. "You can do it. It'll be fun."

Good Lord, was this what we'd sounded like back in high school?

"Fun for you, maybe, but I haven't been on a date in over twenty years. I don't even know how to act. What if he doesn't like me?" I curled my toes into the plush carpet, trying like heck to hold onto... *what?* I didn't know. Most likely my sanity.

"Just be yourself, Zoe. What's not to love?"

The knit material of my shirt slipped off my shoulders. I switched the phone to my other ear and shimmied my arms out, then tossed the item on the bed. "I have a feeling this is going to be the longest dinner of my life. Maybe I'll get lucky, and he'll leave early."

"Him leaving early is your idea of getting lucky?" Tiffany laughed. "Do yourself a favor and don't wear those god-awful granny panties and ultra-support bra you live in." The tone of her voice softened. "I know they're comfy, Zoe, but first impressions are everything, you know."

"Granny?" I huffed. "My panties are not granny, but I'm not you. I can't exactly pull off crotchless undies and transparent bras."

"Sure, you can. All it takes is confidence."

Of which I had none at the moment. I ran a hand through my tangled curls, kneading the back of my neck. "I repeat, this really is a bad idea, isn't it?"

"Try to stay calm. You don't have to do anything, remember? Just go to dinner." A squeal rang through the line on the other end. "No, no, Katy. The TV control does not go in the toilet. Your younger daughter's really... something."

"Hey, I tried to warn you kids aren't easy, but you're the one who insisted on volunteering to baby-sit. I am eternally grateful, by the way. Mrs. Bee is across the street if you need her. Just try to keep Katy in one piece, okay?"

"Only if you try to have fun." The line went dead.

Fun? I hung up and glanced down. *Oh. My. God.* My panties really were granny. I wanted to cry. Darn Tiffany. She would never be caught dead in underwear like mine; then again, she hadn't given birth to four children. She also wasn't nearly as well-endowed as I was. Even if I wanted to look sexy, I wouldn't subject anyone to my Double Darlings unleashed. I should have just stayed in the kitchen. Lighting a fire in my stove I could do. Lighting a fire in a man was a whole different beast.

The knots in my stomach twisted tighter.

Good Lord, I had never slept with any man other than my ex-husband. I didn't imagine stretch marks, cellulite, and saggy breasts were a turn-on for most men. I trembled at the mere thought of exposing them. Maybe the girls were right. Maybe I should stop worrying so much. Change the narrative.

It was my birthday, after all. I could do as much or as little as I wanted.

A morning of sightseeing followed by an afternoon at the spa had been just what I'd needed, even if I had been too distracted to remember most of it. And the thought of dinner without any kids in tow was too tempting to pass up. So long as my date didn't require me to cut his food or wipe his mouth, I didn't care who he was.

Orgasms were overrated.

My inner self called bullshit as terror robbed me of the ability to think straight. I would never make it through dinner at this rate. Maybe she had a point about the underwear, though. My date would never see them, but maybe if I dressed the part, I would have the confidence to get through this evening.

I opened the antique dresser drawer... and stopped... and stared. Okay, more like gaped, but who could blame me? I hadn't seen any of *those* in quite a while. What on earth were they doing in my room? In *my* underwear drawer? My hands shook as I pulled out a pair of royal blue cotton boxers and a white undershirt.

I glanced around the room, my gaze darting everywhere, my

eyelids blinking like a seventies strobe light stuck on high. Then the doorknob rattled, and I sucked in a sharp breath, swallowing my gum. I had to run. I had to hide. But where?

Too late.

The door flew open, and I stood there like a nearly-naked imbecile with hideous taste in underwear. A tall man with sandy blond hair, who looked as though he had stepped straight out of the pages of *GQ* magazine, stood in the entrance of my room. Tan loafers, pressed khakis, sky-blue polo shirt, and perfectly groomed hair. A regular Ken doll come to life.

I looked beyond him for Barbie. A man like him had to be taken, but I didn't see anyone. More important, what in the world was he doing in *my* room? I noticed the slightly different seascape on the wall, and black luggage on the rack, instead of navy blue.

Oh God. This wasn't my room at all.

As my body finally got my brain's message to duck and run for cover, I let out a squeal. Only, there wasn't any cover big enough to hide my goods, and my clothes were on the bed way over by him. I ran around in a circle like a silly dog chasing its tail and did the only thing I could think of: wiggled my granny fanny into his boxers and yanked on his undershirt. Thank God he didn't wear bun-hugging briefs, because at this moment, I don't think I could survive anything of his hugging my buns.

Maybe he hadn't noticed, I thought as I bit my lip, feeling the blood flood my face. I crossed one bare foot over the other and pressed my thighs together. Judging by his sky-high brows and bugged-out stare, I'd say he got quite an eyeful. I mentioned I'm rather endowed but let me repeat.

Double Darlings.

"Housekeeping?" I squeaked, perspiring right through his undershirt, leaving lovely little rings-around-the-pits.

The handsome male specimen cleared his throat and said in

a whiskey-smooth voice I don't think I'll ever forget, "Sorry. Name's Chaz."

Even under the ungodly circumstances, a surprising little zing shot straight to my libido. Until his words registered. If this was the same guy, his online picture did *not* look anything like him. He'd had a beard in that picture. Maybe it wasn't him. I squinted, then my jaw fell open, and I gasped. "Ch-Chaz? As in, swipe right Chaz?" He nodded, and I closed my eyes, my heart bottoming out.

So much for first impressions.

Chaz cleared his throat, and I jumped, whipping my eyes back open. "I'm so sorry," I said. "Your— your— your room looks just like mine. And— and— the door was unlocked, so I— I— I just—"

"It's okay." He spoke in a hypnotic tone and smiled with sympathy. "I stepped out for a minute and didn't lock it. It's my fault."

Heat oozed through my body, sending goosebumps prickling over my skin and my temperature soaring. At that moment, I would have done anything he asked with that voice. His warm hazel eyes held a glimmer of understanding, and crinkled up at the corners as he took in my attire.

My attire!

I snapped out of my trance and crossed my arms over my chest. His t-shirt would be stretched out and ruined beyond repair, unless he didn't care if everyone thought he had manboobs. "Don't worry; I'll take off your clothes in a sec."

He arched a sleek brow, and the corner of his lip tipped up.

"I mean, I'll take off *my* clothes," I stammered.

The smile spread across the rest of his clean-shaven face.

"Oh, God, that's not what I meant at all," I muttered.

"Keep them if you want. I have more than one pair."

"Oh, no, that's not necessary. The shirt's a bit tight, and

boxers aren't my thing. Not that I want you to think the humongous granny panties I'm wearing beneath your boxers is my thing, either. It's just I'm into comfy these days, and I have *no* idea why I'm explaining my preference in underwear to you. I'll go change in my room and return them in a jiffy."

Shut. Up. Zoe.

I bolted to the bed, snatched up my pants and blouse, then turned toward the door. The blocked door. A foot before him, I stopped in my tracks and looked way up. He had to be at least six feet tall, because he towered well over my five-foot-two-inch frame. "Um, excuse me?"

He stared down at me for what seemed like a full minute, the intoxicating green and brown of his eyes swirling together, hypnotizing me, until he said, "You don't recognize me, do you?"

My present predicament snapped me back to reality. Here I was wearing his underwear over mine. Did he actually expect me to engage him in conversation? If he did, then I didn't stand a chance in today's dating world. "Am I supposed to recognize you? I mean, you don't have a beard now. I like the no-beard look."

"My name's Anderson. Chaz Anderson. Ring any bells?"

I tilted my head to the side and studied him closer. Anything to get this conversation over with, so I could go back to my room to change. "Sorry."

"We went to the same high school."

I wrinkled my brow. "Um, no."

"I was a few years behind you."

I pursed my lips. "Still no."

"Everyone called me Chuckie."

I shook my head. "I really am sorry."

"You were a cheerleader, and I was—"

"Oh, my God, the Dorkmeister!" I clapped a hand over my

mouth. My ears burned, and my whole body shook with the need to crawl under something and hide.

He paused. "The *what*-meister?"

"I mean the water boy." Good Lord. "Uh, you were the football team's water boy because you were younger. Four *years* younger, if I remember right." Simon and Garfunkel's Mrs. Robinson ran through my head. Turning forty had never bothered me until this very moment. I needed to go back to my room and die of embarrassment. "Wow... little Chuckie Anderson. I never thought I'd see you again and certainly never like this."

"Apparently." He rubbed his jaw. "The Dorkmeister?"

A bead of sweat trickled between my breasts. "I'm so sorry. We were silly kids, and it was a stupid nickname, but we never told anyone. Besides, look at you now, all grown up." I patted him on the arm. "Why, you're not little or dorky at all. In fact, I — I'd call you hunky," I said, my palm tingling from touching his firm bicep. Why couldn't I just shut up?

He chuckled. "Thanks, I think."

A draft of cool air passed over my bare legs, and a nervous giggle slipped out. I stepped around him. "I, um, I have an awful headache, Chuckie. I think I'll go to my room and lie down."

"Call me Chaz. I haven't been Chuckie in years."

Judging by the lean, athletic frame he now sported, he hadn't been chubby in years, either. I had a hard time taking him in all at once, which immediately made me think of sex. Definitely the wrong way to think of him. "Well, good night, Chaz. I'm sorry to have wasted your time, but I'm sure there are plenty of women your age who would love to have dinner with you."

He looked serious. "But not you."

I backed my boxer-covered, granny fanny out the door and down the hall, clutching my clothes in front of my smothered darlings. "I'm not exactly your age, and under the circumstances, I'm horribly embarrassed. I don't think I could stomach dinner." I couldn't stomach lunch, either, but who was keeping tabs?

"You can't be serious, Zoe. We're in our thirties."

"No, you're in your thirties. I'm officially forty." And freaked out. And *so* not feeling fabulous at the moment.

"Age shouldn't be a factor. Just so you know, it wasn't a random swipe for me." He studied me with kind eyes. "I—"

"Oh, God, you heard about my divorce, didn't you?" I felt the heat climb up my neck and burn my ears. "Great, a pity date." My back bumped into the door to my own room, and relief washed through me. Until Hilda's housekeeper pushed a cart down the hall and shot me a weird look.

"Zoe," Chaz said. "That's not what I—"

"I really need to lie down," I cut him off with a desperate need to disappear. "My head's pounding." I hadn't lied. My head did ache something fierce from my humiliation, and my stomach still ached from... well, let's just say nerves.

He studied me for another full, intoxicating minute with those swirly eyes of his. "Well, it was great seeing you, Zoe. Maybe we'll run into each other again sometime. In fact, I—"

"Maybe." I cut him off as I fumbled for the knob behind me, then slipped into my room and shut the door. I sank to the floor in a heap, as a different answer pounded in time with my headache.

God, I hope not.

Chapter Two

S unday night, safely ensconced in the warmth of my ancient colonial, I prepared for our weekly girls' night. I had tucked my two little ones into bed, and my two older ones were hanging out in their rooms, leaving me to my thoughts, for once. I poured two of the girls a frozen, passion fruit, tropical drink and popped the top to a Diet Cola for the third, then placed their glasses around the antique harvest table in my dining room. I couldn't wait until they showed up.

They weren't going to believe the tea I had to spill.

After Max abandoned us, I was lost and alone for the first time in my life. My family had moved away from our small Massachusetts town, but I refused to put my kids through any more trauma by uprooting them. My mother still called weekly, trying to get me to change my mind. Mayflower was the only home any of us had ever known, but back then, I had been desperate to connect with someone.

I went to my twentieth high school reunion and ran into my best friends. Since we were all in need of a little support, we reconnected and picked up right where we left off over twenty years ago. Only, instead of cheering on a football team, we started cheering for each other every Sunday. For the past two years, we had been celebrating the things that went right and mending the things that went wrong in each other's lives.

As hostess of this week's girls' night, I chose "The Tropics" for my theme. Tropical fruit, succulent roasted pig with my own unique blend of seasonings, and an assortment of pasta, potato and macaroni salads. One of the privileges as hostess was you got to start the conversation, and boy, oh boy did I have something to talk about.

A knock sounded on the door— they knew better than to ring the bell. If they woke my youngest daughter, the evening would be over. They would have to take care of her for the rest of the evening, spending hours trying to cajole her back to bed while I took a bath.

I walked over and opened the door.

They all filed inside and hung up their coats on the wooden coat tree, then took their seats, staring at me in silence, waiting. I took my time serving them before I sat at the head of the table, relishing the anticipation of the tea.

"The Dorkmeister," I finally said, my gaze meeting each of their eyes.

"Wait, I'm confused." Harmony Jones shook her head, her short red spiky hair not moving an inch. Always outrageous and just this side of crossing the line, she owned a New Age shop and was into all kinds of strange things like voodoo. Harm kept life interesting for us. Her exotic pale-green cat eyes stared at me, perplexed.

"I thought you were going to tell us about your date." Morticia Smith adjusted the black knot of hair secured to the back of her head. On the one occasion we caught her with it down, we had been in awe over the waist-length waterfall of the most beautiful strands of black silk we had ever seen. But Morticia, uncomfortable being the center of attention, had never worn it down since. Working in her father's funeral home— her father had a twisted sense of humor in naming his only child— Morti kept life real for us, when her face wasn't buried in a book of fiction.

"I *am* telling you about my date," I said, taking note of the spices bursting over my tongue and blending perfectly with the fruity drink. I would have to remember to add this recipe to my catering menu, but right now I had more pressing matters to attend to.

"Dorkmeister? Who's that?" Tiffany asked, sipping her drink. "I thought the guy you swiped on was a doctor?" She tucked her golden-blond hair behind her ear and raised periwinkle-blue eyes to look innocently at me. Tiff kept life fun for us.

"I have never been so embarrassed in my life," I wailed, usually the boring one of the bunch.

"Why? From the picture you showed us, this dude is gorgeous," Harmony said. "I don't see the problem."

"Yeah, even I'd do Dr. Mc-Screamy," Morticia added.

"Well, I don't want to do *any* men, especially now." I groaned.

"What on earth happened?" Tiffany asked, puckering her brow and looking a little concerned.

In fact, they all were.

"Absolutely nothing happened, and I'm keeping it that way. Being celibate isn't all that bad. If I wasn't sure before, I'm positive now. Sex just leads to complications which I don't need. You girls know what it would do for my business to plan the annual Labor Day Bash, but Mayor Edwards will never choose me if I start making mistakes. Trust me, mistakes are worse than being wound a little too tight. I can't afford any distractions right now." I buried my face in my hands to cool the heat flooding my cheeks. "God, if you were only there, you'd get it. It's just so hard to talk about, even with you all."

"What? Did you have lipstick on your teeth or something?" Tiffany squeezed my shoulder. "Did he at least see you in the slinky black dress I picked out? You're a knockout in that."

"Lipstick would have been the least of my worries, and he saw me, all right, but I wasn't wearing that outfit." I looked up at her. "In fact, I wasn't wearing any clothes, just undergarments."

"Yeah, baby, now you're talking." Harmony wagged her brows, heading to the kitchen.

"Oh, I'm not done. I wasn't wearing cute underwear. I was wearing my old standbys."

"What's wrong with standbys? The older, the better, as far as I'm concerned," Morticia said.

"I agree. Old comfortable underwear is a must for me." I fanned my heated face. "Only, comfort is not sexy."

"I still say comfort would be my first priority." Morticia shrugged.

Harmony walked back into the dining room, handed Morticia a second Diet Cola, and refilled our glasses with another cocktail. "Maybe if you'd stop hiding behind those frumpy comfy clothes of yours, more guys would ask you out." She arched her auburn brow teasingly at Morticia.

"Look who's talking, Ms. Hide-Behind-My-Tattoos-And-Piercings-So-Guys-Will-Be-Intimidated." Morticia spiked her black eyebrow right back at Harmony, but the corners of her lips tipping up gave her away.

"Ladies, you're both beautiful, you just don't know how to showcase yourselves," Tiffany explained. "I'm telling you, if you'd let me help—"

Harmony grunted. "Uh, hello. Easy for you to say, Ms. I'm-Too-Beautiful-For-Words-And-All-The-Guys-Love-Me."

"I hear that." Morticia high-fived Harmony. "I'd have more luck if I gave men a sex massage every day, too."

"It's called sensual massage, and I teach it," Tiffany replied with a smirk. "I don't actually *do* it, because I don't believe in mixing business with pleasure."

"Yeah, well, we'd both have more luck if we were born from her gene pool, that's for sure." Harmony winked at Morticia.

Tiffany rolled her eyes. "I'd much rather have parents who gave a damn, than be blessed with their looks."

I watched them all, loving the fact that we were so open and could talk about anything with each other with no judgement, but still... "Ladies." I slapped my palm on the table until they looked at me. "Remember me?" They sat down and gave me their undivided attention. "I know we all have stuff to get caught up on, but I'm not done yet. It *is* my night, after all, and the hostess gets the mostess time, barring emergencies, of course. That's the rule."

"You're so right, doll, but you can't blame us for this. I specifically told you not to wear your Granny panties," Tiffany pointed out, her blue eyes twinkling.

"I was in the process of changing said panties, but my clothes weren't anywhere to be found."

"I can't wait to hear this." Wearing a Mona Lisa smile, Morticia leaned forward and focused eyes on me so dark I couldn't tell where the iris ended and the pupil began.

Unable to think of a less embarrassing way of explaining the situation, I blurted, "I'd stripped down to my god-awful ugly underwear. You know, the ones your mother tells you never to wear out in public in case you get into an accident. Only, I wasn't in an accident. I was in the wrong room. *His* room."

"Hey, I'm all for skipping a meal and heading straight to dessert." Harmony snickered. "Good for you."

I blinked. "*Not* good for me. Dessert was the last thing on my mind. I was so humiliated; I wiggled my fanny into his underwear and t-shirt. Can you imagine what I looked like wearing his underwear over mine?"

"Awe, I bet you looked cute. And I highly doubt he minded one bit. I have such a visual, though. I wish I could have seen that one go down." Harmony laughed louder.

I cringed. "It wasn't cute, that's all I can say."

"What did you do?" Even Morticia let loose a faint giggle.

"I cancelled the date and hightailed it back to my room to bury my head under the covers." I shoveled a hand through my curls. "That wasn't even the worst part."

"Wait, there's more?" Morticia gaped at me.

"Yes. I repeat, the Dorkmeister."

"I'm still not following you." Harmony sipped her drink.

"Why does that name sound familiar?" Tiffany puckered her brow.

"Do you remember the water boy on the football team who was four years younger than us back in high school?"

Harmony snapped her fingers. "Yeah, he was a little dorky but kinda cute."

"I remember him now," Tiffany said. "He was sweet and endearing. We secretly nicknamed him our little Dorkmeister."

"Chuckie Anderson," Morticia added. "I remember him getting all flustered around Zoe. That and being obsessed with video games and wanting to make them when he grew up."

"Well, turnabout sure is fair play because I was the one who was more than flustered this time," I said. "Because my Dr. Chaz is little Chuckie Anderson the Dorkmeister all grown up."

A pair of green eyes blinked, a pair of blue eyes widened, and a pair of black eyes gaped.

"I know. I was shocked, too. His dating app picture didn't look anything like him. He had a beard. I mean, what are the odds I would swipe right on little Chuckie." I laughed a bit hysterically. "Time to refill my anxiety meds, cuz good ole Panic is here to stay. All I can say is thank God he lives in Boston. I'll never have to see Dr. Chaz ever again."

My MAILMAN, old man Truman Winters, was nearly blind and a bit forgetful these days. Even with his coke-bottle glasses, he still managed to mix up my mail with my perverted neighbor, Lester Bates's, mail on a daily basis. Lester was as weird as they came, but he left us alone, which was all I cared about.

Still, I didn't want anything of his in my box.

Like the time Lester's girlie magazine had wound up in my mailbox, and my home and garden magazine had landed in his. I was sure when he sat down to stretch his mind and actually read something, an article on Martha Stewart wasn't exactly what he'd had in mind. Picture books were more his speed... actual words, not so much.

Truman was the nicest man in town and had been a mailman forever, so no one had the heart to tell him it was long past time he retired. I stepped outside to meet him at the mailbox the next morning, just to make sure there were no more little "mix ups." All I needed was for my boys to get a hold of anything else of Lester's.

Talk about an education.

"Mornin', Mrs. Robinson." Truman tipped his hat as he ambled down Pleasant Street in his gray postal uniform, his canvas satchel slung across his knobby shoulders, looking as though it weighed more than he did.

I'd kept my ex-husband's name so mine would be the same as my children, but I went by Ms. not Mrs. Only no one in town ever picked up on that no matter how many times I corrected them. I'd stopped wasting my breath.

"It's gonna snow," he said. "I can feel it in my bones."

A gust of wind swirled around us, the bare branches above our heads crackling eerily as they punctuated Truman's words. He just grinned. Handing me my mail, he winked on a nod. I discreetly thumbed through the bills that were getting harder to pay, while keeping a watchful eye on what he put in Lester's box.

"So, did you have a nice birthday weekend away?" he asked.

My gaze snapped up to his. Was nothing private in this town? I couldn't help wondering just how much everyone had heard. "I had a nice time, thank you." I fidgeted with the mail.

"Caused quite an uproar in the knitting circle with someone your age on a dating app, and all."

"I'm forty, not dead. Besides, it wasn't like that, really. It was just a date. They don't have to worry. He lives in Boston, and I don't plan on bringing a bunch of men home. I have children, after all." Reputation was everything in this town, and I couldn't afford to lose mine.

"I say it's none of them womenfolk's business. It's high time you found yourself someone special. Like my Lizzy, God rest her soul. She's watching, you know. They always are." He looked to the heavens and smiled such a loving smile, my heart melted all over again. He sure knew how to keep this entire town adoring him, the old charmer.

"I like to think so," I said, and I meant it. "But I don't hold out much hope in finding that bond for myself. I'm just fine on my own, thank you very much."

"Well, I'm sure those gals will find themselves something else to talk about soon enough. Mayflower hasn't seen this much action in quite some time." He chuckled. "Well, I best be going. Gotta finish my route before that snow sets in." He glanced at the darkening clouds and shivered. "It's gonna be a doozy." Then he continued on down the street.

Truman had two speeds: slow and stop. I'd put money on him getting wet before sundown.

"A piece of cherry pie sure would go good with my evening

coffee to warm me up. Maybe I'll stop by the market if I have the energy," he called over his shoulder.

"Don't trouble yourself. It just so happens I made one too many for the church bake sale this week. I'll drop it off later in our usual spot on your porch," I fibbed back in our weekly let-me-know-what-flavor-pie-you-want-and-I'll-bake-you-one ritual. He mentioned a different flavor each week, and I fabricated a different excuse for having made an extra one of that exact kind. What could I say, it worked for us.

"If you insist," he said with a smile in his voice.

"No sense letting it go to waste." I watched him wave as he rounded the corner, then I opened Lester's mailbox and swapped one of his bills for mine with a slight smile and a shake of my head. I hugged my mail to my chest as I jogged back up my sidewalk to go make dinner, only I couldn't stop thinking about what Truman had said.

AN HOUR LATER, I hollered, "Lexi, come set the table, please." I'd made beef stew for my kids and my neighbor, Mrs. Bee, who sometimes babysat for me.

Mrs. Bee liked to eat. She said it showed in all the wrong places. Smooth where she should have lumps and lumps where she should be smooth. I said she was beautiful inside and out. She was just as sweet and a godsend I couldn't live without.

Whatcha got cookin'? was the unspoken question behind her smile. It took a bit of bribery to get anyone to watch my gang these days, but I didn't mind. After all, cooking was my specialty.

Most people were headed to parent teacher conference at the high school tonight, but no, not me. I had a "special" conference scheduled with the principal because of my eldest child's behavior as of late.

"Just a sec, I'm on the phone," said the eldest child in question. Lexi ran a hand through her caramel curls and continued to talk.

"No, not just a sec. Call Mia back and set the table like I asked. Dinner's almost ready. Remember, you're grounded. No cell phone or computer. Are we clear?"

She rolled her amber eyes, made a sarcastic remark to Mia, then hung up and proceeded to set the table in a huff. My shoulders drooped. She looked exactly like me, but we were polar opposites. Her father had been the one she was close to, but since he quit his job, cashed in his pension, and went backpacking across the U.S. to "find himself", things had turned even worse.

He didn't even say good-bye, just left us a note. All he'd found was he didn't want us anymore, and I'd received the divorce papers from Mexico in the mail. None of my kids took that well, but I wasn't about to let them become out of control. Lexi had just obtained her driver's permit and was bugging me to let her take her road test. Until her attitude changed, that wasn't going to happen.

"You okay, Mom? You look tired." Concern creased Troy's forehead as he came strolling in.

I cupped his cheek and smiled. "I'm fine, sweetheart. Go wash up and call Bobby and Katy, please. Don't forget Molly is coming over to study for science tonight."

Troy was all straight blond hair and blue eyes, just like his father. But he constantly tried to keep the peace and take care of everyone, just like me. I wished he would stop trying to be the man of the house and be the thirteen-year-old he was.

"I won't." He looked nervous, and my heart went out to him. Poor kid was having such a hard time in school. His five-week report hadn't been good. Molly lived down the street. She was a year older than he was and had agreed to be his tutor, but nothing seemed to help. I was at my wits' end about what more I could do for him.

At times like these, anger consumed me. I wanted to scream until I was hoarse, bury my head under the covers and never come out. I wanted a Calgon-take-me-away moment on most days, but I'd never follow through literally. What Max did wasn't fair to any of us. I was angry as hell that he left me alone to deal with all of this.

I carried the beef stew to the table, and the smells of spices and gravy wafted through the air. After I tossed the salad and sliced the French bread, I dished up stew for everyone right as two bundles of energy stormed down the stairs, zoomed around the kitchen island, and skidded across the hardwood floor into the dining room.

"Oh, boy, beef stew. I bet that will make me throw the ball real far, Mommy." Bobby shoveled a spoonful of stew in his mouth before he even sat and almost knocked over his chair, his blond hair sticking out in every direction. Bobby had no trouble acting like a six-year-old; then again, he'd only been four when his father left. He didn't remember much, which was sad, yet somehow a blessing.

"Slow down, honey, you've got plenty of time before basketball practice." I smoothed his flyaway strands. He needed a haircut in a big way. "Remember, Mrs. Turner is giving you a ride tonight, so don't keep her waiting. Behave yourself, okay?"

He nodded so hard, his spoon rattled against his teeth, but that didn't stop him from continuing to stuff his face.

"Mommy, I don't like stew. I don't wanna eat." Katy crossed her arms in front of her. She shook her head and stuck out her bottom lip, her brown curls bouncing off her tiny shoulders. My little drama queen was four going on fourteen on a good day, but so darn cute you wanted to eat her up. Poor baby didn't remember her father at all. And that was the only good thing to come out of this mess.

"But if you don't eat, how will you grow big and strong?" I knelt in front of her.

"I'm already big and strong." She stood a little taller. "And I'm *not hungry*." She nodded, punctuating the last two words.

"Hmmm. Are you *not hungry*," I poked her in the belly twice, "because you ate some cake when you weren't supposed to?"

Her amber eyes popped wide, looking like big round frisbees, and her voice came out on a breathy whoosh. "How did you know?"

"Mommies know everything." I winked. "And you have chocolate all over your face, my naughty little princess." I scooped her up and carried her to the kitchen sink to wipe her off when the doorbell rang. "Lexi, will you clean up your sister so I can get the door?"

Lexi grunted but did as I asked. Like she had a choice after what she had done.

Mrs. Bee waddled in with a huge smile on her face, her eyes crinkling to slits until you could barely see them, and her white apron tied high over her belly, looking more like an enormous bib draped over a ruined Jell-o mold. "Whoo-wee. Something smells good, child."

"Thank you so much for helping me out, Mrs. Bee."

"Oh, posh, anytime." She waved her hand through the air, already rocking her way to the dining room.

"The instructions are on the counter in the kitchen, and the cobbler's in the fridge," I hollered over my shoulder as I grabbed my purse and headed for the door.

"Peach?" I heard from behind me.

"Only the best for you, Mrs. Bee."

"Attagirl."

I laughed and said goodbye to the kids, letting them know I would be back soon. I let myself out, then climbed into my mini-van. As I drove to the school, I glanced at the clock on the dash. Not a good idea to be late when you have an appointment with any principal, let alone the high and mighty Brimstone. He was the man in charge, and he liked everyone else to know it.

I parked in the only spot I saw and made a mad dash through the doors of Mayflower High School, my heels sounding like popcorn popping as I power-walked with mini-steps down the hallway. Teachers and parents shot curious glances my way, but I simply smiled and nodded as I continued to pop. I rounded a corner that led straight to Principal Brimstone's office and nearly ran into Bitsy, which was odd because she didn't even have kids.

I didn't have time to worry about what my nemesis was up to. I picked up speed, moving beyond popping corn straight into a fireworks finale worthy of my younger son Bobby's approval, and that was saying something. He used to be the toughest critic in town as he accompanied his dad and the other fire firefighters in overseeing the fourth of July celebration, only now the poor baby refused to watch them at all. Yet another thing I was trying to work through alone. Sometimes the walls felt as though they would cave in on me at any moment.

I'd hated going to the principal's office as a kid, and even more so as a parent. Especially a single parent. Not that I went a lot as a kid or anything. In fact, never, until I'd started dating Max my senior year. Teachers didn't exactly go for passing notes in class, whispering and holding hands in the hall or, God forbid, kissing. Back then, that was the extent of what kids did on school property. Let's just say, times sure were different these days.

"I'm sorry. This won't happen again. I can promise you

that," I said as I entered the office. I'd learned early on, where Brimstone was concerned, it was better to apologize and make promises right off the bat. I sat across the massive metal desk in the sterile room, feeling small under his disapproving glare. Panting for breath, I clutched my purse under my arm as I fiddled with my keys. This was ridiculous. I was a grown woman, not a child, but we were discussing *my* child.

How could Lexi have been so stupid?

Brimstone stared at me in an odd fashion and said, "Technically, nothing happened, but only because we got to them in time, I'm sure. We found them in one of the storage rooms after school. They weren't having sex, just making out, but still. Your daughter's shirt was unbuttoned, her bra, of all things, exposed. I have to say, her actions were highly inappropriate on school grounds." Principal Brimstone finger-combed the long strands of his thin black hair over the top of his bald spot and frowned hard, using his master intimidation techniques. He loved to make people squirm. God, I'd give anything to turn the tables on the judgmental swine just once.

"Highly inappropriate," he droned on. "Cutting class and now this. I know sixteen is a tough age, and with all that she's been through, I'm being lenient. But she has to learn to rein in her hormones if she's going to stay out of trouble." He shook his head, and the carefully positioned strands slipped out of place.

I felt sick, his Aqua Velva not helping matters any. I swear it smelled like Raid. Trust me; it was potent enough to kill something. I shook off the distraction of his bad taste in cologne and focused on why I was here. I couldn't believe we were talking about Lexi.

She had changed so much these past two years, never smiling and becoming angry at the world. The girls had tried to talk to her, but no one could break through her wall, not even the therapist. I sighed, feeling drained. "I'm not letting her stay after school anymore, and she's grounded for two weeks. What more do you want me to do?"

"Talk to her." He raised a bushy brow as though the answer was that simple. He might preside over hundreds of kids, but he didn't have any children of his own. In my book, that meant he didn't have a clue.

"I'll try," I said to pacify him, but I knew it wouldn't work. Every time I brought up the subject, Lexi shut down on me. That didn't mean I would stop trying, I was just being realistic. That way it wouldn't hit me so hard if I failed again. I strove for a smile. "Have you given any more thought to what theme you want for this year's prom?"

His gaze dropped to his clutter free desk sporting nothing but a pen, blotter, calendar, and lamp, as neat and orderly as he was. "About that," he cleared his throat, "I've decided it would be best if I went with someone else, Mrs. Robinson."

"Oh." My smile slipped. "I thought we had an under-standing."

"So did I." His dull gray eyes met mine. "But now all I understand is if you can't handle your own daughter, how can you possibly handle planning something as big as the prom? Maybe you should stick to catering and forget party planning." A phony sympathetic smile spread across his pasty white face.

And maybe you should grow some balls, you lily-livered coward, I thought. He didn't want any backlash from the parents if Lexi got into any more trouble, and the troublemak-er's mom was the chosen party planner. So that's why Bitsy was at the school when she didn't have children. He'd obvi-ously hired her since she was the only other party planner in town.

"Thank you for your time, Principal Brimstone." I left on shaky legs and struggled to inhale enough air all the way to my minivan.

My minivan with a late inspection ticket from Officer Pickles.

What in the world had happened to my life? I'd had everything under control, but now I was losing jobs, getting tickets, my children were having trouble, my house was falling apart, and my mother wouldn't stop hounding me.

The pressures were building. There was a rumbling under my barely-held-together facade, and if I didn't do something about it, Mount Saint Zoe was about to explode, and not in a good way. In hindsight, maybe I should have said yes to the Dorkmeister.

Chapter Three

At the end of the week, I sat on the dreaded metal table in my family physician's exam room for my annual checkup. I pressed my knees together and secured my tissue paper blanket over my legs as I stared at the sock-covered metal stirrups with dread. Whatever guy— let's face it, it *had* to be a guy— came up with the idea of using tissue gowns instead of cotton should be shot.

I had never liked hospitals or seeing doctors, even though I knew it was a necessary evil. Since I didn't plan to have any more children, I combined as many visits as I could. Hence, no more dreaded gynecologist.

Dr. Joy made me feel comfortable. She could give me a complete physical, including a Pap smear and breast exam. So here I sat, waiting for the inevitable, as I attempted to clutch the blue paper gown over my chest. Now, that was a joke. The sucker opened in the front. Dr. Joy was a bit of a germaphobe. She preferred paper gowns you could throw away rather than the cotton gowns you washed. And since she owned the practice, she made the decisions.

I inhaled, and then quickly exhaled the smell of disinfectant. It reminded me too much of a certain someone whom I refused to name in hopes his memory would fade so I could focus on my work. So far, no such luck.

Sarah, my favorite young, perky blond nurse, walked in smelling like daisies and smiled, her polka-dot-covered pink uniform top as cute as her. She loved to chitchat. Fresh out of nursing school, she had already charmed most of the patients in the office. I had known Sarah since she was a child, but I was enjoying getting to know her as an adult.

"Hey, Zoe. How ya doin'?"

"I'm fine, and you?" I responded, feeling almost cheery today. Not "rah rah sis boom bah" cheery, but a definite improvement from last week. Lexi hadn't gotten into any more trouble, and Troy hadn't failed his science test. In my book, that was progress. Things were looking up once again.

Sarah breezed around the room, opening cabinets and pulling out supplies as she prepped the area for Dr. Joy. She even typed in the computer as she talked. Oh, yeah, she'd grown up. Women were pros at multitasking.

"Well, I'm fantastic," she said, then bit her bottom lip and leaned in as though divulging a big secret. "I met the hottest guy, and he's single." She backed away and giggled. "Can you believe it?"

"So, ask him out." I shifted and almost flashed poor Sarah before I adjusted my paper gown. "You're young and pretty. Any man would be crazy not to jump at the chance to go out with you."

"You really think I should?" She glanced at me, her face a mask of insecurity and doubt as she walked by. "I mean, what if he says no?"

"Then he says no. You have nothing to lose."

She stopped mid-stride and smiled, revealing an adorable

dimple in her right cheek. "You're right. I'm going to go for it." She resumed skirting around the room. "Thanks, Zoe."

"You're welcome." A sudden longing to be that young and full of hope again blindsided me. Where had that come from? I didn't want to be twenty-something again. I had loved turning thirty. That was when I finally felt like I knew who I was, and I earned every wrinkle and gray hair I had, darn it. I hadn't planned to be abandoned, but it had caused me to think about what I really wanted and make something of my own. I liked my life just the way it was.

I frowned, deepening said wrinkles, as I realized exactly where that longing had come from. I was no longer thirty, and so far, turning forty had brought me nothing but trouble. Sandy blond hair flashed in my mind, but I suppressed the image and forced a smile. "You can pay me back by filling me in on all the details after the big event."

"Oh, that's a given."

A knock came on the door, so she excused herself. Not two minutes later, she poked her head back in the room, with a frown marring her face. "I hate to tell you this, but Dr. Joy had to leave for a family emergency. Her appointments are backed up. If you want to reschedule, it will take about a month to get in, or would you rather see someone else today?"

I had been coming here for four years now, right after I'd given birth to Katy. I'd seen all the doctors in the practice several times anyway, and I didn't want to have to don another paper gown until next year, so I said, "I'll stay."

"Great. Someone will be in to see you as soon as they're free." She disappeared, closing the door behind her.

I blew out a puff of air that fluttered my bangs as I browsed the magazines on a nearby table, and then chose one on entertainment. Crossing my ankles and swinging my heels between the stirrups, I held up my magazine and began to read.

Or tried to. The print blurred before my eyes, making it impossible to see what the hottest celebs were up to these days. Great, now I needed to get glasses. I held the magazine closer and struggled to make out the words.

At least optometrists didn't make you wear paper gowns.

Speaking of eyes— no matter how hard I tried, I couldn't get a certain pair of hazel ones out of my head. Brown and green and gray with flecks of gold all swirled together, creating a mesmerizing effect nearly impossible to look away from. And that voice laced with smooth undertones that made liquid heat ooze through my loins had awakened urges I didn't even know existed.

Me with urges... in *my* loins, no less.

I didn't dare tell the girls and prayed the urges would go away. I had lost out on another job this week, and I couldn't afford to lose out on any more. Gas and electricity had gone up to an insane amount, and since when had kids' sports become so darn expensive? When I went to school, we didn't have to do all these extra indoor and outdoor year-round camps and travel teams to get noticed. We played for fun, but today, everything revolved around competition.

Kind of like my job, I admitted.

I tried to focus on the words and stop thinking about things I couldn't control when someone knocked on the door again. "Come in," I called as I set the magazine down and rubbed my blurry eyes, adding, "Thanks for squeezing me in."

"My pleasure."

I stopped breathing, and my hands stilled. "Come again?" I managed to croak out, afraid to lower my hands and look.

"I said my pleasure, Ms. Robinson."

That was *not* a female voice.

In fact, it was... oh, dear God in heaven, a whiskey-smooth voice who had no problem calling me Ms. not Mrs. I yanked my hands away from my face and stared past my tightly pressed knees and those hideous stirrups. My mouth fell open, but I couldn't breathe. Dr. Hunkorama was here? In Mayflower? In my doctor's office? He wore the oddest look as he tried not to stare at my slightly exposed....

I clutched my gown together and gasped for air, then wheezed, "Y-You're not a woman."

He glanced down at his long, lean frame. "Not the last time I checked." A grin tugged at the corner of his firm lips. He wore a white lab coat with a stethoscope draped around his neck, a long cotton swab thingy in his left hand, and a pair of scary looking tongs in his right. That could only mean one thing.

Dr. Hunkorama was Mayflower's new family physician.

"Ready to get started?" he asked.

"Oh, I, uh, um... no!" I jerked into motion, jumping off the table. As I yanked my stupid paper gown together even tighter, I heard it rip clear down one side.

"Zoe, it's okay. I'm a doctor."

"Not *my* doctor," I muttered as I darted around the room, searching for someplace to hide. My traitorous Double Darlings had sprung to attention at the first sound of his voice, so I slapped the stupid paper blanket over them. Two layers of paper were no match for my awakened darlings who, at the moment, insisted on saluting the cause of their stirring.

"Just calm down, and we'll sort this all out." He took a step closer, his eyes fixed firmly on my face.

"Stay where you are," I blurted. "Please." Running to the chair where I had folded my clothes, I repeated, "Sooo not my doctor." I scooped up the garments.

"Okay, I won't come closer." He stepped back by the door. "But you have to relax, or you're going to have an anxiety attack."

"Going to? Already there, Doc." I fought to catch my breath

and ducked behind the curtains hanging from the window. Not trusting he couldn't see through the ultra-thin drapes— they *had* to have been made by the same idiot who'd created the paper gowns— I yanked my pants and shirt on over what I wore. Forget the underwear. Those suckers had caused me enough trouble. Besides, I was kind of in a hurry to escape.

"Zoe, this is ridiculous. Just talk to me."

I poked my head out. "Nothing to say." Then I emerged fully and stuck my keys in my mouth so I could grab my coat and undergarments. As I charged past him, I could hear the tails of my gown that stuck out of the end of my shirt, flapping in the breeze behind me. "Gotta wun. Ewwands. Wots and wots of ewwands." My bra strap snagged the doorknob and yanked me back into Chaz's arms.

Chaz's firm, oh-so-delicious arms.

"Whoa, hey, easy there." The heat of his fingers burned through the layers of my shirt and gown, clear to my shoulders, as the muscles of his chest pressed tight against my back. I felt his heartbeat pick up pace, and his musky smell engulf my senses. "Here, let me." He reached out a hand, still holding me close against him, and unhooked my bra strap from the doorknob.

Too bad I wasn't wearing it. I blinked. Oh, boy. Escape, remember? I jerked away and said, "Uh, Wank you, Waz. Wee ya."

Sarah gaped as I flew past the reception desk and waiting room full of slack-jawed patients, my humongous bra dangling from my fingertips. Someone had made millions by creating cute bras for large-breasted women and hiring full-figured glorious models to display them, but cute bras in my size usually sold out quickly. Not to mention when your ex-husband abandons you, all you can afford are these hideous torture devices.

I dropped my keys by accident as I said, "Reschedule my

appointment with Dr. Joy only, Robin. I don't care if I have to wait a whopping year. Dr. Joy only."

"Will do," Robin replied, eyebrows all but gone beneath her nest of teased brassy red hair.

I bent to pick up the keys and heard my pants rip clear down the crack of my... well, my non-underwear clad fanny. That was it. Time to join the gym first thing in the morning.

A male voice cleared his throat. I straightened, keys in hand, and started powerwalking with my butt cheeks clenched tight. Hopefully, the rip wouldn't gape open, because my hands were too full to worry about covering up my jiggling bottom.

"Ms. Robinson, wait. You forgot...." said a familiar voice from somewhere behind me.

To heck with this. I picked up the pace, wiggling all the way, but I didn't care. Whatever Chaz had to say couldn't possibly be as important as me escaping another humiliating situation. Who was I kidding? The draft blowing over my dimpled bum spoke volumes.

Wait until the girls heard the new town doc was none other than Dr. Chaz.

THAT AFTERNOON, fully clothed with an extra layer to boot, I headed into town and parked my van at the beginning of Light-house Lane. After a long cold winter, rays of sunshine warmed the day, giving the citizens of Mayflower spring fever. People milled about everywhere. The lunch crowd had picked up, but I'd lost my appetite after this morning's doctor's appointment. Right now, I was on a mission, and it had nothing to do with food.

Walking two doors down, I barged into *Peace, Love and Harmony*, ready to let the owner know that "Chaz, the Boston

Doc" was in Mayflower. But the owner was nowhere to be found. A giant of a man sporting a red flat top and a faded *Where's the beef?* t-shirt— one of Harmony's seven older brothers— stood behind the counter. He looked out of place and decidedly uncomfortable surrounded by all sorts of new age items, incense candles burning, and bizarre music filtering through the sound system.

I nodded and smiled at Gerty and Gabby Rogers, the town's resident busybodies and notorious hypochondriacs, who waved and smiled back. I was surprised to see them any place other than the doctor's office. They usually didn't emerge from hibernation until the temperature hit seventy. They leaned their gray heads and pressed their equally gray cardigan sweaters together, pretending to be deep in conversation over which soothing aromatherapy kit to buy.

They were no more into aromatherapy than I was. More like they were tuned into my every word, just waiting for a tidbit of gossip like hungry dogs waiting for a treat. If they had tails, they would be wagging for sure. In fact, if I could see their faces, I was pretty sure their tongues would be hanging out.

Given how fast the rumor mill spread in our lovely little "small town," they must have heard about my doctor's appointment this morning during their daily I-think-I'm-going-to-die-because-I-have-everything-under-the-sun visit. Now, they were obviously hoping to get the scoop as to why I fled. Sorry, busybodies, but I wasn't about to let that cat out of the bag for them to chase all around town.

"Hi, Denny, is Harm around?" Harmony's mother conceived one child per year until she finally delivered her girl, naming each boy alphabetically so she wouldn't forget who came next. Denny was number four, a truck driver who helped Harmony out between runs, and big as a grizzly. All of Harmony's brothers were intimidating, to say the least, but this particular one was nothing more than a big ole teddy bear.

"Nope," he answered.

A teddy bear who didn't talk much. "Do you know where she went?"

"Nope."

Ugh. "Do you know when she'll be back?"

"Nope."

Double ugh! "When you see her, will you tell her I need to talk to her?"

"Yup."

I bit back my frustration and shot him a smile. "Thanks, Denny." He didn't deserve my frustration, Dr. Hunkorama did. Where were the girls when I needed them? I sent a group text, but no one was answering.

I headed six doors beyond that to the middle of Lighthouse Lane, right across from the park with the gazebo in the center. A jazz band played a lively beat, giving a midday concert. I liked Jazz. Normally, I might stop and listen.

Not today.

Narrowing my eyes, I marched through the doors of *Tiffany's Titillating Touch* and headed straight to the reception desk to wait my turn. Glancing around the plush waiting room decorated in different shades of relaxing blues, with sounds of the ocean filtering through the sound system and a waterfall trickling against the far wall, I had to stifle a laugh. All of her clients were men. That did not surprise me one bit. But the waiting room seemed unusually full today.

"I'm sorry. Something important came up and Ms. Eisenhower had to step out. I can squeeze you in with Lucy if you'd like, Mr. McGinnis," Trixy, the receptionist, said.

My gaze snapped to the man beside me.

"Thanks..." the curly-haired, big strapping blond Irishman

glanced at her name tag, "...Trixy. I'll come back another time when Ms. Eisenhower is in. No need to give her a message." He flashed me a deep-dimpled smile, and I nearly gasped out loud over the bluest pair of eyes I'd ever seen.

So, this was Matt McGinnis, the new pub owner in town and Tiffany's latest conquest. I almost felt sorry for him. He wasn't my type. I tended to go for the clean-cut all-American guy like— I paused, not ready to go there— but this guy was definitely right up Tiffany's alley. What Tiffany wanted; Tiffany usually got.

It wouldn't last, her relationships never did, but that was by her choice. She had given up on finding a decent guy after divorcing her loser of a husband and getting stuck paying palimony for the past five years. Although, this guy looked like he could handle himself just fine.

Matt left, and I turned to Trixy. "Something important came up? Ugh, I wanted to fill her in on my doctor's appointment." Whoops, I hadn't meant to say that out loud.

Trixy's face flamed bright red, her bleached-blond pigtails looking unusually pale next to her skin. "Something happened at your doctor's appointment? I hadn't heard."

"Right." I bit the inside of my cheek. Shoot, my kids were better actors than that.

Her gaze dropped to her monitor, and she scrolled through the screens. "Ms. Eisenhower didn't say who called or what came up. She just said she had to step out for a minute and to reschedule her appointments."

"Well, thanks anyway." If Trixy had heard about this morning's freak show, then Tiff and Harm had to have heard. So why didn't they answer my text messages? Maybe they were out looking for me. "Did she say how long she would be gone?"

"Nope, sorry." Trixy checked the appointment screen once

more. "There's nothing updated here. Would you like to leave her a message?"

"That won't be necessary. I'll find them."

Heading outside, I stormed down eight more buildings to the end of Lighthouse Lane but wasn't surprised when *Smith's Funeral Home* was closed. Morticia's father was absent, and since it was just the two of them, she pretty much ran the place when he was gone. Come to think of it, he'd been gone a lot lately. How convenient. Morticia could do whatever she wanted, and apparently, that included teaming up with the girls. The sign read, "Sorry for the inconvenience, but an important meeting came up." Ha! Bet I knew the topic of *that* discussion. But why not include me?

"Ugh. This is not the time to be left out of a group chat." I checked my cell, but no new messages from any of them.

A flock of gulls flew out of a tree, soaring high above the funeral home out over Freedom Lake. Must be nice to let your worries fly away. Some of the birds landed on the water, startling the resident swans who flapped their wings in anger. Boy, could I relate. I needed them, and they were nowhere to be found.

Having no choice, I gave up on giving my girls the scoop. I headed to the party store and browsed the supply aisles for baptismal items. I wanted to be prepared with ideas when I stopped by the Morgans' house. They had chosen me to plan their son Jimmy's baptismal party, and I wanted to make sure we were on the same page as far as ideas went.

The bell over the door chimed, and— speak of the devil— the Morgans walked in. They chattered on excitedly as they headed to the same aisle I stood in, but they ceased speaking as soon as they saw me.

"Oh, good, just the people I wanted to see. This will save me a trip to your house this afternoon." I smiled wide.

They did *not* smile back.

"Um, well, about that. We need to talk." Mr. Morgan shot a serious look at Mrs. Morgan, who pressed her lips together in a stern line and nodded for him to continue.

Obviously, they were on the same page, but I had a strange feeling I was in a completely different chapter. "Fire away, I'm all ears," I said.

"We've decided to go with someone else for Jimmy's party." Mr. Morgan swallowed hard, and Mrs. Morgan patted his arm.

I inhaled sharply. "Why? Was it something I said?" I couldn't for the life of me fathom what had brought this on. Had they heard about the trouble Lexi had gotten into at school? Lord only knew, given how old-fashioned this town was.

For two years, I'd been trying to get them to see me as something other than the wife the fire chief abandoned, with no luck. They loved to gossip and lived for drama, but they hated change. Resisted it on all levels. In their eyes, Bitsy Beaumont was the party planner, while I would forever be poor Mrs. Robinson. I wasn't even sure half of them knew my first name.

"No, ma'am, it was something you did." Mrs. Morgan pursed her lips tighter.

Guess the rumor mill had spread faster than usual today, and the stories always ended up embellished beyond belief. "I can assure you, nothing happened with Dr. Anderson this morning. I only ran out of his office half-dressed because something urgent came up." Their eyes sprang wide, and I suddenly realized I wasn't on a different page, or even in a different chapter. I was in a whole other book.

"Half-dressed?" Mr. Morgan looked at Mrs. Morgan as though this confirmed their decision to go with another party planner had been the right choice.

"We chose not to use you because we found out you have

nude paintings in your house," Mrs. Morgan explained as though I were a bit slow.

Admittedly, I didn't have a clue what they were talking about. My jaw fell open as I tried to comprehend. I didn't own a single nude thing, except nylons, maybe.

"Nude paintings and baptisms just don't go together," Mr. Morgan added in an even slower voice to be sure I understood.

All of the sudden it hit me. I snapped my fingers and laughed. They took a rather large step back.

"No, no. You don't understand," I quickly added. "I know what happened. I'm remodeling my house, and I bought nude paint the other day. I wanted to paint my living room the same neutral shade as my panty hose; so technically, my living room is nude, not my paintings. Or my legs, at the moment." I slapped my pant leg on a laugh, albeit, sounding a bit hysterical to my own ears. I couldn't help it. I needed this job. "So you see, everything's fine, right?"

"Wrong. Nude 'anything' and baptism just don't mix. And, quite frankly, neither do half-dressed women running out of doctor's offices. Good day, Mrs. Robinson." Mrs. Morgan took Mr. Morgan's arm, and they left the store at once.

Go figure. Now I was out of yet another job. I really needed my girls.

I was about to try their cell phones again when my phone rang, so I glanced at the caller ID. Why on earth would *she* be calling me? We were competitors, after all. I flipped it open and said, "Bitsy, how nice of you to call." Yeah, right. She was up to something. Perfectly put together Bitsy Beaumont with nary a hair out of place never did anything "nice." On the surface, she oozed sugar, but beneath her poised exterior bubbled pure venom. Whatever she had to tell me couldn't possibly be worse than anything that had happened today.

"Zoe, darling, you poor thing. You must be a wreck."

Like she cared. "I'm fine, Bitsy. An emergency came up, so I had to cut my doctor's appointment short. It had nothing to do with Dr. Anderson."

"My, my, I never said it did. Though it must have been some emergency for you to flee with that silly little gown waving to all of Mayflower as you scurried out the door."

"Yes, well, you can rest easy now. Everything's fine. I really have to—"

"Oh, but darling, your little 'episode' in the doctor's office isn't why I called so concerned, though it is rather alarming in and of itself." Bitsy loved to play this game. Dance around the issue, pretending to actually care, then deliver a blow when you least expected it.

"Ah, well, the Morgans deciding to go with someone else to plan Jimmy's baptism had to do with a difference of opinion, that's all," I countered, playing my role. Turn a blind eye, be the bigger person, and don't take the bait. But I couldn't help thinking that had to be a record for the rumor mill, considering the Morgans had just walked out the door. I glanced outside and could still see them window-shopping further down Lighthouse Lane.

A pause hovered over the phone line. "You lost the Morgan job?" Bitsy sounded thrilled as her voice went up an octave.

Well, fiddlesticks. One of these days I would learn to keep my big mouth closed.

She deepened her tone and spoke softly. "Oh, my, oh, dear. I'm so sorry. What a day you've had. First the doctor's office, then the Morgan job, and now this. You should take the rest of the day off and relax. Take a hot bath, read a book, and forget all your worries."

Right. I stifled a snort. Obviously, she didn't have children because she had no idea what my days were like. I was a single parent of four kids. There was never any 'take a hot bath, read a

44

book, and forget all my worries' time. I was lucky if my fanny hit a chair before ten, let alone find the time to put my feet up and relax. Through my amusement, something she said nagged at the back of my brain, filling me with an inexplicable trepidation I could no longer deny.

What "now this" was she talking about?

"Bitsy, if you didn't call about the doctor's office or the Morgan job, then why did you call?" I forced the words out and swallowed, attempting to wet my suddenly dry throat.

"Why... the other thing, of course."

"Of course. And that would be?"

"The thing that's circulating all around town. Surely, you've heard by now."

I ground my teeth, though now that I thought about it, I had been getting some strange looks all day. I'd just assumed they had to do with the 'episode.' Now, I wasn't so sure. "Apparently, I'm the only one not in the know. Would you care to enlighten me?" *Since I know you're just dying to,* I wanted to add but didn't. Though I had to repeat, *Don't rise to the bait, Zoe,* five times to refrain from doing so.

Bitsy hesitated an inordinate amount of time before finally blurting, "Apparently, inappropriate pictures of a scantily clothed anonymous teenage girl are circulating around town. But they think they know who it is."

I let out the breath I'd been holding. "Oh, well, that's good they know who it is so they can put a stop to it."

"Good for the town, not so good for you, I'm afraid."

"What on earth does this have to do with me?"

"Because they think the girl in the photos is your daughter, Lexi."

The last thing I remembered was "That's the night that the lights went out in Mayflower," playing through my mind as my head hit the floor.

Chapter Four

That evening I stood in my tiny themeless kitchen, using my mismatched dishes— years of garage sale replacements for the broken ones— to make chicken and dumplings. I sighed as I held an ice pack to my head. One of these days I'd find the time to create my dream kitchen. Right now, I'd settle for creating dinner without passing out.

According to Dr. Joy— she had hospital duty when Officer Pickles escorted me into the emergency room— I didn't have a concussion, thank God. Just a bump the size of Principal Brimstone's enormous nose.

Anyhow, I never did get to tell the girls about the hellacious day I'd had with the Dorkmeister moving back home to become Dr. Hunkorama. Women loved doctors, but not ones who examined their— as my four-year-old daughter Katy would say— coochies! Good Lord, talk about intimidating.

Not that all family practice doctors did that, but mine did. All the more reason not to date Chaz. Thank God he hadn't been at the hospital to witness yet another one of my humiliating episodes. I swear these things could only happen to me, but those inappropriate pictures circulating would be enough to make any mother faint.

I carried the slow cooker over to the table and filled the plates, then called the kids for dinner. They all came barreling in and sat down to eat, except for Lexi. She dragged herself in at barely more than a crawl, picked at her food, and refused to even look at me. I cleaned up the kitchen, my appetite evaporating along with my trust in my daughter.

Losing the Morgan job and finding out Lexi was being accused of sending nearly nude photos into cyberspace had been a fitting end to a crappy day. The police were involved, for crying out loud. I didn't know what to believe. Lexi had denied everything, saying it wasn't her in the pictures, but she'd been on a downward spiral for a long time. Once photos like that were sent or posted anywhere, they never truly went away, even after being deleted. I'd stressed that multiple times as soon as she hit puberty. No boy was worth the risk. Something didn't add up. Sending sexy pictures didn't sound like my daughter. Then again, neither did making out half-naked with a boy on school property. If they hadn't caught her, would she have gone all the way? Had she already?

I wasn't ready for any of this.

The doorbell rang, and I dried my hands on a corner of my food-speckled apron. The *kiss the cook* writing was no longer visible, not that anyone had kissed *this* cook in a long time. I shook my head, having no idea where that thought came from. I removed the tattered garment and focused on answering the door. Who in the world could it be? None of my girls had answered their cell phones or responded in the group text. I still hadn't seen them all day, which was so not normal.

I was beginning to get worried.

I wasn't worried about some psycho being on the streets. I had lived in Mayflower, Massachusetts all my life. While the tight, close-knit town drove me crazy with its citizens' unsolicited opinions and advice, I knew they were there for me if I needed anything. They were set on watching out for me, or at least they had been before all of my latest disasters, and now the scandal. They meant well, but it was exhausting living up to their expectations.

I opened the door, and even though a gust of frigid air swept in, intense heat replaced my smile in a heartbeat. Wide shoulders filled my entryway. My eyes crept higher, but I already knew whose head belonged on those shoulders.

"Chuckie?" I gaped.

"Chaz." He grinned.

He looked oh-so-sexy in his black trousers, olive-green dress shirt with the sleeves rolled up and top two buttons undone. His matching tie hung loose around his neck. He stood like a *GQ* centerfold with one hand dangling from his pants' pocket, and the other hand holding his suit coat slung over his shoulder.

It took everything in me to keep from fanning my face. I tore my gaze away from the blond hairs poking out of the vee of his shirt and tried not to sigh as I inhaled his musky scent. A far cry from Brimstone's eau de Raidiness.

"Wh-what are you doing here?" I managed.

"Freezing. I left my overcoat at the office."

He couldn't be too cold with his suit coat hanging over his shoulder and his sleeves rolled up. I peered beyond him to see the windshield of his BMW splattered with snow, shimmering under the streetlamp like glitter. Looked like Truman was right again. I smiled slightly, picturing him eating the cherry pie I'd dropped off in "our spot" on his front porch and sipping his coffee by a warm fire. The old charmer. I shook my head, and then caught Chaz staring at me with a puzzled pucker on his forehead and a slight grin on his lips.

"Oh, I'm sorry. I must have left my manners back in your office, along with my dignity. Come in."

He stepped inside and ran a hand over his head, slicking back his sandy strands. "Nothing to be embarrassed about. Happens all the time."

"I doubt that."

He chuckled, his gaze sweeping through the house until it landed on the table. A genuine smile spread across his face all the way to his eyes. "I heard you had your hands full, but it looks like you're doing fine to me."

I followed his gaze to see the kids, for once, all behaving like human beings. Probably because they didn't see too many strangers come through town. If I had known that was what it took to get them to mind, I would have recruited a few two years ago when my life had been a mess. Not that it was much better now.

"We manage."

"I can see that. They're beautiful."

"Thank you. Why are you here, Chaz?"

His eyes returned to mine and held me captive. "To apologize. I never meant to embarrass you, Zoe. I hope you believe that."

"You didn't do anything wrong. Seems I have a horrible sense of direction, awful taste in undergarments, and I'm the bearer of the biggest wardrobe malfunction your office has ever seen. I take full responsibility."

"It wasn't as bad as you think it was." He lifted one shoulder in a shrug. "At least you have your friends to lean on. I feel like I've been gone so long no one remembers me. How are the women, anyway? I haven't seen them in years."

I huffed. "I wouldn't know. They haven't answered their phones all day. I'm not mad at you, by the way. I just had no idea you were moving back to town. I'm embarrassed, given the fool I made of myself the last time we met, and now today."

"I tried to tell you on the Cape, but you left before I could. If it helps any, I'm sorry for your embarrassment then and now just the same. And I completely understand your reservations about letting me examine you."

"Oh, I think I've given you plenty to examine already, but thank you."

"You're welcome." He stood there, staring at me in that intoxicating way he had about him. Back in high school, I thought he was a little awkward. Now, I thought he was mesmerizing, and...

I cleared my throat, stepping toward the door. "Well, if that will be all...?"

"Actually, that's not the only reason I'm here." He placed his hand on my arm, and I sucked in a sharp breath at the electric pulse that shot through my skin every time he touched me.

Good Lord, what else? "Oh?" I squeaked, praying he would leave soon.

A bouquet of something purely Chaz, no eau de anything necessary, captured my senses once more. Warmth spread through my extremities and drew my attention to his clean-shaven face. He had a square chiseled jaw, and I itched to stroke the length of it with my fingertips. Just once. But I didn't need to prove myself any more of an imbecile by acting on impulse, which basically meant he had to leave.

Now.

"I tried to catch you on your way out of the office, but you must not have heard me," he said.

Oh, I'd heard him, all right, but nothing he had to tell me could have been more important than my escape. "Well, whatever it was, it must have been important for you to make a house call. I didn't think doctors did that sort of thing anymore." I crossed my arms over my cardigan, which covered both a blouse and turtleneck, wishing I had added a fourth layer even though the temperature outside had risen. Or maybe my temperature had risen. Whatever the case, I was burning up.

"You dropped these on your way out, and since I know how important comfort is to you, I felt it my duty to return them right away." His eyes twinkled, and he reached into his suit coat pocket. To my horror, he pulled out the ugliest pair of granny panties I owned.

Big, stretched-out, tan monstrosities.

I gasped, then snatched them right out of his hands and shoved them under my sweater. "Oh, those silly things. I've been meaning to throw them out. I only wore them because I haven't done the laundry yet."

His gaze shot to the full basket of clothes at the bottom of the stairs. Clean, folded clothes. "I see." His mouth twitched at the corners.

"Except for one load," I blurted. "Speaking of laundry, while you're here, I have something of yours." I ran to the basket and stuffed my panties down deep, then lifted his white under-shirt and blue boxers from the top. Returning to the foyer, I thrust out my hands. "I believe these are yours."

"Mommy, why did that man have your underwear?" Katy tugged on my pant leg.

"Well, you see, I... I...." I had no idea what to say.

Chaz knelt down to Katy's level and calmed her with a heartwarming smile. "It's okay, sweetheart. I'm a doctor. I work with your mommy's doctor, and I stopped by because she forgot those at the office today."

Her big brown eyes widened, and her little pink lips parted while she stared at him, transfixed on every word he said. "I left my teddy at my doctor's one time, but he never brought it back to me. Mommy had to go all the way back there and get it for me." She grinned up at me and said, "I like him, Mommy. Wait until I tell my teacher the nice doctor brought your big girl undies all the way home."

"Katy, I really don't think...."

Katy took off down the hall, the conversation long since forgotten.

"Why do you have *his* underwear, Mom? You don't even know him." Troy appeared by my side, squaring his shoulders, and lifting his chin a notch as he scowled at Chaz.

"Um, well, I...." And I sure as heck didn't know what to say to that. It had taken two years to get my life under control, yet it only took two run-ins with Dr. Hunkorama to completely mess it up.

"Your mom and I go way back." Chaz stood and stuck out his hand. "I'm Chaz."

Troy glared, until I nudged him, then he shook Chaz's hand. *Barely.* "Troy."

"Well, Troy, it's nice to meet you. Your mom and I went to high school together."

"Then you must have known my dad."

Chaz's eyes softened. "He was a few years older than me, but I knew him. Although I wouldn't call him a friend. We didn't exactly have much in common."

Troy's shoulders relaxed a bit, and he nodded.

"Hey, mister, wanna play King of the Castle? I got Mom's armor, and everything." Bobby whipped out a cardboard sword and stood proud wearing my... dear God in heaven... my bra. The funny thing was it really did look like armor on him.

Only I wasn't laughing.

"That's quite the armor, young man. Looks like it could protect you from just about anything." Chaz glanced at me and winked. "Except your mom, maybe."

My stomach hit my throat, but I managed to say, "Bobby, I've told you a million times my bra is not your toy."

"But, Mommy, it's perfect."

My gaze shot to Chaz's. I could tell he fought off a grin as he pressed his lips together and forced a serious expression. I rolled my eyes and heard a slight chuckle slip from his lips, so I focused on Bobby. "That's not the point. Now, go take that off and get ready for basketball. Troy, would you please help him?"

Troy's gaze swept from me to Chaz, then back to me, and he sighed. "Sure, Mom."

"Lexi, would you please clean up the kitchen? I'll be there in a minute to help."

Lexi shrugged, still not speaking to me, but she did as I asked without an argument, for once.

It had stopped snowing. I walked Chaz out to the front porch and said, "Thank you for bringing my underwear here, and for tolerating my personal circus. They haven't had it easy."

He searched my face. "And what about you?"

"I'm okay. Really."

He reached out and tucked a loose curl behind my ear, and I jumped over the contact. "Really, huh," he said.

I cleared my throat. "I'm just not used to someone touching me. It's been a long time."

I hadn't expected to feel desire for another man. Max had been everything to me. The love of my life. When he decided he didn't want me anymore, I was afraid to take a chance with any man. What if I fell for another man, and he changed his mind down the road, too? I couldn't take that chance no matter what feelings Chaz had awakened within me. Besides, the thought of acting on those feelings scared the hell out of me. Let's just say I no longer had the body of a high school cheerleader.

Chaz slid his hand back into his pocket, letting my comment

go. "How's your head?" I should have known he would hear all about my fainting.

"I always knew I needed my head examined, but I never thought literally." I gingerly touched the knot on the back of my skull and winced. "I'll live."

"Good, and for what it's worth, I don't believe Lexi sent inappropriate pictures to anyone. Any daughter of yours has to be a good kid."

"Thanks. Wish I was as confident." I immediately felt guilty for thinking that, but I couldn't help it. Something was going on with her, but she wouldn't talk to me. What was I supposed to think?

An uncomfortable lull fell in the conversation, and then Chaz tried again. "Have dinner with me. You owe me a dinner from the Cape. I promise, there will be no touching involved. I won't even hold your hand." He slipped his own hands behind his back and grinned. I figured he wouldn't forget my comment about being uncomfortable with someone touching me and it having been a long time since I'd had sex.

"Don't worry, Chaz. I'm not holding you to the pity date. Trust me, I don't want another man in my life. I'm not in a good head space for that." There, I said it. I let him off the hook, so why didn't he look relieved?

"I'm not here because of pity, Zoe. I tried to tell you that as well back on the Cape, but you ran out before letting me finish. Kind of like today. Do I detect a pattern?" He studied me. "I'm here because I like you, and I want to get to know you again. It's that simple. Just have dinner with me. Dinner doesn't have to equal sex, Zoe. Not that I don't find you incredibly attractive, but I get it. You're not ready."

Mount Saint Zoe started churning again, building up even more major steam and pressure at the mere thought that Chaz might want to have sex with me. Why me? He could have any woman he wanted with his good looks and that voice. My knees knocked, and my volcano began to quake. I couldn't do this. Chaz rattled me, and with the future of my career hanging on the line and the mess Lexi was apparently in, I couldn't afford to be rattled.

"I-I don't think dinner is such a good idea."

"Why not? Everyone has to eat. You just said you and your kids were fine, so why not go out on a date with me?"

He would never give up if he knew I was attracted to him, so I lied. "I'm sorry, Chuckie. I don't think I'll ever be able to think of you as anything other than a friend."

He searched my face once again, looking disappointed, and then he lifted one shoulder. "Fair enough. Can't say I didn't try." He held out his hand and smiled, but this time it didn't quite reach his eyes. "Friends it is."

I slipped my hand into his, and as our warm palms slid together, I felt that little zing again right down to my core. He squeezed, and I shivered, then pulled my hand from his, rubbing my palm on my slacks.

"All righty, then. I'd better get inside. That air has a definite chill to it." I rubbed my arms.

He stared at my three layers of shirts, his eyes crinkling at the corners, and then he glanced at the driveway. A couple of inches had accumulated. "Want me to shovel before I go?"

"Thanks, but I just bought a new snowblower. I'm all set." I made a mental note to buy a snowblower first thing tomorrow morning.

"Okay, then. See you around, Zoe. Stay warm."

"Right. You, too." I hurried inside and shed one of my layers before I melted. Chill, my behind. I was on fire, and *that* was the problem. I had good ole Dr. Hunkorama breathing down my neck. Literally. And I liked it way too much.

Only one thing left to do other than join the gym, buy a new snowblower, and shop for new underwear. I had to get to the bottom of the inappropriate pictures accusation against my daughter, and I had to focus on landing more party planning jobs so Mayor Edwards could see all I had to offer. That basically meant staying out of trouble, which definitely meant staying far, far away from one Dr. Chaz Anderson.

~

"WE'VE BEEN over this a million times, Mom. I'm not moving to Florida," I said into the phone that evening as I put away the last of the clean dishes from the dishwasher. I glanced at the clock. Nine, and I hadn't even sat down yet. Another typical night, I sighed, throwing out a chipped glass.

"Zoe, your dad and I are worried about you, especially after what we heard. Your poor babies are having some serious problems, and little Chuckie Anderson got you half-undressed? Dear, what's going on?"

Good grief, how far did the rumor mill travel? I glanced out the window at the house across the street, and my eyes narrowed. "You've been talking to Mrs. Bee again, haven't you?" I dove my hand into my Miss Piggy cookie jar and stuffed an Oreo in my mouth.

"Well, can you blame her? She's as worried as we are."

"Lexi hasn't been in any more trouble in school, Troy has a tutor, and there's nothing going on with Chaz— uh, Chuckie. Really. Now, stop worrying."

"How can you possibly expect me to stop worrying after what I've heard?"

"And here it comes," I muttered under my breath, snatching another Oreo. Talking to my mother warranted comfort food, and Oreos were my favorite.

"People are saying there are inappropriate pictures of our

Lexi floating around in cyberspace everywhere!" she screeched, her voice rising to near dog-ear level.

I yanked the phone away with a wince.

"Dear God in heaven."

I could still hear my mother talking from a foot away, and I mentally pictured her making the sign of the cross. Out of habit, I made it with her. After I deemed it safe, I brought the phone back to my ear.

"I told you social media was no good. Lexi may be doing fine in school for now, but that won't put an end to the picture rumors. What are you planning on doing about that?"

"The police and the school board are already looking into it, Mom. I'm already monitoring her phone calls."

"I meant what are you going to do about the town. You can't possibly believe Lexi is capable of that, can you?"

The now familiar stab of guilt slammed into me. What kind of mother was I? A worried one, I admitted, since I still couldn't shake the feeling something was going on with my daughter. "I said I'll handle it, Mother."

Her voice grew quiet. "It's okay to admit you can't do this alone, you know."

I massaged the back of my neck, attempting to work the kinks out. "It's been two years, Mom. I think I've done fine."

"I think your little catering thing is adorable, dear, but getting Max to pay his fair share of support for you and the kids has proven nearly impossible. Don't you think it's time you took things seriously? Let us help you, Zoe. That's all we want to do."

I bit my tongue on 'little catering thing' because I knew she genuinely cared. As a parent, I understood her worry, but that didn't mean I would change my mind. "I know you do, Mom, but it's not necessary. I don't need help."

"Kids are expensive, you know."

I almost laughed over that one. Times had changed since I

was a kid. She didn't have a clue how expensive kids were in this day and age. Clothes, toys, sports. If it wasn't cool, it was out. Admittedly, I'd given in a lot more than I would have if Max were still here. Now that I was striving to rectify that, they were fighting me tooth and nail. But I'd never admit that to Granny I'm-On-My-Way-To-Save-The-Day.

"I have things under control. I've expanded my 'little catering thing' into a party-planning business. We're fine." I clamped my jaw so tight my molars ached.

My mother meant well, but she didn't understand how much it mattered for me to do this on my own. I wanted— no, I *needed*— my independence. I needed to have something of my very own, and I didn't want anyone taking care of me. Not even her.

"But I heard you lost the prom job, and the Morgans pulled out. That doesn't sound fine to me, dear."

Darn Mrs. Bee. My mother's own personal spy. I yanked my curtains closed, and the light in Mrs. Bee's kitchen went off as though she'd read my mind and didn't want to be caught watching me. "I have plenty of other prospects, Mom, now stop worrying."

She sighed long and hard, and I rolled my eyes. It wasn't too difficult to see who my little drama queen took after. "For the record, this never would have happened in Florida." When I didn't respond, she added, "Well, if you change your mind, you know where we are."

How could I not know where they were? She reminded me every day with her catch phrase about nothing bad ever happening in Florida. I had news for her. The last trip I took to Florida, she convinced me to let her friend's son and his wife take me out on the town. Turned out they were swingers. I thought I was safe— given I was a family friend and all— but that didn't stop them. They claimed a threesome was the next best thing, and I feigned a migraine worthy of an Oscar.

"I love you, Mom. Tell Dad I love him, too."

She harrumphed, undoubtedly exasperated over not winning again. She hated losing, but she especially hated not having the last word. She had convinced both my brother and my sister to move to Florida, but I was the stubborn one. Probably more like her than I cared to admit. Until she felt I was truly okay, she wouldn't give up, no matter what I said.

"We love you, too, dear. Call if you need anything."

Or just tell Mrs. Bee, I thought, shaking my head.

After I hung up, I reached into Miss Piggy for another Oreo, but they were all gone. I frowned. I couldn't possibly have eaten all of them, could I? Sighing, I admitted, after talking to my mother, anything was possible. I searched the liquor cabinet but couldn't find anything appealing. I would kill for an ice-cold glass of Pinot Grigio but was too tired to go out and get one. As I contemplated my next move, someone knocked on the door.

My heart skipped several beats, taking on an erratic rhythm that sounded suspiciously like, *Don't you wish your girlfriend was ME! ME! ME!* Could it be Chaz again? Passing a hall mirror, I smoothed my hair and checked my makeup, then scowled at my reflection when I realized what I was doing. I forced the rhythm back to a nice normal, *Hit the road, Chaz, and don't you come back no more, no more, no more, no more.*

I marched over to the door and yanked it open, but no one was there. Nothing, expect a large white wicker basket that smelled like homemade cinnamon rolls— my favorite— and was filled with two bottles of Pinot Grigio, grapes, cheese, crackers, chocolate, and— joy of all joys— Oreos. Taped to the top was a card. Reaching down, I snatched up the card and read it.

Surprise!

We've been planning this all day after we heard the news, but it took longer than we had anticipated. We didn't want to spoil the surprise. That's why we didn't text you back. We're so sorry, Zoe. Screw the Morgans and screw the town. There's no way Lexi is the girl in those pictures. We're so sorry Dr. Joy was called away, but not sorry Chaz is back in town. He's a great guy and might be just what you need. But no worries. As much as we would love for that to happen, we realize it's none of our business. We're here to support you in whatever way you need. Please say you'll forgive us for not being around when you needed us.
Love, The Squad

I couldn't keep the smile from spreading across my face. Their timing was impeccable, as always. "Just what I needed, ladies, although I wouldn't have minded someone to talk to," I murmured to myself, a lump forming in my throat as I reached for the wine and a cookie.

"Yes! Better late than never." Harmony popped out from behind my van.

I jumped a foot, and tossed my cookies, literally.

Morticia appeared from the side of the house, carrying a six pack of Diet Cola. "She still hasn't said she's forgiven us for not being around yet."

"Please, Morti." Tiffany glanced at me and winked. "She smiled and wished we were here. That's enough for me." She scooped up the basket and headed straight into my living room. "Let's take this party inside before Zoe changes her mind."

I snapped my jaw closed. You'd think they wouldn't be able to surprise me anymore, but they always did. I tried not to smile, but it was pointless. They all knew I loved them for it, and right now, I needed them.

"Right behind ya, babe." Harmony flashed her pearly whites.

My eyes welled up with tears. What a day.

Morticia slipped her arm around my shoulders and rested her head against mine. "Come on. Let's go drown our sorrows."

Two bottles of wine, a whole bag of cookies, a facial, a mani-cure, a pedicure, a henna tattoo, and a whole lot of laughter later, I finally felt like myself again. None of the kids came down. The little ones were fast asleep, and the older ones had better things to do. Thank God for my girls, I thought, until someone decided to turn on my computer in the corner of my living room.

"What are you doing?" I asked, feeling the full effect of the wine.

"Checking out Lexi's social media." Harmony straddled the chair and went to the site.

"Why? Last time I checked, everything was fine."

"And how often do you check?" Tiffany asked as she walked over to stand behind Harmony and peer over her shoulder.

"Daily. What aren't you guys telling me?"

"Ever Google her?" Morticia joined Harmony and Tiffany at the computer. "People steal pictures all the time."

"No. What is going on?"

Harmony looked at Morticia. "What do you think?"

"She's probably drunk enough." Morticia turned to Tiffany.

Tiffany looked at me briefly before focusing back on the computer. "I don't know, maybe one more glass."

"*She* is standing right here, and *she* doesn't need any more drama for one day. Dammit, what the hell is up?"

"Oh, shit, she swore," Harmony said.

"Twice, and she never swears," Tiffany added.

"Can't be good," Morticia chimed in.

"Ladies," I snapped.

"It's probably nothing," Morticia said.

"If it has to do with my daughter, then it's not nothing, so out with it."

"Well, doll, the rumor goes there might be some rather, um, even more revealing images... that is to say some people might see them and think... so you see...." Tiffany rambling and at a loss for words was worrisome all by itself.

"No, I don't see. What are you talking about?"

"There are pictures of Lexi's ta-tas on the Internet," Harmony blurted. Tiffany glared and Harmony shrugged. "What? It's the truth."

"Can you say blunt? Geez, Harm." Morticia winced.

"Blunt is better than rambling like Tiff." Harmony grunted.

"Let me see." I shoved them aside and stared in disbelief at the screen before me, my jaw falling wide enough to fit a fist in my mouth. "Oh, my God," I breathed as I stared at my daughter. My *grown* daughter on a questionable website. When had she gotten so big? How had I not noticed? Her face wasn't clear but looked enough like her to ramp up my fears.

"Damn, she is definitely your daughter." Harmony focused in on the picture.

Tiffany glared. "Harmony Jones, honestly."

"Again... the truth. You're a perfect C, and Zoe is an impressive Double D. Lexi looks to be following in her mama's ta-tas, lucky girl."

"Again... bluntness." Morticia shook her head. "Just because you're an A—"

"Oh, like you're much bigger, Ms. B."

They rambled on with more nonsense, but I wasn't listening. I couldn't take my eyes off my daughter's picture, and more doubt settled into my mind. No wonder the town was pointing the finger at Lexi. I would have to confront her first thing in the morning. Right now she was sound asleep, and I was in no shape to hold a coherent conversation.

"Enough." Tiffany swiped her hand through the air. "A, B, C, whoopty flippin' D... who cares. Zoe, are you okay?"

"How did I not see my daughter grow up?" I sat down hard on the chair. "How could I have let this happen?"

"Sweetie, no one can control questionable websites like that. The minute they're shut down, new ones pop up. Besides, we can't be positive that's even Lexi." Tiffany squeezed my shoulder.

"Yeah, we'll catch the sucker behind this mess. Whoever this girl is, she doesn't deserve to be ogled by perverts." Harmony patted my other shoulder.

"What they said," Morticia added from behind me.

"You guys don't understand." I turned around to face them all, guilt clogging my throat. So far, I had thought it, but I hadn't actually voiced the words out loud. "I should be my daughter's biggest champion, yet I don't believe her. Isn't that horrible of me? I know something is going on with her, but she won't talk to me. I think my daughter might actually be the girl in those pictures, and I have no idea what to do about it."

Chapter Five

"I assure you, Mr. Caputo, there are no mouse droppings in my apple dumplings." A gust of snow whipped in my face, startling me as I stood outside in my driveway. My cell phone slipped, but I managed to hold onto it through my bulky mitten.

"Now, I'm not saying you're lying, but..." He took a breath through the line, then plunged into a full-fledged ramble. "... Maria said Suzy's best friend's father heard from the guys at the barber shop that Pete's wife, Veronica, sat by Mrs. Bee at bingo, who said her niece LuLu heard from a friend of a friend at the Legion's party you catered, that something was dumped in the dumplings, all right, but it sure wasn't apples."

"Mr. Caputo... Vinny... you know me better than that. Yes, I prepare my food at home, and yes, my house is ancient, but I do not have mice." I threw my hand up in the air. "You know how the rumor mill is in a small town. What was undoubtedly nothing more than an apple seed suddenly becomes a mouse dropping."

The Caputos were late baby boomers, having Suzy in their forties after years of trying. Since Mrs. Caputo wanted everything perfect for her only child, I had assumed the job was mine.

Especially since they had been good friends with my parents before my parents retired to Florida. Now, I wasn't so sure they would still use me.

A long sigh came through the line. "Look, Zoe, if it were up to me, I wouldn't have anyone else plan Suzie's sweet-sixteen birthday party. But Maria, well, you know Maria." He grunted. "Once she gets an idea in her head, there's no changing her mind. I'm sorry, but I'm sure you'll get the next gig. Hang in there, kiddo."

"Thanks." *For nothing.*

I hung up my cell and stuffed it in the pocket of my ski coat. What a crappy day. Lexi wasn't even speaking to me after I confronted her this morning about the pictures of her on the Internet. She'd denied everything, but I doubted her, and she was hurt.

And now, I'd lost another job.

What in the world was going on here? Yes, Lexi's scandal with the pictures was affecting me from landing any current jobs, but that didn't account for the other jobs that fell through before the scandal. Last week I lost out on planning two jobs because of misunderstandings, and now this. Not outright lies, just simple twists of the truth. I lowered my eyelids to slits.

Twists that began after the mayor made his big announcement.

Starting this year, he would throw an annual Labor Day Bash for the entire town. The biggest party of the year, and he was looking for someone to plan it. Winning that bid would mean a whole lot of clout and tons of business. But I wasn't the only party planner in town. I knew exactly who was behind these latest setbacks.

Bitsy Beaumont.

I tugged my mittens on tighter, zipped up my coat further, and hoisted my chin for good measure. Then marched my granny fanny clear across the street and five houses down. Climbing the steps, I rang the doorbell.

No answer.

"I know you're in there, Bitsy. Open up." I pounded on the door.

The door opened, and a wave of some expensive perfume clouded my sinuses with the beginning of a headache as a tall, trim, picture-perfect-in-every-way blond woman turned up her nose at me. "Oh, it's you."

"That's right, it's me," I hissed, dying to wrinkle her Vera Wang clothes and mess up her two-hundred-dollar hairdo right after I popped some ibuprofen. What was it with people bathing in their cologne? I breathed through my mouth and focused on the reason I was there.

My target.

Just once I'd love to see her frazzled. Heck, I'd even settle for plain old human. Why, I'd bet an entire party job she slept looking just as perfect. No wonder she couldn't land a man. Men were messy, and Bitsy would never stand for that. Well, I wasn't about to stand for anymore interference from her, either. Now I knew exactly why she had been at parent-teacher conference. She *had* been convincing Brimstone to give her the prom job instead of me.

"Where do you get off scaring my customers away? Don't deny it, because I know it's you," I growled.

"Darling, have you looked in the mirror? You're perfectly capable of 'scaring' all on your own."

I glanced down at Max's old beat-up black ski pants and orange coat. They didn't exactly go with the hot pink hat and green gloves, but I couldn't afford to buy anything new. Besides, I hadn't planned on anyone seeing me. I'd only wanted to stay warm while snowblowing the foot of fluffy white flakes the freaky March storm had dumped, but I had gotten the call before I'd had a chance to start. I certainly hadn't planned on talking to Ms. I-Don't-Even-Get-The-Newspaper-At-The-Crack-Of-Dawn-Unless-I-Look-Perfect.

Dammit, she'd gone too far this time. "You won't win. No one will want you once they discover what you're really like." I glared.

"What no one wants is a phony, my dear. Have you forgotten who you are, Mrs. Robinson?" Her icy blue gaze ran over me from head to toe with obvious disdain. "You might be able to cook, but you are not a party planner. I, on the other hand, have been planning parties for years."

"Exactly. The same parties over and over. This town needs something new and fresh. Besides, there's enough business for the both of us. Why can't you just focus on planning your own parties instead of sabotaging mine?"

"But, darling, you give me such good material to work with. You expect me to pass that up?" She made a tsking noise. "I think not. I'll deny it, of course, so save your breath. You'll only look like a sore loser. Now, if you don't mind, I have loads of work to do. Besides, you're letting the cold in."

She had loads, all right. Loads of bull pucky.

She started to push the door closed, but paused as she added, "The mayor's going to make up his mind by Memorial Day. You can't exactly showcase your so-called talents if you don't have any parties to plan. Save yourself more heartache, sweetheart, and admit you've lost." Then she shut the door in my face.

"This isn't over, *sweetheart*," I yelled through the closed door.

Ooooh, the woman made me want to pull my hair out, but she wasn't worth the bald spot. Winning the bid for the mayor's Labor Day Bash, however, was. Not the hair loss, but the effort, that is. I had to do something, but what? I had to find a way to stay in the game, but how? I set my shoulders and squared my jaw, knowing exactly what I had to do. I had to find a party to plan, now.

But who in this town would still have me?

~

I SLIPPED and slid all the way back to my house and decided to tackle snowblowing the driveway. Maybe the cold air and exercise would help me let off some steam and figure out what to do about Bitsy. My best ideas often came to me when I focused on something else. So I read the directions, adjusted all the knobs, pulled the cord five times until my arms burned, and finally the engine roared to life.

"Admit defeat?" I set my jaw with determination. "Never."

I squeezed the trigger on my left, and the blades started churning. Looking around, I saw a sea of men blowing out their driveways. No women in sight, except me. That needed to change. Women could do whatever men could. I was discovering that more and more each day. Feeling the engine vibrate beneath my gloves, I suddenly understand why so many men got off on machinery. The feeling of power coursed through me. I could do this. I squeezed the trigger on my right, and the machine started to move.

Okay, *move* was a huge understatement.

I let out a yelp as the turbo-charged contraption zigged and zagged all over the driveway, yanking me along at an insane speed. It took a lot of strength to control this hunk of steel. I slid into the road and spun on my heel just in time to keep from running over Mrs. Bee's mailbox. Poor old Truman was confused enough, I didn't need to add to it by putting up a new box.

Thank God no cars drove by. Jaws of Death here would

have eaten them for lunch. It was bad enough several heads had turned my way, and even Bitsy had pulled back her living room curtains. Loads of work, huh. Yeah, right, even if she'd stolen every one of my jobs.

I glanced next door and— oh, yay me— now Lester stepped out onto his front porch, wearing a gap-toothed smile and a "Twisted Sister" t-shirt.

Why hadn't I just confessed I could have used Chaz's help yesterday? Because I was too darn proud and afraid to depend on him, that was why. All winter, I had used a shovel, but Troy had broken the shovel the other day. Chaz caught me off guard. Now, here I was feeling like a maniac as I ran back and forth, making whacked-out patterns across the snow, my arms straining at the sockets, just to prove a point. At the moment, the only point I proved was I had been reduced to the status of moron.

The snow whipped into my face over and over, and I blinked like crazy to see, but I refused to give up. My fingers tingled and stiffened with numbness, so I slipped them out of the finger holes and made fists, using my whole arms to keep the levers pressed, looking like the hunchback on Pleasant Street.

One hour later, I finished the blasted driveway, ready to take the awful machine back to the store and pay someone to keep my driveway plowed. I should have done that in the first place, but I couldn't really afford it. Besides, I preferred to take care of everything myself. I thought about that. Good Lord, Tiffany was right.

I *had* become a control freak.

Breathing heavy, I cut the engine and heard the distinct sound of a car idling behind me. Great. Could my day get any worse? Plastering a smile on my stiff face, I turned to see Chaz grinning from ear-to-ear, looking too hot for words.

He rolled down his window and said, "You know, they make

shields for those things," and his grin broadened, if that were possible.

"Really, I'll keep that in mind."

"I hear they work great to keep the wind out of your face."

"Is that so? Have you ever tried one?"

"Nah. I prefer to shovel. Besides, I'm not the one who needs a shield."

"And you think I do?" I stood straighter. "Do you see my driveway? I did this myself. Without a shield, I might add."

"I know. I pulled up just as you were finishing." He scanned the driveway and chuckled. "Interesting technique. And on high speed, no less. Impressive."

My mouth unhinged. "This thing has more than one speed?"

I could tell he struggled not to laugh. "You mean you didn't know?"

I put my hands on my hips, thinking for a way out of looking dense. "Of course, I knew. I was being sarcastic. I like to move fast."

"Really, now?"

Okay, so I'd walked right into Stupidtown with that one. I would be better off just ending this discussion now before I moved on to Idiotville. "If we're done discussing my blowing technique, I really have to—"

"I didn't come here to talk about your, um, what did you call it? Blowing technique?" I closed my eyes, and he did laugh this time. "Hey, your words, not mine," he said. "I didn't come to discuss whether or not you need a shield, either, which you do. I came here to ask you to lunch."

My pulse throbbed in my neck, and the thought of eating made me sick. Every time I was around him, my appetite hit the highway. Best diet I'd ever been on. "I thought we discussed this, Chaz? We're just friends."

The sun reflected off his eyes, and the green swirls stood out as he stared at me for a long moment, his smile dimming. I squirmed, wondering what was going on behind those studious eyes, until he finally spoke. "I did agree to being just friends, but I didn't say it wouldn't be difficult. I'm trying my best, but this isn't a date, Zoe, this is a business lunch. I need to talk to you about a catering job."

"I'm not just a caterer anymore, Chaz, I'm a party planner."

"Good, because I need that, too."

"Oh." Well, what could I say to that? He had obviously heard the rumors, and now he was coming to my rescue. I hated relying on anyone, and I'd never be able to eat in front of him. But at the rate I was going, I couldn't afford to turn down any job, even one that involved Mr. Make-My-Volcano-Quake. No one else would hire me now. "In that case, give me five minutes."

"Done." His eyes roamed over my face, and his smile resumed, full force. "Take your time."

I wondered what that look had been about as I wheeled Jaws back into the garage. Heading into the house, I stripped off my gear and jogged upstairs to change for lunch. I couldn't deny my heart raced like the front runner in the Kentucky Derby, but I blamed it on the excitement of a new job, not that Chaz's smile did unmentionable things to my insides. And that voice. God, that voice made me want to rip off his clothes and jump him. I shivered over my own thoughts. This wasn't me. At all.

What had turning forty done to my brain?

He wasn't the only one having a hard time remaining just friends. I shook off any thought but business as I ran into my closet and changed into the infamous nude pantyhose, a basic brown skirt, amber blouse that matched my eyes, and brown pumps, with a matching brown jacket. Appropriate business attire, even if it was my most flattering suit. Then I headed into my bathroom to touch up my makeup.

I looked in the mirror, dropped my makeup bag, and let out a scream. Oh, dear God in heaven. What must Chaz have thought as he sat in his car, talking to that creature staring back at me? I needed more than a shield. I needed a bag over my head. I could see the Mayflower Gazette headlines.

Attack of the Rabid Raccoon, starring Zoe Robinson.

Huge, runny black circles framed my eyes, with black smudges streaking down my cheeks. Major lesson learned: never wear non-waterproof mascara on a windy, blustery day while snowblowing the driveway. I was surprised Chaz hadn't tried to trap me and relocate me in the woods somewhere.

This took moron status to a whole new level.

MAYFLOWER, Massachusetts was your typical small, picturesque New England town. Trees lined the sidewalks, while Cape Cod and Colonial houses with white picket fences framing their front yards sat back from the curb. Brick buildings with gorgeous architecture and churches with beautiful steeples dotted the town, adding an element of charm. And a quaint college sat on the outskirts of town.

The citizens took their history seriously and refused to allow overbuilding or commercializing to take place. It was one of the main reasons I loved living there, but it wasn't cheap. Mayor Edwards just had to choose me to plan the Labor Day Bash, that was all there was to it.

I could give this old-fashioned town a bash its citizens would talk about for the whole year. A bash filled with excitement, fun, and different activities, without taking away from the charm that was Mayflower. Bitsy couldn't do that. Why, she would undoubtedly stick with the same old boring, predictable stuff she always did. The problem was the town liked boring and predictable. Traditional.

It suddenly dawned on me I needed this job as much for me as for the town. I needed to show them, and me, that it was okay to change, be different. To give them the spontaneous, carefree part of me dying to break free.

I stared out the window of Lolita's Place, contemplating that revelation as I waited for Chaz to return from the men's room. A few minutes later, Sarah walked by in her nursing uniform. "Hi, Sarah. You on your lunch break?"

"Ohmigosh, yes, and I'm so nervous." She bounced on the balls of her feet, wringing her hands, nearly jumping out of her skin.

"Nervous why? Lolita's food is fantastic."

"Oh, it's not the food I'm worried about."

Only one thing could have the outgoing adorable Sarah nervous. "You didn't." I grabbed her arm, my eyes scanning the restaurant for her mysterious new man.

Morticia's father was having lunch with some woman I'd never seen, probably working out the details of a funeral. Brimstone was studying some paper— undoubtedly gossip related— at Gerty and Gabby Rogers' table in the far corner. Father O'Dority and Sister Mary Agnes sat by the fireplace, discussing some church-related issue, judging by his serious expression. He didn't fool around when it came to sinning, and any type of sex other than marital he considered a sin.

Sexy pictures and quaking volcanoes be damned.

I shivered and looked back at Sarah. "So where is this hunky guy of yours?"

She laughed. "You're right, I didn't, and he's not mine yet, but I'm hoping to change all of that today. I'm taking your advice, and I'm going to ask him out. That's why I'm nervous."

I shot her a smile. "You'll do fine. You're cute, and sweet. Really, you have nothing to worry about." I surveyed the room again as more people filed in. "So, is he here?"

"I'm not sure yet, but I hear this is where he loves to eat." She searched the growing crowd of people, and then her face lit up, her smile spreading wide. "Oh, God, he's here, and he's headed right this way. Wish me luck."

I looked in the direction she stared, and then sucked in a sharp breath.

She glanced at me. "I know, he's hot. Kinda takes your breath away, right?"

My heart darn near stopped beating. I couldn't say a word. I tried, but my vocal cords froze as tunnel vision consumed me, and waves of dizziness made me nauseous. My peripheral vision faded to black, allowing my eyes to focus solely on Chaz as he stopped right in front of Sarah. "Hey, Sarah. You here for lunch?"

"Um, yes." Sarah's cheeks turned pink, and she shot me a little smile. "I, well, you're just the person I was looking for. I wanted to talk to you about something. Join me?"

"Can't." He slid into the booth across from me. "I'm having lunch with my friend Zoe today." He sent me a smile. "But my last appointment of the day cancelled if you want to meet me in my office later. We can talk then."

Sarah's eyes inflated, the whites expanding to twice that of the blue as they traveled from him to me. Her jaw opened and closed as though she was attempting to speak under water. A few garbled noises emerged, but I wouldn't call them actual words. Her cheeks darkened to a ruby red, and she cleared her throat.

Three times.

Why now? Why this? *Why me?* I thought. "Sarah, I—"

"No problem, Dr. Anderson. It's not important. I'm sure I'll find someone else to, um, talk to about this matter." She wouldn't even look at me.

"Sarah, please." I touched her arm, but she stepped away.

"I forgot there's something really important I have to do." She spun on her heel and made a beeline for the door, not once looking over her shoulder.

I wilted as I watched her leave, her back ramrod straight.

"Care to tell me what that was all about?" Chaz asked.

The waitress walked up at that moment. "All set to order?"

"Not—" Chaz started to answer.

"Yes, we're ready." I cut Chaz off and ordered a salad, ready to get this catastrophe over with. Besides, that was about all I could stomach.

Chaz rattled off his order. When she left, he leaned back and crossed his arms over his chest... waiting.

He never let anything drop. I met his gaze, not sure what to say. If I told him, Sarah would never forgive me, but I had to say something. Maybe I could help her. "Don't you think Sarah is pretty?"

Chaz arched a brow. "Sure, she's an attractive woman, but what—"

"And isn't she the sweetest thing?" I ripped tiny little pieces off my napkin, staring down at the table and stacking them in a neat little pile as I talked.

"Absolutely. The friendliest person in the office, in fact, but that still—"

"She's young and perky and so...." my voice trailed off.

He slid his warm hand over mine and squeezed gently. "Zoe, look at me. What's this really about?"

My eyes met his, and my mind went blank for a moment. I peeled my gaze away to snap out of it and licked my dry lips. "I think she may have gotten the wrong impression about our having lunch together."

His eyes dropped to my mouth, then he pulled his hand away. "And what impression would that be?"

My pulse kicked into overdrive, and my hand felt suddenly cold. "Um." Now, I was the one clearing my throat. "Well, that we're interested in each other romantically."

He sat back and searched my eyes. "That's true in part, but—"

"Chaz." I frowned as I cut him off.

"Zoe." He smiled all the way to his eyes. "If you had let me finish, I was going to say but I respect your wishes to just be friends."

"Oh." I let out a frustrated sigh because I was the one having issues respecting my own wishes.

He eyed me curiously.

"You just *think* you're interested in me, but you're holding onto a childhood fantasy of dating the older cheerleader. It's not real, Chaz. Trust me; I'm not the same person mentally or physically." I sucked in my stomach, not that he could even see it beneath the table, but I knew it was there. Time to lay off the flipping Oreos.

"No one's the same, Zoe, including yours truly. Thank God." He patted his now flat stomach and chuckled. "I just want to get to know you. That's all I ever wanted, even then. Even though I agreed to be just friends, that doesn't change the way I feel about you. I can't just shut my feelings off, but I won't act on them. You have my word on that. Though I can't imagine why Sarah would care about our relationship status one way or another."

This time I arched my brow. For such a brilliant doctor, he didn't have a clue.

His eyes widened. "Ohhh."

"Yeah, oh. I knew she was interested in some guy, and I encouraged her to ask him out." I groaned. "I thought maybe he was Matt McGinnis, that new pub owner. Or maybe some guy she met at college. I mean, she's still taking classes to get her RN, so it was a good assumption, right?"

"Sure."

"Oh, God, who am I kidding? The guy had to be you, of all people. *You*. She'll probably never talk to me again."

"Don't worry about it, Zoe. Even if I wasn't interested in you romantically, or just your friend right now, it doesn't matter. I don't date women I work with. I'll handle it."

Even friend Chaz made me nervous, but I wasn't ready to admit to any feelings. And I definitely didn't have the guts to act on them. I had to stay focused on work. But I also couldn't let him 'handle' anything. "Oh, yeah, that will go over really well. You don't say a word. I will talk to Sarah myself later."

The waitress brought our food and drinks, so we dug in and ate in silence. Okay, so I only picked at mine, but I'd learned my lesson after the lobster cramping, roaring, and blasting fiasco. My stomach twinged, so I set down my fork and focused on the reason I was here. Reaching into my purse, I fished out my tablet and opened a screen to take notes. "About that party planning job, what did you have in mind?"

"Well, my parents just retired. They've been prominent members of this community for a long time, so I want to plan a retirement party where everyone who's anyone will be there."

Prominent was putting it mildly. They chaired a lot of events and gave more money to the town than anyone else, even though they couldn't always afford it. Dr. Chaz had plenty of money and was picking up where they left off. Everyone knew and loved all the Andersons, especially the mayor.

I jotted down notes. "What type of place were you thinking of?"

"I wanted something a little more intimate and personal. Like the house I had built, maybe." He stroked his clean-shaven jaw, looking as though he were warming to the idea. "Yeah, why not? There's plenty of room, it just needs some decorating."

I tucked my hair behind my ear and nodded. "That could work. What time frame were you looking at?"

"Soon. How about the weekend before Memorial Day?"

My eyes collided with his. Mayor Edwards had said he would make his decision on Memorial Day. "Chaz, you don't have to do this for me. Besides, it will be tough to pull off a party that size in two months. Pick the date you really want."

"I have every confidence if anyone can pull this off, you can. And that is the date I want. May is a good month for me. Come on, what do you say?" He stared into my eyes, looking so handsome in his olive-green suit. A sandy lock of hair slipped out of place, and I had the strongest urge to reach out and fix it.

"I say we've got our work cut out for us, but you've got a deal."

"So when do we get started?" he asked.

"Yesterday."

"Good. Come over, and I'll make you dinner."

Oh, boy, my stomach gurgled. Time to exit, stage left. I clenched and said, "Chaz."

"What? We both have to eat, and we have a lot to go over, and you seem to be concerned with being seen with me in public. A business dinner sounds like the perfect solution." He reached out his hand. "What do you say?"

I stared at the long fingers and neatly clipped nails, then slid my palm against his. Damn that stupid tingle. "Deal. Just business," I repeated more for myself.

He dropped his hand immediately. "What time?"

"Tonight?" I clenched harder.

"Don't you need to take a look at my place, throw some ideas around?"

"Well, sure, but I have children, if you've forgotten."

"Children who need to eat, and I make a mean spaghetti. Say six?"

I chewed my lip, thinking it through, more worried about myself than him. I couldn't afford to turn down this job, but I couldn't afford to spend more time alone with Chaz, either. And I'd never be able to eat spaghetti of all things, but I could fake it. Trust me; after twenty years of marriage and four kids, any woman could learn to fake anything at least once.

I didn't want my children getting attached to him. Then again, if they knew this was strictly a business dinner, they would be okay with the idea. Maybe I had been approaching this situation wrong from the beginning. Maybe having four kids around would be the perfect buffer, and maybe they would work their magic and scare him out of thinking he was interested in me. Maybe dinner was his best idea yet.

Or maybe I was making the biggest mistake of my life.

Either way, I didn't have much of a choice. If I didn't get out of there soon, something was bound to burst, and it wouldn't be pretty. I took a deep breath, looked him in the eye, and said, "You're on."

Chapter Six

B efore I went to Chaz's house for dinner, I had to make peace with Sarah. The problem was, I had been trying to reach her all afternoon, but she wouldn't return my calls. Not quite ready to walk through the doors of my doctor's office anytime soon yet needing to make it home in time to meet the school bus, I was desperate.

Thank God their office was on the first floor. I stepped through the slushy snow and hid behind a bush, right next to one of Dr. Joy's exam rooms, and waited. I might not own Vera anything and my shoes were hardly Jimmy Choos, but nevertheless, I doubted they would ever be the same. I did my best to make sure no one saw me, but with the rumor mill in this town, I didn't hold out much hope. However, even the threat of being *The Mayflower Gazette's* front-page headline tomorrow morning wasn't enough to make me do the sensible thing and go inside.

Instead, I kept popping up out of the bushes and peeking inside the window as Dr. Joy examined patient after patient. She pulled the curtain closed around the exam table for each person, then opened it in between patients. I couldn't see or hear anything about Mayflower's citizens and didn't care to. Finally, my patience paid off. The room was empty, except for Sarah.

I picked up a pebble and tossed it at the window, but she didn't look. Glancing around, I snatched up a stick and tossed it against the window. Again, she didn't look. Desperate, I hefted a rock and tossed it at the window; albeit a bit harder than I had intended.

The glass cracked right down the middle.

Sarah's eyes locked on mine, and I felt my face flush. She mouthed, "Are you crazy?"

Oh, boy. I was either going to get a ticket or arrested and couldn't afford either. At the very least, this crazy idea needed to be worth it. I put my hands in a begging motion as I pleaded, "I need to talk to you."

She stood there for what seemed like an eternity, until Dr. Joy came in. I ducked back behind the bushes, the heel of my shoe sinking into the mush. After a minute, I stood up, but Sarah was gone. I felt as though I hadn't accomplished a thing except getting into more trouble. They were probably calling Officer Pickles this very moment.

I opened my cell to call and confess when from behind me I heard, "Oh, my word, sister. No wonder her daughter's sends inappropriate pictures to porn sites. She's got Peeping Tom for a mother."

"Peeping Tom indeed. Why, the streets of Mayflower aren't safe to walk anymore. Whatever happened to the good ole days when doctors made house calls?"

I closed my eyes and pressed my lips together. Only I could get caught peeping through a window by the gossip queens. Then I pasted on a bright smile and turned around as I trudged back through the snow to join Gerty and Gabby Rogers on the sidewalk. They stepped back and huddled together in their drab clothes, their enormous matching black purses nearly obscuring them.

"I'm not a Tom and I would never dream of peeping, I assure you. I saw some trash over by the bush below the window. I simply picked it up in my small effort to keep Mayflower clean."

Gerty still looked wary as she leaned to the side and stared at my flat coat pockets. "Trash you say? I don't see any trash, do you, sister?"

Gabby's gaze followed Gerty's. "Indeed not." *Tsk, tsk.*

I shoved my hands in my pockets and pulled out a tissue. "Trash is still trash, no matter how small, right?"

"That's always been my thought. All trash should be cleaned up, don't you agree, sister?"

"Precisely. And how is your daughter doing these days?" Gabby switched her bag to her other shoulder, wincing.

I narrowed my eyes. "Lexi's coping, thank you." I took a step forward, and they took another step back simultaneously, as though we were dancing. "Here, let me help you carry your bags inside. They must weigh more than both of you put together."

"No," they blurted in unison.

"Okay." If I didn't know better, I'd swear we were dancing around something.

"I mean a woman's purse is sacred. You must know that, Mrs. Robinson." Gerty's face looked paler than usual.

"I understand, but you might want to consider a smaller purse. That can't be good for your shoulders and back." I knew all about sore shoulders and bad back issues from lugging around heavy— ahem— things. Double Darlings were not exactly light.

"We'll do. Come along, sister. We mustn't keep that nice Dr. Anderson waiting."

"Indeed." Gabby smiled, and I swore a bit of color crept into her cheeks, but they hustled away faster than I'd ever imagined possible. What a pair. Lord only knew what gossip they'd spread now. I headed for my van and unlocked the door.

"You're crazy, you know that."

I whipped around and slapped a hand to my chest. "Sarah, thank God. I thought the less embarrassing thing to do would be to get your attention from outside instead of going back inside that office."

She grinned wide, not appearing angry like I had expected her to be.

"Yeah, I know. I thought wrong." I smiled back, worrying about how I was going to replace a window I couldn't afford.

"Ya think?" Sarah giggled.

"I really am sorry, Sarah, but you have to understand, there is nothing going on between Cha— Dr. Anderson— and me. We're just friends from back in high school, and now he wants me to plan his parents' retirement party. If I had known he was your mystery man, I would have made that clear before I had lunch with him."

"Fair enough." She flashed her dimples. "By the way, I wasn't avoiding your calls today. We've been swamped. If you'd checked your messages before you threw that rock, you would have seen I had just returned your call. You could have saved yourself several hundred bucks." She shook her head. "I repeat, you're crazy. Thanks for making me smile, though, and for explaining. It means a lot to me."

"In that case, I'm having dinner with Chaz tonight." I wanted to be right upfront this time.

Sarah blinked, surprise registering on her pixie face. "You go, girl." Her smile reached all the way to her eyes.

I frowned. Why was she smiling? "Strictly business," I clarified. "So I can get a look at his place since that's where he wants to hold the party. My kids will even be present, but you know how fast and twisted the rumor mill in this town is. I just wanted you to hear it from me first. I can even put in a good word for you if you want."

"Thanks, but that won't be necessary. It was a stretch anyway. I'm pretty sure I heard other women say he won't date anyone in the office."

"Well, he did say something to that affect." I winced, feeling bad for her. "It's okay. I've got my sights set on a younger guy on campus, now. Well, toodles. Gotta run before they miss me. I'll come up with some excuse for the window, but I'm sure you'll still get a bill."

"That's fine. Say hi to Dr. Joy for me."

"Oh, I almost forgot. Just so you know, Gerty and Gabby Rogers have formed a petition. They've been making the rounds all day, getting the citizens of Mayflower to sign it. Since your daughter is rumored to be the girl in the pictures and they were scandalously taken outside after dark, they're campaigning for the town to lower the current teen curfew of ten p.m. to dusk instead."

"It's March. Dusk is practically right after dinner. I can't imagine all the parents agreeing to this." That must have been what Brimstone was studying so carefully at lunch today. I was sure he gladly signed. No wonder those little busybodies didn't want me to help them with their bags. Unbelievable.

"I don't know, those sisters can be pretty persuasive. They have half the staff believing they're on death's door with their daily visits." She chuckled. "I really do have to go; I just thought you'd want to know."

"Thanks." I stood there, numb, not knowing quite what to do. Ever since I saw those pictures of Lexi on the Internet, I'd doubted her innocence. Yet a curfew that early was a bit extreme and affected all the town's teens. Everyone would blame Lexi, and she didn't need that right now. It was bad enough older boys kept calling the house and giving her more attention than I was comfortable with.

Speaking of unwanted attention and poor judgment. My judgment had been off with throwing the rock at the window among other things. Doubts about tonight's dinner consumed me like a bad case of heartburn after a hot and spicy meal. Something I did not need right now. What I needed was to be sure Chaz and I stayed just friends. I needed to be sure I wouldn't give Chaz any ideas that I'd changed my mind.

I needed a plan.

I PULLED into Chaz's brick driveway at six pm sharp and cut the engine to my minivan, ready to put my 'plan' into action. Wow, I thought, staring up at the enormous, brand-new Victorian with the wraparound porch. It had to be five thousand square feet. What on earth did he need with a house that big? Soft almond siding with hunter green shutters decorated the outside, and the mansion— compared to my falling down colonial, that was what it looked like— sat on a lot twice the size of any other house on the block.

Talk about clout. Looked like the zoning board had made more than a few allowances for their beloved Dr. Anderson. It didn't hurt that his parents were former members of the board, current members of the historical society and town council, and his father had even been mayor years ago.

"Must be nice to be rich." Lexi gazed up at the house while twirling a long caramel curl.

"Yeah, really. Look at that Beamer," Troy said with longing in his voice as he stared with stars in his baby blues. I hadn't seen him that excited about anything in quite some time.

"And look, Mommy, he even has a basketball hoop." Bobby

bounced on the bench seat in the back, his blond hair flopping about as the whole van shook. "Can I play, Mommy? Can I, can I, pleeeeease?"

"We'll see." I made eye contact with each of them. "Now, remember, this is a business dinner, but Chaz is very down to earth. He wants you to be comfortable, so feel free to be yourselves, okay?"

Lexi's gaze met mine, and her eyes formed little amber slivers. "What if my self wants to talk on my phone as much as I want?" She paused. "Even during dinner?"

Smart cookie. The sly vixen knew cell phones were forbidden during dinner, not to mention she was still grounded, but she also knew exactly what I was up to. I should have known she wouldn't agree without something being in it for her.

I ground my teeth and bit out, "Sure, honey. I just want you to feel comfortable." I felt something, all right. My cheeks growing warm. I cursed my fair complexion and prayed the sky would stay cloudy and the light dim.

Lexi shrugged. "What-ever."

"You're kidding." Troy gaped. "She gets to bring her cell in?" When I nodded, he added, "No way. Then I'm bringing my iPad in. I mean, *my self* can't be comfortable without my music and videos to relax to." He shot a look in Lexi's direction and wagged his brows as he threw in, "Especially during dinner."

I had to take a slow deep breath. Even smarter cookie. But letting some of my rules slide for the sake of my sanity would be worth it if they scared Chaz out of thinking he might ever want to have a romantic relationship with me. Because there was no 'me.' Only us. And 'us' could be quite overwhelming, on a good day.

"Like I said, whatever makes you comfortable." I tried for a smile, but it felt stiff.

"Oh boy, oh boy, oh boy. I'm gonna go exploring. I wonder if he has anything to make a sword out of, or even real big armor like yours, Mommy?" Bobby's bouncing grew faster, his front toothless smile spreading wide across his ruddy cheeks.

"You never know what you might find at a bachelor's house," I muttered and glanced at the windows, wondering which bedroom was Chaz's. Blood throbbed through my veins. I smoothed a hand over my curls, then turned back to Bobby. "Make sure you explore every nook and cranny, now. And don't worry if you make a mess. I'm sure the doctor has a maid with a house this big."

Katy started to cry. Okay, more like wail. It had always amazed me such a loud, high-pitched sound could come out of such a small body.

"Shhh. What's wrong, sweetie?" I reached back to her booster seat and rubbed her tiny hand.

"My self don't have no phone cell or pad with eyes or swords." She looked down at her chest and wailed even louder. "And I don't ever think I'm gonna have armor like you. How's my self gonna be comfy?"

I bit back a laugh. Her real tears ripped my heart apart, but I knew my daughter, oh queen of the drama. I cupped her pink cheek and swiped the crocodile tears away with my thumb. "Would your self feel comfy if it had a few cookies?"

Wet amber eyes blinked back at me, and the sobbing hiccups ceased in an instant. She nailed me with a toothy smile and nodded so hard her brown curls flew in twenty different directions like an out-of-control bobble head. "Does my self get to have my cookies during dinner, too?"

I did laugh out loud at that one. "Why not," I answered. There goes my smartest cookie yet.

"Well, *my* self can't wait any more. Ready, Mommy?" Wound tighter than the Tasmanian Devil, Bobby squeezed past everyone. The second the sliding door opened, he whirled out of the van like a tornado.

Chaz didn't stand a chance.

I almost felt sorry for him, but then I remembered the way he made my insides feel. I couldn't afford for Mount Saint Zoe to go off with the future of my career on the line. And I couldn't afford for my kids to get attached to the charming doctor, only to have him disappear from their lives as well. But most of all, I couldn't afford to go through that kind of heartache ever again.

The rest of us got out of the car just as Chaz opened the door. His eyes connected with mine, and that darn Ping Pong match started up in my chest again. Oh, yeah. Something told me if I let him in, I would have my biggest heartache yet. I could only pray my kids would work their magic. Bobby charged through the door and bolted straight up the stairs, snow covered shoes and all. I smiled, feeling my confidence return.

Chaz's mouth fell open, but I had to give him credit. He recovered quickly and smiled back in my direction, waving for us to join him.

Showtime.

"Come on, guys, let's go get *comfy*."

I led the way to the door with the rest of my brood following close behind, while Chaz stepped back and ushered each of the kids inside. And then there were two. We just stood there, staring for a moment, until his lips tipped up in such a warm, genuine smile, I couldn't help but return the action.

"Zoe." He tilted his head.

"Chaz." I tilted mine.

Then he cleared his throat, and I blinked. What the hell was wrong with me? I swear, no matter what mindset I approached a Dr. Hunkorama situation with, the minute I laid eyes on him, my set mind went poof, and I turned into a dimwitted buffoon. I knew this was hard for him, and I sure wasn't making it easy.

"May I come in? It's freezing out here." I rubbed my arms through my coat. Nearly half the snow from that late March nor'easter had melted, but the temperature still hovered a breath above the freezing mark. An odd contrast to the sound of robins chirping on the roof.

"Sorry." He stepped back and pushed the door wider.

I knew his house would be beautiful, but nothing could have prepared me for the enormous windows, cathedral ceiling, massive chandelier, and sweeping staircase. And that was just the foyer. The houses people owned around here were mostly renovated old Cape Cods and colonials. Nothing this grand or modern, especially right in town. Hope Lane ran perpendicular to Lighthouse Lane, where the heart of Mayflower existed. A fantastic location, to say the least.

"Wow," I said on a breathy sigh. "This is amazing, Chaz."

I took off my coat and hung it in the closet, then picked up the pile of coats my kids had dropped on the floor and did the same. They had taken me at my word, that was for sure. This never would have happened at home. I slipped my shoes off, noticing none of my kids had. Another thing they would never have gotten away with at home. I had to remind myself this was a necessary evil to keep my sanity intact. He wasn't the problem. I was. I needed to convince him I wasn't worth the trouble. Still, second thoughts penetrated my brain as the gleaming hardwoods and top-of-the-line light fixtures registered.

Chaz's whiskey-smooth voice cut through my thoughts. "Care for a tour?" He was on his best behavior and hadn't done anything inappropriate, yet searing heat scorched my system, obliterating those second thoughts.

I cleared my throat and stepped forward. "Sure. Lead the way, Doc."

Such a bad idea.

I couldn't help staring at the nicest, firmest butt I'd seen in way too long to remember. He had worn casual pants and dress slacks before, but the jeans he had on now were snug enough to show his glutes flexing as he climbed the stairs. Meanwhile, my gluts— or lack thereof— wiggled as I walked behind him. Oh, yeah, those darn Oreos went straight to my big ole behind.

The upstairs consisted of five large bedrooms and two huge bathrooms with double sinks. White paint covered the walls, that "new" smell still lingering, and none of the rooms were furnished. I ran my hand along the windowsill as I looked down at the street below.

"The rooms are spacious, but I see you haven't gotten around to decorating them yet."

"I'm not really good with that stuff." He shrugged, glancing back at me. "I thought maybe one day I would have someone in my life to help with that."

I had the strongest urge to offer my services. I blinked. *Where... are... my... kids?*

When I wanted them to disappear, they were always underfoot, but when I needed them, they were nowhere to be found. I broke eye contact and moved out into the hallway. Resting my hands on the half wall, I stared down into the living room, but only saw the massive fireplace with the enormous plasma TV above it and genuine black leather U-shaped couch in front of it.

"The kids are awfully quiet," I said.

"Isn't that a good thing?"

I laughed. "Um, no." Poor guy grew up an only child. He didn't have a clue when it came to kids, so scaring him away should be a piece of cake. If I could find the little monsters, that is. "We'd better go check on them."

"Sure. I'll show you the rest of the house along the way."

We passed a formal living room, with a bay window overlooking Hope Lane, and floor-to-ceiling bookshelves. I had always wanted a library-type room just like this. Longing rippled through me, but I tamped it down. My renovations were coming along, albeit as slow as Grandma Robinson with her walker, but progress nonetheless.

The dining room contained a trey ceiling and a chair rail made out of the most intricate crown molding I had ever seen and hosted a real oak table with a matching hutch. But when we turned the corner, I stopped in my tracks and gasped as I gazed upon my dream kitchen come to life.

Tons of counter space, tiled backdrop, quartz countertops, an island the size of my harvest table with a flattop range built right in. A large black iron wagon wheel hung above it, with cast iron pots and pans dangling. A second oven and microwave were built into the wall beside the cabinets, right next to the wine bar and breakfast nook. And all the dishes matched.

My self could be very comfy spending the rest of my days in a kitchen like this.

This was exactly how I would remodel my kitchen, if I had the money. I closed my eyes and inhaled the scent of oregano, basil and garlic oozing from the pot of sauce simmering on the stove and felt myself swoon.

"Zoe? You okay?" Chaz placed his hand on my back.

I jerked into motion. "The kids. I need to check on the kids. Now." I headed in the direction of noise, desperate for my children to misbehave, then shook my head over that thought.

Poking my nose into an office, I wilted in relief. Attagirl. Lexi didn't even hear us since she had made herself at home, chatting on her cell phone while simultaneously surfing the Internet on Chaz's computer without even asking. Normally, I would have a fit, but today, this was just the type of behavior I had hoped for.

"Oh...." Chaz said from behind me.

"I'm sorry, she seems to have forgotten her manners. I'll tell her she has to get off."

"That's okay. As long as she doesn't go into any of my medical files, she's fine." He patted my arm.

I frowned. "Okay, then." I bit my lip and continued to search for my other children, hoping they would have more of an effect on him.

Troy had plopped his butt in a comfy-looking chair with his feet up on a glass coffee table, shoes and all. He had his iPad blaring, and the TV even louder, surfing the endless streaming services.

"I can have him turn that down if you want." I peered up at Chaz, waiting.

Chaz stared at Troy's sneakers dripping on the glass table, and looked as though the volume on the TV was the last thing on his mind. His sandy brows formed a deep V and he pursed his lips, then seemed to make up his mind about something. "It's only glass. It'll wipe clean. And you can't hear this TV in the kitchen anyway, so he's fine. Really." Chaz smiled at me.

I frowned harder.

He didn't seem to notice as he continued down the hall and entered the half bath before I did. He must have found Katy since he knelt down and spoke in soft tones. "What's the matter, angel?"

I peeked over his shoulder and saw Katy standing there with her bottom lip trembling as fast as one of her happy meal, wind-up toys. Uh, oh. That could only mean one thing. I plugged my ears two seconds before her loudest wail yet poured out of her.

Chaz jerked back, falling over. He recovered quickly as he rolled to his knees and rubbed Katy's back. "Whoa, hey, now. Whatever happened can't be that bad." He stared up at me with the most adorable helpless expression, and my heart melted.

Having pity on him, I said, "Come here, baby." As I held out my arms, Chaz's mouth fell open, and I bit back a laugh. When Katy climbed over him to get to me, his face took on a sheepish look and a twisted smile. "Did you have an accident, sweetie?"

"I was playing dress-up and looking for armor with Bobby. I didn't want to stop, but then I didn't make it to the potty." She wailed even louder.

"Accident?" Chaz's face paled and he gaped down at the floor, just now realizing what he was kneeling in. "Oh, shi-uger." He jumped to his feet.

"I should probably go home and change her," I said, relieved my plan had worked. I didn't think I'd last a whole evening with Charming Chaz.

Katy wailed louder still. "I don't want to go. My self didn't get my comfy cookie yet."

"I have a t-shirt she can change into, and you could tie a knot in my boxers. They'll be more like pants on her, but they should work," Chaz offered.

"Y-Your t-shirt and boxers?"

His eyes crinkled up at the corners. "My dresser is at your service again, my lady."

"Funny."

"I try."

I thought about my daughter's naked bum in the good doctor's boxers. Yeah, not gonna happen. "How about draw string gym shorts. Have any of those?"

"Even better. They're in the drawer below my t-shirts and boxers. Help yourself."

"But what about the mess on your floor? Aren't you dying for us to go before some other catastrophe happens?" I grasped for straws. No matter what happened, he seemed to roll with it. Not what I had expected in the least.

"Not a chance. It's no big deal, Zoe. My bedroom is down the hall. Go change her, and I'll clean up the mess in here."

"Okay, but don't say I didn't warn you. My brood can be a

whole lot more than a handful." I headed down the hall. "Sooo not what I'd expected," I repeated under my breath.

At the end of the hall, I entered what had to be the master suite. "Oh. My. God!" The room was enormous, housing a massive four-poster king-sized bed and a sitting room, for crying out loud. It smelled like Chaz— musk and man, combined in an intoxicating mixture of eau de yumminess— but what caught my eye were the piles of clothes all over the floor. Chaz was neat and orderly. This had to be the handiwork of one bouncy little devil.

I picked up a t-shirt and a pair of gym shorts to change Katy into, tamping down the urge to yell at the guilty culprit. This was what I had asked for, even though they had all broken just about every rule I'd ever set. It would undoubtedly take me months to set them straight again.

Bobby came bouncing out of a huge walk-in closet, wearing a pair of Chaz's tennis shorts and shirt while carrying... oh, good Lord in heaven....

"He didn't have any armor, Mommy, but I found something better. A sling shot." He held up Chaz's jock strap and pointed it away from me, toward the door. "I even found a ball." He hooked the straps over one hand, put a tennis ball in the cup, pulled back hard and....

"Bobby, put that down. It might not be clean," I said a little too late.

Chaz stepped in the doorway just as Bobby let her rip.

"Ooomph." Chaz doubled over and dropped to the floor like he'd gone a round with an MMA fighter. "He found a ball, all right," he ground out through clenched teeth, then let out the most painful moan I'd ever heard.

Katy began to wail again.

Bobby started to cry.

Troy bolted in with his jaw hanging open.

Lexi ran in and let out a giggle beneath her clamped hand.

And I realized things had gone... way... too... far.

"Oh, my God, I'm so sorry, Chaz." I sprang into action, tossing the t-shirt and shorts at Lexi and dropping down to Chaz's side. "Lexi, change your sister. Bobby, get out of those clothes. Troy, get some ice."

An hour later, after a surprisingly productive business dinner and the most delicious homemade spaghetti sauce I had ever tasted, Chaz stood at the door, waving goodbye to my kids through the van window. I kept my eyes locked on his, trying in vain not to stare at his bull-legged stance and baggy running suit that didn't quite hide the huge bulge between his legs. Bobby's sling shot had come in handy as an ice pack holder. I just prayed we hadn't done any permanent damage.

"I really am sorry, Chaz."

"Zoe, I said it's okay. Your children were perfect angels all through dinner, same as the day I met them. Nothing at all like the little heathens who invaded my house earlier." He narrowed his gaze. "Can't imagine what got into them."

"Me neither." My eyes skirted away.

"Right," he said. My gaze snapped back to his, and I saw the twinkle as he continued, "Seriously, though. Kids will be kids, and you've got a pretty great group, if you ask me."

"Thanks." We stared at each other for what seemed like a full minute, and I suddenly didn't want to go. I had even managed to eat in front of him, no cramps or clenching in sight. He didn't look like he was in any hurry for me to leave, either.

Well, shoot. So much for scaring him away.

Chapter Seven

"What am I supposed to do now?" I asked the girls on Sunday night in Harmony's apartment above her New Age shop.

It was her night as host, so her night to vent. She was too frustrated with her mother to talk about her problems. That's where I came in. Tonight's theme was Mexican, and with the way things were going, I was more than ready to drown my woes in another margarita. Though the incense candle burning in the kitchen was giving me a whopper of a headache.

"You're supposed to lighten up and have some fun. Why can't you just roll with it? Dating doesn't have to lead to marriage. If it did, I'd never go out, and I go out all the time." After Tiffany's marriage to a lazy, freeloading bum had ended in a bitter divorce with her making monthly alimony payments, she had vowed never to marry again. From then on, she had been the one doing the using.

"I like men. They're purty. At least I make them purty," Morticia said, sitting crisscross applesauce on the faux fur rug in front of the Ouija board painted wooden slab that sat atop a couple of milk crates. Basically, Harmony's idea of a coffee table. "But the ones I like always leave on a permanent vacation, six feet under."

"And you wonder why men don't ask you out." Harmony shook her short, red, spiky head of hair, then sank her teeth into a gooey beef and cheese burrito. Harmony made a mean burrito, loaded with chili peppers and hot sauce, her cooking as tough as she was.

"It's not her fault the living don't get her sense of humor." Tiffany reclined on the tie-dye, throw-covered couch with her bare feet tucked under her. She ran an elegant finger around the rim of her margarita glass, then took a dainty sip.

"Doesn't help that Lolita loves to convince every man who's ever talked to me that I'm weird. She never did get over me beating her out of that cheerleading spot. Grow up, already, right?" Morticia shrugged. "I wouldn't normally care, but the dead ones can't give me a baby, and that's what I want more than anything." She raised a black brow above big dark eyes. "Or can they?"

"That's sick." Harmony snorted.

"Apparently you don't get my sense of humor, either." Morticia frowned. "I'm just kidding."

"I know, me too. Love ya, honey, but your sense of humor can be a bit morbid." Harmony winked.

Morticia sighed and nodded simultaneously. "Yup, that would be it. You're definitely not morbid," she pointed to Harmony, "but you sure as hell aren't normal."

Harmony barked out a laugh. "Touché, sister." She walked through the hanging beads to get to the kitchen, then returned with the margarita pitcher for us and a Diet Cola for Morticia.

"As for me, I'd settle for some sex. To heck with a baby." Harmony refilled our glasses, then set the pitcher on the coffee table. "Men. They say they are okay with women calling the shots, making the plans, and deciding on everything. But the men I've met really aren't. Why can't any of them— living or dead— deal with a woman being in charge?" She huffed out a breath, her frustration evident. "And my mother is driving me insane."

"What mother doesn't," I said, thinking of my own mother issues as I sipped my margarita. Add in my ex-mother-in-law— who refused to believe the 'ex' part and was still very much my children's grandmother— and I could relate to Harm's 'driving me crazy' statement.

No matter how old children grew, mothers never stopped mothering.

"I love your mother, Harm." Tiffany sucked a margarita drop from her fingertip and finished with, "Wish mine was more like her." Okay, so I take that back. Some mothers actually did stop mothering and never looked back. Good thing for Tiffany she had her grandmother.

"Well at least you didn't grow up an orphan." Morticia held a hand to halt our protests. "Being raised by a crazy mortician for a father doesn't count."

"I'm not saying I don't love my mother, but if she calls one more time trying to get me to go to another fashion show and tea party, I'm going to drag her to a monster truck rally and pour a beer down her throat." Harmony licked the salt off her wrist, tossed back a straight shot of tequila, and bit into a slice of lemon without so much as a wince. "I mean, what the hell does she expect? I have seven older brothers, for crying out loud, and she wants me to be more 'girly'."

"Yeah, that ain't happenin'." Morticia chuckled.

"Like you're a regular ballerina, there, Tinkerbelle." Harmony smirked.

"You both have so much potential, if you'd just—" Tiffany started to say, but the other two were having none of that.

"Spoken like Cinderella herself." Harmony rolled her eyes. "Guess that makes us the wicked stepsisters."

"Wicked." Morticia nodded once. "I can live with that." They laughed and reached out to high-five.

Harmony and Morticia lived for sparring with each other and thrived on thinking up a better comeback, but especially loved joining forces to team up against Tiffany. She was the smoothest of our friend group, only she didn't rattle easily. One of these days she'd meet her match, and I for one, couldn't wait to see how she would handle falling off her pedestal. Still, we all loved each other immensely, and we all had each other's backs, no questions asked.

"As much as I hate to break up this fairy tale, I need help, ladies." I downed the rest of my drink. "I'm so out of my element here."

"Yes, mother," Harmony and Morticia said in unison, then shot each other devilish grins as they added simultaneously, "Great minds," then broke out into peals of laughter once again.

Tiffany shook her head, but her lips tipped up a hair as she looked at me. "Ignore them, step-mummy, the floor's all yours."

"Very funny." I wrung my hands, then jumped into my current issue. "I just have no idea what to do."

"About the petition?" Morticia studied me as she wiped her hands on a napkin. For someone so quiet, not much got by her.

I nodded. "The Rogers sisters are organizing a town meeting for everyone to vote on the curfew next month. The little old biddies think our whole generation has fallen apart, and our children have run amok."

"Think about it, doll. I'm sure people from their generation didn't take intimate pictures, let alone have much sex. Naturally, they're scandalized." Tiffany patted my hand in sympathy. "I'm surprised they haven't gone to the emergency room for heart palpitations. Hell, they've certainly gone in for everything else."

"I know, but I can't say I totally disagree with them. Although, I don't think the answer is lowering the curfew to that extreme. The backlash is going to be awful for Lexi. She's already lost some friends."

"Well, that sucks." Harmony chugged another shot, wiping her hands on her jeans. "Seems to me there's only one thing we can do."

"Clear her name." Morticia stretched out on the fur rug, crossing her sweatpants-clad legs at the ankles.

"Exactly," Harmony said.

"I'd love to, but...." I couldn't finish my sentence.

"I know you have doubts about Lexi's innocence, Zoe." Tiffany fixed me with a baffled look that said she had no clue why.

None of them did, because none of them had children. The pressure to raise kids right in today's world was overwhelming enough, but as a single parent, it was simply terrifying. My greatest fear was at least one of mine would end up on reality TV, saying I turned out this way because of her, pointing the finger at me.

"Look at it this way," Tiffany continued. "In trying to clear her name, you'll find your answers once and for all."

She had a point. They all did. While they might not know anything about parenting, they knew me. If I didn't do a little digging, then I would never know what was going on with Lexi, which basically meant, I would never be at peace. Besides, at this point, I had nothing left to lose. I couldn't lose any more business than I already had, and Lexi was still furious with me.

We spent the next half hour, throwing out ideas on how we were going to go about the investigation, until we came up with a plan.

"Thanks, guys, I don't know what I would do without you." I sighed. "I'm beginning to think Bitsy's going to win. With all that's going on in my life right now, I'm off my game. Let's just say Chaz throws me *way* off my game, yet I can't avoid him. He's the only person giving me work these days, and planning his parents' retirement party is just the break I need to get the mayor to take me seriously."

"So plan the party." Tiffany looked at me as though the answer was that simple.

"How am I supposed to do that? I told Chaz I just wanted to be friends. He's been so good at respecting that. I'm the problem. I don't want to give in, so I need him to stay strong. Shoot, I even let loose my kids on him as a reality check, thinking he wouldn't want anything to do with me ever. I'm telling you, nothing works. The guy's a hero." I grabbed the bottle of tequila and took a swig, then went into a major coughing fit. How did Harmony do that?

Harmony whacked me between the shoulder blades. "It comes down to one thing in my book." She paused until she had my full attention. "Does he flick your Bic?"

"Flick my what?" My face puckered as though I had just bitten into a lemon.

Her green cat eyes pierced me, and she spoke slower and louder. "Does... he... turn... you... on?"

"I'm not deaf or dumb," I snapped.

"You're not happy being celibate, either," Morticia observed, and three pair of eyes locked onto mine like piranha moving in for the kill.

"Oh, all right, I admit it." I felt the blood flood my face, regretting the words the instant they came out.

"Yes!" Harmony got up and danced a little ditty. "I win, ladies." Morticia and Tiffany scowled but each handed over a twenty to Harmony.

"You guys are terrible, wagering money on me." I tried to appear outraged, but it didn't surprise me. We had done this sort of thing to each other since we were kids.

"Oh, please, like you haven't done your share of betting in the past." Harmony stuffed the money in her jeans pocket.

"Yeah, but you have an unfair advantage. From here on out, no more using your tarot cards or Oujia boards to predict the future, okay?" Tiffany nailed Harmony with a serious look.

"Fair enough." Harmony turned to me and grinned wide. "Don't think you're getting off that easy. Details, babe."

There was no turning back now, so I closed my eyes and conjured up Chaz, then let the words spill out. "Every time he looks at me, I melt like a blob of ice cream and he's the hot fudge oozing all over me until nothing is left but a puddle. When he talks, my insides quiver like guitar strings stroked by his voice, only they're coiled way too tight. And when he touches me, I... I... oh, hell, all I know is I can't take the pressure anymore."

I opened my eyes and found them all staring at me, mouths agape and faces slightly flushed.

"Ladies, I'm about to snap at any moment, and I'm terrified of what will happen when I do. You have to help me!"

Harmony fanned her face. "Damn, woman, you've got it bad." She looked as though she were giving the matter serious thought. "I think Tiff is right. If you can't beat him, join him. You have to sleep with the guy and get him out of your system, that's all there is to it."

I got up and started to pace, the burrito and margarita doing a bad imitation of the salsa in my belly. Way too much shaking going on. "Nope, no way, not a chance," I managed.

"Why not? It's just sex." Tiffany uncurled herself from the couch and stretched into another pretzel-style, yoga pose. "It was your idea before when you thought he was a complete stranger."

"And look how that turned out. Now that I know who he is, there's no way I could go through with it. I don't know what I was thinking before. I don't do 'just sex.' I haven't done 'just sex' in years. I don't even know if I remember how."

Tiff paused mid-stretch and smiled gently. "Honey, that's not something *anyone* forgets."

"Okay, so even if I remember how, I don't have the body I used to. What if I disappoint him?" I rubbed my stomach. "Good Lord, Harmony, what did you put in those burritos, anyway?"

"I don't know, a little of this, a little of that, and a whole lot of kick, why?"

"Because they're thisin' and thatin' and kickin' their way through a spicy mambo as we speak." I headed to the kitchen. "Got any antacids?"

"Top drawer on the left beneath the beer nuts. Right next to the book on hexes."

"Geez, Harm, what are you, a witch?" I asked as I found the antacids and chewed a couple, then chased them with water, praying the music would change to a nice calm waltz as I headed back into the living room.

"I wish, then I could put a curse on all my lame dates."

"Better not be putting a curse on me." Morticia grunted.

"Honey, you were cursed the day you were born." Harmony snorted.

"Said the pot to the kettle." Morticia turned to me. "You look great, Zoe. You've earned every mark." She smiled, adding, "Besides, he'll be focused on a pair of your biggest assets. The rest will fade away. Trust me."

"Chaz is a doctor. He sees women all the time," Harmony said.

"That's my point. I don't want to be compared to other

women and come up lacking. He looks like a model. Sleeping with him is *not* an option."

"Well, there is one other solution." Tiffany's gaze met the others, and they all turned to me with wide grins and mischievous eyes.

"Oh, God, I'm going to have to use one of those, aren't I?" My whole body shook at the mere thought.

"You want to clear Lexi's name and win the mayor's bid, all while keeping your sanity, yet you won't sleep with Chaz. Yeah, you're gonna have to use one of those." Tiffany laughed. "Don't look so appalled, doll, once you try it, you're gonna be hooked. It's really not that big a deal."

"But I don't even know where to get one without everyone in town knowing."

"I know the perfect place in Boston," Tiffany said. "Anyone up for a road trip tomorrow?"

"I'll get Denny to cover for me. No way I'm missing this," Harmony said.

"Oh yeah, count me in. My dad owes me. He's been gone so much, he'll cover for me," Morticia said.

"It's up to you, Zoe. We could leave right after your kids get on the bus, and you know Mrs. Bee would take Katy to preschool and pick her up, so what do you say?" Tiffany asked.

Three determined sets of eyes on a mission stared at me, waiting to see what I would do. Sex with Chaz, or shopping in an adult toy store for my first vibrator, and then finding the courage to actually use the stupid thing.

"Let's do it," I said without hesitation, and nearly passed out. What in God's name had I just agreed to?

"You've got to be kidding me," I said, sinking lower in the passenger seat of Tiffany's bright red convertible. At least she'd left the top up. Still, nothing like standing out in a bad section of Boston, but the alternatives were worse. I should have just bought the stupid thing online, but I wouldn't have a clue what kind to get. There were so many options. Not to mention, I would be mortified if Truman mixed up that piece of mail. So I sank down lower in Tiffany's car.

Mrs. Bee needed my minivan to take Katy to school, and no way was I riding in Morticia's hearse or Harmony's rust bucket tie-dyed love bug with holes in the floor. The red convertible had been the least conspicuous, but still... what had I been thinking? "I can't go in there."

"Sure, you can. The sign on the door says no one under twenty-one, not forty-one," Harmony chimed in from the back seat. "I'll bet they love women on the verge of menopause."

"Thanks for the reminder my eggs are practically dead before I even have a chance to hatch them," Morticia added from right beside her.

Harmony snorted. "Your eggs might be, but I'll bet your libido isn't, or you wouldn't have tagged along."

"Look who's talking." Tiffany glanced in the rear-view mirror.

"Hey, I'm not denying it. I plan on getting acquainted with a few new friends in there." Harmony gripped the door handle. "Let's go, ladies."

"Wait." I started breathing heavy, and my libido had *nothing* to do with it. "Look at that place. There are no windows, no advertising, no bright colors to draw attention. Just a shady-looking cement building with a big sign on the door that says, 'No cameras allowed.' I haven't seen a single woman go in there, just a bunch of old men, and none of them have come out." My palms began to sweat. "What if they don't let you leave?"

"Oh, look, there's a man coming out now." Tiffany leaned forward and squinted. "What's he got in his hand?"

A well-dressed man with white hair ambled out, carrying a long, bagged item stuffed between two newspapers, his eyes shifting left and right before he ducked into an expensive-looking car. Two more gray-haired men followed, also carrying bagged items hidden between newspapers. Then a couple of bald older men emerged, again with the newspapers and nice cars.

"What is this, lifestyles of the rich and infamous?" Morticia asked.

"More like a retired newspaper convention." Harmony laughed. "Must have some interesting headlines today. Let's go see."

"I'm in. Reading's good for your mind." Morticia opened her door and climbed out, allowing a swirl of spring breeze in, the chill of winter struggling to hang on.

Harmony buttoned her coat and followed suit." And I'm banking that whatever's inside will be damn good for your body."

"You expect me to go in with them?" I squeaked, as I watched them practically skip with the excitement of children about to receive a special present.

Tiffany laughed. "Come on. I've got your back."

"It's not my back I'm worried about," I muttered, but stepped out anyway. Might as well get this over with because I knew they would never let me leave without at least going in.

Harmony and Morticia must have gone inside already because they were nowhere to be found, but at least I still had Tiffany.

Halfway there, Tiffany said, "Hold up, Zoe. I forgot to tell you to lock your purse in the car. Trust me, you only want to bring some cash with you in a place like this." She took my purse and headed back to the car, hollering over her shoulder, "Go on in, I'll catch up in a minute."

Like it mattered anyway. If someone wanted to break into her convertible, all they had to do was slice through the vinyl top. So much for not being on my own. I pulled the hood of my red cloak up over my head and started walking again. This was ridiculous. I was a grown woman afraid to go into a toy store, for crying out loud. Based on the size of those newspapers, the toys had to be big and scary, but still. How bad could it be?

As I neared the building, I noticed there were two doors. One had a No Cameras Allowed sign and no windows, where the other said, "Gentleman's Club." So far, I had only seen men enter door number one, and a lanky blonde had just gone into door number two. Besides, anything with the word 'gentleman' on it had to be better than 'no cameras allowed,' so I chose door number two.

Big mistake.

As soon as I entered, I noticed the only women behind this door were employees. From what I could see through the dimly lit room, they sure were working their goods on those poles, and the so-called gentleman were enjoying the show from the peanut gallery down below the stage. Not a job I ever cared to have. And I could only imagine what was going on in the curtained rooms against the back wall.

From behind me, a male voice said, "Hey there, Little Red Riding Hood, your big bad wolf is ready for a nibble. Don't worry, honey, my teeth aren't the only thing that's big."

A familiar male voice. I gasped, and I turned around to gape. *Oh. My. God.*

"Principal Brimstone?" I stuttered, breathing through my mouth to avoid the ever-present raid smell.

He stood there frozen like a wax statue, his eyes all bugged-out like a cartoon character, and all I could hear in my head was *ahoooga*! Maybe he thought I worked here, since there were no women around except employees. My gaze dropped. Oh my, he wasn't kidding when he said big. He wore a thong, but still. I shook my head to clear it, and snapped my eyes up to his, forcing them to stay put.

I really didn't want to know what big 'anything' he had, but I couldn't stop the words, "What the devil are *you* doing here?" from slipping out.

He jerked into motion, fidgeting all over the place. "Oh, I, um...." His eyes darted left and right, then he threw his hands up in the air. "I got nothin'." He backed up toward the door, looking desperate to escape. He wasn't the only one who wished he'd never gone over the river and through the woods, and this sure as heck wasn't grandma's house.

And he thought my *daughter's* actions were highly inappropriate? Ha! He had some nerve.

"You know, you really need to learn to rein in your hormones if you're going to stay out of trouble." I couldn't resist throwing his words back at him.

His eyes widened, then he blurted, "The prom job is yours."

"Oh, no, that's not why I said that. I was just making a point," I finally got out. I would never resort to blackmail, even though Bitsy had resorted to all kinds of tricks to steal party planning jobs away from me. I wanted to win by my merits, not by sinking to her level. "You don't have to—"

"I insist."

"But what about Ms. Beaumont?"

"Bitsy— I mean— Ms. Beaumont will just have to deal with it." His eyes looked wild, and he grabbed the door handle. "Remember, what happens on the boulevard, stays on the boulevard, right?" He was single, and he was of age. I really didn't care to know about his sex life, as long as it didn't involve my children... or me. I shuddered.

"Trust me," I said. "I don't want anyone to know I was here any more than you do."

Most of the citizens of Mayflower thought of me as this pure innocent woman who'd been wronged by her ex-husband. They would never understand my trip to Adult World, any more than they had understood my daughter posing for inappropriate pictures. I didn't quite understand how I had ended up here, either, other than my girls were a force to be reckoned with— harmless on their own, but when combined, literally unstoppable.

Principal Brimstone disappeared, and not ten seconds later, that unstoppable force barged through the door like Charlie's Angels meets Arnold Schwarzenegger. If any one of them said, "I'll be back," they could darn well come back on their own.

"I can't leave you alone for five minutes, doll." Tiffany took my arm and steered me toward the door, while Harmony and Morticia backed her up, giving the men who had emerged from the curtained rooms a look that sent them scurrying back inside.

"How was I supposed to know this was the wrong door?" I muttered as I allowed them to lead me outside and through the correct door. The scary 'no cameras allowed' door, which turned out to be a whole lot less scary than the 'gentleman's club' door.

"You really have been sheltered if you've never heard of a gentleman's club." Harmony headed to the shelves in the back.

"Now, how would I have heard about that? I was with Max since high school, and it's only been two years since he left. All I can say is there was nothing 'gentlemanly' about what the guys behind those curtains were doing, according to the grunts and moans I heard." I shook my head and scanned the inside of this toy store. Rows of magazines and books lined the shelves, with aisles and aisles of God knew what. I was afraid to look and wouldn't dream of touching. "There has to be a better way," I muttered.

"As your friends, we'll support you no matter what you decide you want to do." Morticia squeezed my arm then headed toward the back to join Harmony.

"Thanks. You guys are the best friends." I followed close behind, not about to be left alone in the front and still unsure of what I wanted to do.

Harmony turned around and held up her hands. "Say hello to *my* little friends."

I let out a little scream and hopped back a good foot, knocking over a whole rack of the freakiest-looking adult toys I could have ever imagined. She might not be holding a machine gun like Al Pacino in *Scarface*, but those 'things' looked just as deadly. I glanced at the paraphernalia strewn about on the floor surrounding me.

"Why on earth do they sell necklaces in a place like this?" I asked, picking up a strand of beads.

"Doll, those are beads, but they don't go around your neck." Tiffany struggled not to laugh, soon giving up the futile effort.

"Then where do they go?" I couldn't help asking, curiosity getting the best of me.

"Try down south." Morticia pressed her lips together.

"In the va-jay-jay?" I arched a brow.

"Va-nay-nay, babe." Harmony chuckled.

"Oh, my God." I dropped the beads and scrambled to my feet with a desperate need to wash my hands, even though the *butt-laces* were still in their wrapper. "That's downright scary to me." I shuddered.

"Hey, to each his own." Harmony put the beads back on the shelf.

"Max and I never used anything like this. I, honestly, didn't even realize these kinds of things existed. We never watched sexy movies together. Maybe he was bored and that's part of the reason he left."

"More like he was the boring one if he never even asked you to try something new," Tiffany said, shaking her head in disgust.

"He was lazy." Morticia shrugged. "You deserved better."

"Damn right she does," Harmony said, "and we're about to show her how to play."

I was an adult, but I had no desire to *play* with any of those toys. They were far too intimidating and made me feel old. "I can't do this. It was a big mistake. Can we just get out of here?" I didn't wait for an answer and headed for the door, out to the car, not even bothering to put up my hood.

Ten minutes later, the rest of the girls joined me, and every single one of them carried a package wrapped in newspaper. My jaw fell open, and I shook my head as they all grinned from ear-to-ear.

"Like I said, great headlines." Harmony chuckled.

"And great minds think alike." Tiffany winked.

"Gotta love reading." Morticia laughed.

They got in the car, and I joined them. Like I had a choice. But when they handed me my very own newspaper wrapped surprise, I gasped. "No way."

"Yes way." When I wouldn't take it, Harmony set the package in my lap. "Don't worry, there's no 'jewelry' in there. Even *we* wouldn't do that to you. It's just a little friend of your very own. You don't have to use it if you don't want, just keep an open mind."

"I'm telling you. I'll never be able to use one of these, you know." I stuffed the package into the canvas bag I brought.

"Set the mood, and you'll be fine," Morticia said.

"But what if someone finds out?"

"No one is going to find out, Zoe. You really are making too big a deal out of this. Use it or don't. The choice is yours." Tiffany started the car and headed home, for once, leaving me to my thoughts.

Could I actually do this? My stomach churned, and my throat felt like I'd eaten dirt during a dust storm. This was ridiculous. Women used vibrators all the time. Up until two years ago, I'd had weekly sex. I had thought it was good because I didn't have anything to compare it to. I was beginning to realize our sex life had been basic at best. Now I felt old and past my expiration date to start over— another thing Max had taken away from me— so it was only natural I had newly discovered needs. The alternative was sleeping with Chaz, which really wasn't an option. Once again, I asked, could I actually do this? Then I came to a simple conclusion.

There was only one way to find out.

Chapter Eight

Later that night, after Bobby's last basketball game, helping Troy struggle through his homework, bathing and tucking Katy into bed, cleaning up the dinner dishes, working on the house repairs for about an hour, and brainstorming ideas for Chaz's party... I'd about had it. The phone rang, but I let the machine get it. I was not up to talking to my mother, and the last thing I needed was to get into yet another argument with Lexi, but the universe didn't care about what I needed.

Life had a tendency to go on no matter what. I had learned that the hard way after Max left. What I resented most was he hadn't even said anything to my face. Just left me a note, took off, and sent quickie divorce papers from Mexico in the mail. All those years together, and I hadn't even warranted a court battle.

I would've even settled for an argument. I'd never been able to tell him how I felt even through a letter because he never stayed in one place long enough. And tracking down child support was nearly impossible. He occasionally sent money when he felt like it, but it was never consistent and never enough.

There had been no closure, and I was afraid there never would be. I had four children who needed me, so no matter how much I wanted to curl up in a ball and die of self-pity, I knew I couldn't. No more than I could give up on Lexi now.

"I can't believe you're saying no. I've been so good lately. Principal Brimstone even let me out of in-school suspension." Lexi crossed her arms and glared at me as she leaned against the kitchen counter.

"I'm sure he did." But I doubted her being good had much to do with it. "The answer is still no." I walked into the dining room and wiped off the harvest table. Putting the candle center-piece back in the middle, I maneuvered until it sat at the perfect angle. Order gave me peace, even if the rest of my life insisted on remaining in a constant state of chaos.

"Oh, sure, Mom. It's okay for you to change the rules, like at Dr. Anderson's house the other night." Lexi followed right on my heels, hands now on her hips. "That's just not fair. There's no reason Scott can't take me driving. He's eighteen and has his full license."

"The person you ride with has to be twenty-one."

"When will you stop treating me like a child?"

"When you stop acting like one," I said, striving to remain calm. "I don't care for the attitude you've adopted or your tone of voice right now. Besides, we've been over this before, Lexi. You're only sixteen, and you just got your permit. Like I said, he's not twenty-one, so he legally can't take you driving. I don't feel comfortable with *anyone* taking you driving except me, and I especially don't feel comfortable with you riding in the car with an eighteen-year-old boy you got caught making out with. I'm sorry, but that's the way it is."

"Yeah, well, that sucks."

"And your mouth isn't helping your cause, either." I stared her down, but she raised her chin in defiance.

"Like you're helping my cause? That's a joke. You're my freaking mother, yet you don't believe I'm not the girl in those stupid pictures. I wouldn't be that dumb. Real cool, Mom." Her posture radiated anger, but I could see the hurt beneath. I felt like such a heel. Wanting to make her pain go away, I reached out to her, but she jerked her shoulder away and took a step back.

I dropped my hand to my side. "The whole town suspects you of sending those pictures into cyberspace. The last thing you need to do is fuel their fire by being out after dark," I snapped, taking several calming breaths. I'd learned from years of practice losing my temper would get me nowhere with her. "I want to believe you, Lexi, but you make it hard when you don't confide in me. I know you too well. There's something going on, but you won't talk to me."

"I can't talk to you. God, can't you see you're ruining my life?" She threw her hands up in the air. "If Dad were here, he'd believe me, and he'd let me go driving with Scott. You just hate me. You made him go away. It's all your fault."

A sharp pain shot through my chest. Max had always been the one she'd confided in, even when she was little. She was the ultimate daddy's little girl, and I'd never been jealous. Anyone with more than one child knew kids tended to gravitate more toward one parent than the other, and each child was different. I knew it didn't mean she loved me any less. It just broke my heart her daddy, who supposedly loved her so much, had abandoned her, sending an occasional postcard and presents. Like that made up for his absence. She needed him, and I had no idea how to help her.

"That's not true," I said. "I'm doing the best I can on my own, and it's out of love that I want to keep you safe."

"What-ever. I don't care anymore." She stormed upstairs, her curls bouncing as she stomped her feet all the way.

I sighed and poured myself a big ole glass of Pinot Grigio. Taking the bottle with me, I locked up and headed upstairs to my own bedroom. I thought making it through Max's abandonment had been tough. Surviving the teenage years was going to take a miracle. I sat down on my bed and stared at the empty pillow beside me.

Life was so unfair, I thought and let the tears fall.

Two more glasses of wine and a couple hours later, my tears had long since dried and a nice warm feeling buzzed through my body. I glanced at the end table beside my bed. I might not have a miracle, but I did have a new friend, and I was in dire need of some stress relief.

Just do it, ran through my head.

Did I dare? I glanced at the clock. Midnight. The kids were sound asleep, and like my girls said, who would know? Everyone did it. It was no big deal, just set the mood. I could do this. I had to do this. If I didn't find a way to relieve the tension soon, my volcano was going to blow its top, literally. The way I saw it, for the safety of all those around me, I really didn't have a choice. Did I?

Just do it.

"Okay, already," I snapped, turning off the censor in my head, and deciding to go for it.

I dimmed the lights and put on some soft music. Lighting a few lilac scented candles and filling the tub with bath salts, I soaked for a good half an hour until I felt my muscles relax. This wasn't so bad. Maybe I actually could just do it.

I had thrown all my negligees— that was the height of our adventurous love making— out after Max left, so I chose a tank top and panties, instead of my usual flannel pajamas. That was about as sexy as my wardrobe got. Slipping back under the covers, I took a deep breath and leaned over to get my little 'friend' out of the end table. I had left it wrapped in newspaper and stuffed inside the canvas bag. I pulled the vibrator out of the bag and unwrapped the newspaper. Holding the gadget up to examine it, I felt my eyes spring wide.

"Holy Mother of God," I said in barely more than a whisper.

It was huge and had two heads, for God's sake. Two heads! What on earth did any woman need with two heads? For that matter, what had the ladies been thinking? This had to be a joke. There was no way— *no way*— I was using that. I started to wrap it back up, when the stupid thing turned on. I jumped a foot and dropped the shaking monstrosity on the bed.

Well, shoot. Guess I had to touch it again if I was going to get any sleep. So I picked the sucker up and hit God knows what, because it started twisting and rotating as it continued to shake at high speed. I let out a little scream and dropped it on the bed.

That was a friend I could do without, ever!

Katy chose that moment to walk in wearing her Hello Kitty nightgown, the 'y' long since worn off, and dragging her pink fuzzy blankie behind her like Linus's long-lost sister. I whipped the covers up over the convulsing gadget.

"What's wrong, honey," I asked as the stupid thing took on a life of its own, slithering about under the covers of my bed.

Katy's eyes, still puffy from sleep, grew huge as she stared at the moving covers, her bed-head hair sticking out in a million directions. She dropped her blankie— that was saying a lot since Katy didn't let go of her blankie for just anyone— and held her hands out in front of her in a stop motion.

"Mommy, don't be scared. I think a mouse is in your bed." My little protector took a step forward. "I save you. Let me see."

I grabbed her arm. "Oh, that's something Mommy doesn't ever want you to see. Besides, I think it's a snake."

Her jaw dropped open. "A real live snake? But I like snakes. I'll get him for you, Mommy." She took another step. I should have known she would like snakes. My fearless little drama queen was not your average girl.

"No!" I grabbed her arm again, and her face took on that stubborn look that said, 'I'm not going to stop until I get my way.' No way was I giving in this time. "Um, sweetie, I love that you want to protect me, but the snake might be poisonous." She blinked and looked as though she was having second thoughts, so I pounced, "That's right. That sucker is very dangerous. It spits." Lord only knew that was the God's honest truth. "Let Mommy handle this, okay?"

"Okay, Mommy." She stood back to watch. Of course, she wouldn't go to her room, that would be too easy.

I searched the recesses of my room for something to put the 'snake' out of its misery. Perfect. Bobby had left his bat in the corner by my dresser, no doubt when he'd been stealing my armor again. For once, I was grateful. I picked up the bat and lifted it high, preparing to smash the snake to smithereens.

"Don't kill it, Mommy!" Katy screeched, her bottom lip wobbling.

Wonderful. "What do you expect me to do?"

"Set Snaky free. Please don't kill it, Mommy." One big crocodile tear hovered on her long brown lashes, then tumbled down her cheek.

Oh, for the love of God, I thought, but said, "Okay. We'll set Snaky free."

I scooped up my covers, the snake still convulsing deep inside, and marched all the way down the stairs and out the back door. Katy followed me every step of the way. She stood on the back deck, while I slipped on a pair of boots and trudged through the wet grass in my tank top and underwear to where the edge of my yard met the woods.

Thank God it was the middle of the night and my whole street was asleep— at least I prayed they were asleep; one never knew with Lester. I shook out the blankets, and the convulsing two-headed snake went sailing into the woods. I heard it thrashing about in the bushes. Those had to be energizer batteries— they just kept going and going and going. A giggle slipped out. This could only happen to me.

"Is Snaky free, Mommy?" Katy called from the deck.

"He's safe and sound, right where he belongs." Out of my bed for good.

I marched back inside, knowing as soon as Katy fell asleep, I would have to go back out and retrieve good ole Snaky. I didn't need one of the neighborhood kids— or worse, Lester— stumbling upon that sucker, but there was no way I would bring it back inside, either. The only place that puppy was going was straight into the bottom of my garbage can, beneath as much garbage as I could find.

Just do it?

I had a good mind to tell the girls what they could do *with* it, that was for sure. From now on, I was sticking within my comfort zone, which meant no adult toys for me, and no men. Renewing my vow of celibacy, I would simply have to find another way to work off my stress.

"THAT DOESN'T LOOK RIGHT," I said to Harmony, who was on an exercise machine at the gym a couple days later. She had Denny open her shop for her so I wouldn't have to go to the gym alone the first time.

"It doesn't feel right either," she said, attempting to get the high-tech contraption to move.

I leaned over and read the directions. "Harm, you're on it the wrong way." I laughed my butt off.

"No wonder." She rolled off the machine and snorted, cracking up right along with me.

We had messed up almost every machine we'd tried, but we were having a blast. Considering the stress I had been under, fun was what I needed right now. Planning the prom would help my cause, but planning an amazing retirement party for Chaz's parents was my best bet at convincing the mayor I could handle the Labor Day Bash, only I was blocked. I couldn't think of a single idea for either event. The ladies were right. I needed to relieve the tension in a big way, only nothing I tried had worked.

"Things sure have changed since I last belonged to the gym," I said, trying to take my mind off my troubles. I looked around and noticed mirrors lined the walls everywhere. You couldn't avoid your reflection, except the image appeared distorted. "I swear there's something wrong with these mirrors. I know I don't have *that* many wrinkles, and I can see my pores from clear across the room. They had to have gotten these from a fun house."

"Wait until you get on this machine and look at your profile. Talk about a bubble butt. My ass looks twice the size it does in my mirror at home. It has to be a gym conspiracy."

"A what?"

"A gym conspiracy. The owners distort how their patrons look to keep them coming back."

"Ya think?" I glanced in the mirror, thinking I didn't look that bad.

"I know." She hopped off the machine so I could take a turn. "Hop on, and you'll see what I mean."

I climbed on and craned my neck to the side, then gasped. "Oh, yeah, major bubble butt. I've seen enough, thank you."

"Actually, bubble butts have been all the rage for a while now. Maybe you should embrace the fad. Be proud of your body. It's given you four healthy babes. Besides, Chaz doesn't seem to mind your butt one bit."

"Maybe," I said, seeing my butt through a different lens for a moment. Then I shook off the thought that Chaz liked any of my assets. I couldn't go there, so I focused my energy on my workout.

I had soaked my t-shirt by the time I finished my set, and we headed into the aerobics room to stretch since the kick boxing class had finished and the room was empty. I wasn't the only one sweating. A ripe smell permeated the air. Most of the people here were stay-at-home moms who came as soon as their kids were on the bus. That was why I chose this time. Early morning and late afternoon tended to be the working crowd, not that I was trying to avoid a certain someone. I forced my thoughts elsewhere.

"Oh, good Lord, these mirrors are even worse. Look how tight our clothes look," I said, staring at my distorted reflection. I ran a hand over my stomach to make sure I didn't pop and sink in odd places like the mirror reflected.

Harmony laughed. "This is usually my pre-workout work-out, but what the hell. We're the only two in here, so who cares, right? What better way to work the kinks out and cool down than stretching out our workout clothes." She squatted one two, squatted one two. Then grabbed the waistband of her spandex pants and yanked out to the side one two, side out one two. Her red spiky hair never moved an inch, but I'd thought maybe during a workout it would. Not so much. She must use a gallon of product. "You can do it. Stay with me now."

I chuckled and joined in, my crooked ponytail halfway down my head. It wasn't like anyone could see us.

"Really work it now." She slid her hands under the fabric of her pants and onto her thighs, then pushed out one two, out one two.

I did the same, but the stupid things insisted on bouncing right back into place. "There's a reason they put Lycra in spandex, ya know." There was also a reason why I didn't participate in aerobics classes. My pants weren't the only things bouncing. There wasn't a sports bra on the planet big enough to contain my Double Darlings.

"Yeah, no kidding. Gotta hate spandex. Okay, onto the shirt. A nice loose shirt can cover any imperfection, but if your dryer is like mine, it's plotting against you, so really work this." She grabbed the front of her *Go green! Save a tree, ride a lumberjack* t-shirt and pulled forward one two, forward one two. "You got it." Then she grabbed the edges and stretched to the side one two, side one two. "Now the other side and repeat."

"Oh, my God, we look like morons." I couldn't stop giggling, really working my *Big Mama* t-shirt, thinking I desperately needed to go shopping for some new workout clothes.

"Yeah, but we're hot morons." Harmony's green cat eyes sparkled as she dragged me over to the wall containing waist-level hooks with bungee cords over them. "And last but never least, slip the back of your t-shirt over the hook and run. Run hard. Run fast. Run that man right out of your system."

I did as I was told, laughing hysterically now.

"Come on, faster now. Don't stop, unless," her voice trailed off and she stopped running, "unless said man is standing in the doorway, wearing a shit-eating grin."

"Don't stop on my account, ladies, I'm thoroughly enjoying the show."

I let out a squeak and ripped my t-shirt in my haste to break free. Whipping my head to the side, I saw Chaz leaning against the doorframe with corded arms crossed over his chest. Even in gym shorts and a muscle shirt, he still looked perfectly put together. Like he should be posing as the centerfold for some athletic magazine. It wasn't fair.

Women aged. Men became distinguished.

"That would be my cue to leave." Harmony hugged me as she whispered in my ear, "I still say he's much more appealing than Snaky."

I gave her "the look", and she just laughed. "See ya, Doc." She swatted Chaz on the ass with her towel as she walked by.

Chaz chuckled, turning the full wattage of that shit-eating grin on me. "*What* was that?"

"Um, stretchy-robics?" I laughed, and he joined me. "Seriously, you don't want to know."

"I'll take your word for it." He kept staring at me, still grinning wide.

A warm sensation spread through my extremities, fogging my senses. *Just do it*, filtered through my brain, and I shivered, only not from fear. Blinking rapidly, I cleared my throat. "Aren't you supposed to be at work?"

"I took this morning off. Thought I'd get in a workout. Guess we had the same thing on our minds."

If he only knew what I had on my mind, he'd be shocked. "So, um, have you given any thought to what theme you want to go with?" I asked, needing to change the subject in a big way.

He ran his long fingers over his smooth jaw, looking pensive. "Well, since both my parents worked for the railroad, I'm thinking trains would be a fitting touch."

"Trains it is. I'll pull some ideas together and call you as soon as I have something concrete to go over."

"Sounds like a plan. Just do whatever you want to, and I'm sure I'll love it."

I chewed the inside of my cheek, attempting to mimic Harmony by saying, "Okay, then. See ya, Doc," as I sauntered past him, only I wasn't going anywhere near his ass. Although I never wanted to 'just do something' more in my entire life, the million-dollar question was: Did I actually have the guts to do anything?

Probably not.

A half hour later, showered and ready to head to my next appointment, I peeked in the gym for one last glimpse of Chaz. My spine stiffened.

Bitsy Beaumont.

What was *she* doing here, and in a suit, no less? And why was Chaz smiling at her as she yammered on about something?

Oh, my God. She was trying to steal this job from me, too. I had to find a way to stop her. I started in their direction, but I was too late. Chaz headed into the men's locker room, and Bitsy zeroed in on the door. Just before she left, her gaze met mine. She looked startled for a moment, and then a bit guilty before she hoisted her pointy chin and marched out.

I couldn't lose this job to her as well. Maybe they were talking about the weather. Or maybe they were just being friendly. I set my jaw and pursed my lips. Maybe it was time I found the guts to actually *do* something before someone else did.

"Yup, that's definitely poison ivy." Chaz squatted down to Katy's eye level and tweaked her nose, while she soaked up every bit of the attention.

Dr. Joy didn't have any slots open today, so we had to see Chaz. I had to admit, he was wonderful with Katy. My heart ached at the thought of what she was missing out on by not having a daddy around.

"You been playing in the woods, angel?"

Katy shot a guilty look in my direction, then slowly nodded.

"Katy, you know better than to play in the woods. You can't go outside without someone with you, honey. You could get hurt." I wagged my finger at her. Good Lord, I was turning into my mother, I thought and dropped my hand.

Katy's bottom lip wobbled. "But I didn't go far, Mommy. I just wanted to check on Snaky."

I sailed into a coughing fit like a ship into a storm and choked on a mint, sinking fast.

"You okay?" Chaz jumped up and searched my face with concern, ready to save me in true hero form.

Breathe. Just breathe, Zoe. I wiped the tears out of my eyes and strove for calm as I rasped, "I-I'm fine." Calm? Dear God in heaven. How could I be 'calm' after Katy had just dropped the Snaky bomb. He drew his sandy brows together, so I unscrambled my brain enough to add, "Really."

He relaxed, and the corner of his lip tipped up. "Snaky?"

I stood there with my mouth opening and closing like a blowfish, not having a clue what to say.

Katy, on the other hand, had no trouble whatsoever. "Mommy's pet snake. It has two heads and spits. Right, Mommy?"

"Um, uh, er...." I giggled, sounding a bit hysterical, and still stood there like an imbecile.

"He's not really our pet, but he was in Mommy's bed. Mommy wanted to bash him with Bobby's bat, but we set him free."

Chaz's blond brows disappeared into his perfect Ken Doll hairline, yet he still managed to maintain that cockeyed grin.

I shrugged. "What can I say? I hate snakes."

"Was it big?" he asked.

"Oh, yeah. Very big," I answered.

"And scary?" His lips twitched.

"Way scary." I shuddered.

"I admire your courage." He patted my arm, and a tingle raced along my nerve endings.

"Trust me; I'm still recovering." I strove for a serious expression.

Chaz turned to Katy. "So, was Snaky in the woods?"

"Nope." Katy shook her head so hard her brown curls bounced. Hopping off the exam table, her pigtails swung along with her every move.

"I made sure of that," I muttered.

Chaz studied me with a perplexed, amused look as Katy slipped on her backpack, and then he said, "Sorry, angel, no school for you today. And try not to scratch."

"But, Mommy, I want to see my friends," she wailed. "Today's show and tell." And the award goes to the child prodigy. She knew exactly how to work every situation.

"Not this time, sweetheart." I focused my attention on Chaz. "I have to stop by Sacred Heart Church because the sisters are having their annual banquet tonight, and I'm the party planner, if you can believe it." They were one of the few groups who hadn't fired me after news of Lexi's scandal. Then again, they were nuns. I would hope at least *they* would give me the benefit of the doubt. "Their oven is much bigger than mine, so do you think it would be okay if Katy went with me? No one will be in the kitchen."

"That's fine as long as she just watches. Now, how about a lollipop, angel?" Chaz held a huge bowl of lollipops in front of her and winked at me.

Katy's face brightened in an instant, show and tell all but forgotten, bless the man.

After making a quick stop home for my supplies, we headed

for the church. I was married in Sacred Heart and baptized my children there. It held a lot of special memories for me, despite what had happened, and I was thrilled the sisters had decided to keep me as planner of their banquet. Hopefully, this would make another wonderful memory for me and bring in more business.

Katy helped me carry the supplies past the noisy preschool classes. We continued by Sister Mary Agnes who stood on the altar, surrounded by beautiful spring flower arrangements as she practiced her keynote speech. Prisms of light lit up the church as rays of sunshine filtered through the colorful stained-glass windows. I nodded to Father O'Dority as I descended the flight of stairs to the huge kitchen in the basement.

Katy sat on a stool watching me unpack my supplies. "Pleeease can I help, Mommy? I won't get nobody poisoned ivied."

"You're not contagious, honey, but you heard Dr. Anderson. You only get to watch because you need to rest, but if you're a very good girl, I'll bake you some cookies when I'm done making this cake, okay?"

Her pout intensified, but she didn't climb down off her perch. She loved to help me bake, especially when it came to beating the eggs, but it couldn't be helped. Maybe next time she wouldn't break the rules and wind up sick.

"Why don't you play with your Barbies? I put a couple in your backpack."

"I took them out." Her pout remained in place, and she crossed her arms tight over her chest.

I glanced at her and frowned. "Now that I think about it, I haven't seen you play with your Barbies in a long time. How come?"

"Cuz I don't know where to put the daddy no more, and the mommy's too busy to play with me. She just works all the time."

The knife pierced my heart.

I had no idea what to say to that, so I found some paper and a pen. "Here, honey, why don't you draw your teacher a picture? You can give it to her when you go back to school."

"Okay, Mommy." Just like that, her pout disappeared, absent daddies and neglectful mommies forgotten.

But it would be a long time before I forgot her words.

After all the prep work was done for the party and stored in the refrigerator, I started on the cake. Katy sat quietly on her stool, drawing, but I knew my Katy. Something wasn't right. She was being too good, which meant she was up to *no* good. I added the eggs and was getting ready to question her when my cell phone rang.

Wiping my hands on my apron, I walked over to my purse and checked the caller ID. Mrs. Hurley the guidance counselor. What now? I answered my phone with dread.

"Hi, Mrs. Robinson. I'm just following up like I told you I would about last week," she said.

"Thank you, I appreciate that." I rubbed my eyes with a thumb and forefinger. Mrs. Hurley loved to chat, but I had so much to do before the kids got out of school.

"Troy failed another test," she said with a thick New England accent.

My fingers stilled as my heart sank. "But I thought he was doing better?" I massaged my throbbing temple.

"Molly told me he hangs on every word she says, but it doesn't seem to be helping. You might want to consider something more aggressive like a learning center after school. Or maybe he's getting teased because of his sister posing for the inappropriate pictures."

"Allegedly." It was one thing for me to have doubts, but I wasn't about to let others go around stating it as fact. "There's no proof."

"I'm just saying kids can be cruel. This whole scandal might be affecting him more than you think. Have you tried counseling?"

"Right after Max left, he went to a therapist. We all did. She helped us then, but maybe he needs to see someone new. I'll find someone, I promise, and I'll look into a learning center as well."

A buzzing sound rang out from behind me. Katy. I whipped around, and sure enough, Katy had scrambled up on the counter like a naughty little monkey and was mixing the cake batter. Only, the hand mixer sounded like it was on its last legs. I would have to remember to change the batteries when I got home.

"Mrs. Hurley, I have to go. Something just came up, but thanks for calling." I flipped my cell closed and stuffed it in my purse. "Katy Ann Robinson, you know you're not supposed to use the mixer," I said, marching over to her.

"But I'm not using the mixer, Mommy." She grinned a toothy grin. "I'm using Snaky."

"Snaky!" I screeched. I swear to God my heart stopped for a full minute. "B-B-But you said you didn't find him in the woods."

"I didn't. He wasn't in the woods." Her grin grew wider, if that were possible. "He crawled into the trash can all by himself, and I rescued him before the trash man came. I thought he was dead, but when I tickled him, he moved, so he's all better now. That nice lady Bimsy Beaubos saw me when she was taking out her trash. I showed her Snaky, and she said I should bring him to show and tell." Pride radiated out of every pore on Katy's small frame, while raw untamed fury bubbled within me.

Bitsy!

"Mrs. Robinson, that doesn't look like a snake to me," Father O'Dority said from behind me.

I jerked and turned toward the open doorway, my stomach in my throat.

"Or an eggbeater, for that matter," Sister Mary Agnes stammered, her face paler than the white on her habit.

Please God in heaven get me out of this one. "Give that to mommy, Katy." I reached for Snaky, hoping to hide him from full view, but the monkey had mischief in her eyes.

"But it *is* a snake." Katy set her jaw and pulled the bowl away. "A special one, too." She lifted Snaky high out of the goop, the batter dribbling down her arm and back into the bowl. "See, he has two heads and everything. Just like my picture for Mrs. Turner."

I heard a gasp and closed my eyes, afraid to look. Wincing, I peeked over my shoulder. Sister Mary Agnes had fainted, and Father O'Dority was fanning her with one hand and making the sign of the cross with the other.

I could just see the Mayflower Gazette headlines tomorrow....

Party Planner, Zoe Robinson, Uses Two-Headed Vibrators To Bake Her Cakes!

Chapter Nine

"You've got to be kidding me," I said to Tiffany as we sat on the bleachers, the spring breeze blowing our hair and carrying with it the smell of new grass.

Basketball season was over and baseball season had arrived. Troy's sport. I loved to watch Troy pitch, but I didn't think I could focus if I tried.

"What's the matter, doll?" Tiffany asked me, the sun reflecting off the jewels in her ears and on her neck.

She looked completely out of place at a ballgame, but at least one of my girls always attended the games with me. They had come to love watching my kids play sports as much as I did. The kids appreciated having someone other than me there to support them, since they were one of the few whose family lived away.

"What *doesn't* that man do?" I zipped up my fleece jacket and scowled. "I heard he does charity work and volunteers for just about everything, too."

"What man? You're starting to worry me." Tiffany drew golden blond brows over puzzled periwinkle-blue eyes.

"Chaz." I tucked my hair behind my ears so I could see

better, still half in disbelief. "Chaz is the umpire. Can you believe it? I thought he didn't like sports. He was the water boy, for Pete's sake, he never actually played."

"Things change. *People* change." She shrugged, shielding her eyes with her hand to get a better look. Her lips formed a slow, sensual 'mama likes what she sees' smile. "Boy, do people ever change. Doll, he looks sexy as hell in that uniform."

I swatted her on the arm. "You are *not* helping matters."

"Sorry, but it's true." She squinted and looked at the other set of bleachers. "He's not the only one I'm surprised to see here. Since when does Bitsy go to the ballgames? She doesn't have kids."

I looked to where Tiffany pointed, and I gasped. Bitsy was talking to Gerty and Gabby, who were circulating that blasted petition for all the people to sign.

"Unbelievable. First Bitsy showed up at the gym the other morning, then I saw her at the hospital the other day when Chaz had rounds, and I was catering a couple of staff lunches. Now this? Give me a break."

Troy threw a pitch, but the batter hit a home run with bases loaded. "Shake it off, Troy. You'll get the next one," I shouted.

Chaz glanced in my direction.

My heart fluttered like a bird desperate to head south, and at this moment, I'd give anything to hitch a ride. I turned away to check on Katy and Bobby at the playground, then Lexi who was chatting with a couple of boys over by the dugout. Figured, she was gaining boys as friends and losing girls. If this petition went through and the town lowered the curfew, everyone would blame her. Then she wouldn't have friends left of any gender.

I had taken away her phone and Internet, and she wasn't allowed out of the house after dark, all in an attempt to keep her out of trouble. The girls and I had done some homework. There was no indication that Lexi had ever done anything inappropriate before. In my heart, I don't think I ever truly believed Lexi was capable of such behavior. I just knew she was keeping something from me, but the damage had already been done. Now, *she* no longer trusted *me*. If I could only find out who had posted those pictures of her on the Internet and get them to admit it, then maybe we could start repairing our relationship. In the meantime, there wasn't anything more I could do, and Lexi's troubles were not my only problem.

I focused on Tiffany. "Bitsy's trying to steal the Anderson job, I just know it."

"Sure, she is. She's not about to give up without a fight. She might have won most of the parties in town, but none of them are as big or as important as Chaz's party because the mayor loves his whole family and relies heavily on them for support. If you pull this off, then the Labor Day Bash will be yours for sure." Tiffany's eyes met mine, and she frowned. "You'd better be on your guard with that one. You make a mistake; she'll be all over it."

I blew out a breath, thinking about all the 'mistakes' I had made lately. "You aren't kidding. Last week, I put Troy's gym shoes in Bobby's bag. Poor baby didn't want to miss bowling, so he ran around gym class looking like a clown. He didn't talk to me for the rest of the night. And I got a call from his gym teacher, asking if I was feeling all right."

"You're kidding." She laughed. "It's not funny, but, oh my."

I shook my head. "Then this week, I made them all salami sandwiches for lunch, but I completely forgot to put the meat on. Just bread with mustard. None of them were happy with me that day, and they made a point of letting the lunch lady know. You can guess what happened next. I got another call that night from the guidance counselor recommending a good therapist."

"Oh, no."

"Oh, yeah. And the other day, when I saw Bitsy at the

hospital while I catered the two staff lunches I told you about, I had a major screw-up. Everything would have been fine if I hadn't run into Chaz making his rounds. I gave beef to the Indian doctor and seafood to the doc with a major shellfish allergy. I could have sworn I had them straight, but now that I think about it, Bitsy probably had something to do with it. By the time I got home, the news had already reached my mother."

"Oh, doll, you poor thing."

"It gets better. Just yesterday morning, I woke Lexi up for school. She was so tired, but I made her scoot her butt into the shower. The girl takes thirty minutes just to shower." I huffed. "Anyway, I made coffee and sat down to watch the news, but none of my shows were on. Know why?"

"I can only imagine."

"Because the local news isn't on at one a.m."

Tiffany gasped. "You didn't."

"I did." I swiped my hands over my face. "I don't think Lexi has forgiven me yet."

"No wonder the poor baby was tired."

"Ya think?" I sighed. "Now, after the episode with the vibrating cake, people are looking at me like I'm the one with two heads. Not to mention the Rogers sisters told everyone I'm a Peeping Tom. God, what a mess. I wouldn't blame Chaz if he fired me and went with Bitsy."

"You know he wouldn't do that. He wants to help you. Anyone can see that." Tiffany rubbed my back.

"I don't think he'll help me at the expense of his parents. They deserve a great party, and I'm beginning to doubt I can give them one." I looked up at her. "What the hell is happening to me? I had everything under control, and now I feel like my whole life is unraveling all over again."

"Because you won't let anyone in," she said matter-of-factly. I started to protest, but Tiffany held up her hand and cut me off.

"I'm serious, Zoe. You can't do everything alone. What I don't understand is why you'd want to when you don't even have to. So many people love you and just want to help you out a little. Is that so bad?"

"I know it's hard to understand, but I just don't want to depend on anyone ever again. What if I come to rely on someone, and they change their mind like with Max? I don't think I'm strong enough to go through that again."

"Oh, Zoe, no one knows what life has in store for us, but you can't live in fear. You have to let down that wall sometime."

"I have." I kept my gaze out at the field. "I let you and Harm and Morti in."

"That's not what I mean, and you know it," she said gently. "I'm not saying you have to get married, unless that's something you want, but you can't shut yourself off from opening your heart to a man again."

"I know, and you're right. I will when I'm ready." My gaze wandered to the backstop where Chaz stood behind the catcher. He called a strike for Troy, and my heart ached. "I'm just not ready."

Tiffany followed my gaze. "Whatever you say, doll, whatever you say."

Bobby and Katy ran up to the bleachers. "Aunt Tiffy, will you get us some candy, please, please, pleeease?"

Tiffany glanced at me and winked. The kids knew I made them eat dinner first, and so did Tiffany. "Dinner first, kiddos." She picked up Katy and took Bobby's hand. "I'm going to get the kids some hotdogs from the stand. You want anything?"

"I'm all set, thanks," I said, sitting back and focusing on what really mattered.

I whistled and clapped from the bleachers as Troy pitched a no-hit final inning and won the game. He and the rest of the players headed over to the refreshment stand for hotdogs and sodas on the coach, and Bitsy stopped to talk to Chaz. He said something to her, and then his gaze shot to me. I could see Bitsy's spine stiffen from way over here. She stormed away, while Chaz walked in my direction with long mouth-watering strides.

Good Lord, times *had* changed.

I licked my lips, pressing them together. What he did to that uniform made my insides quiver. I could barely think straight to say what needed to be said, but I had to. I liked Chaz a lot, and he deserved for me to be honest with him.

When he stopped right in front of me, I said, "So you've probably heard about the mistakes I've made lately and are here to tell me you've changed your mind. It's okay if you've decided to go with Bitsy, Chaz. I mean it's your parents we're talking about, and—"

Chaz placed his finger against my lips, and the breath caught in my throat as butterflies flittered about in my belly. "Bitsy relished filling me in on all the gossip, and I let her know exactly what I thought," he said, his voice husky.

"Y-You did?" I asked from behind his finger, and his gaze landed on my lips.

He blinked, then dropped his hand. "I did."

"And wh-what do you think?"

He paused for a long moment, staring deep into my eyes, the green in the hazel swirl of his mesmerizing me. "I think you're amazing," he finally said.

"Chaz...."

"I know, I know. Friends. I get it, and I'm trying like hell to honor that, but this is about more than you and me." He took a deep breath and looked around. "I think you're an incredible woman, and I think you're an amazing party planner." His eyes locked onto mine, seeming angry. Not at me, but *for* me. "I don't want anyone else planning my parents' party, Zoe. If you won't plan it, I won't throw a party for them. Simple as that."

I frowned. "You can't do that, Chaz. They deserve a party."

"I agree. But I also think you deserve to plan it. People haven't given you a fair shake recently, and to be frank, it's pissing me off. As far as I'm concerned, you've done nothing wrong, and Bitsy's done nothing right."

My heart burst with something warm and tender, and I felt lighter than I had in years. It felt wonderful having someone believe in me and my abilities for a change. "Thank you. That means a lot."

"Then stop worrying and show me what you've got, woman. Other than your vibrating cake mixer, that is." He smiled. "Deal?"

Heat radiated up my neck and out my ears, but I smiled back, feeling renewed confidence in my abilities. "Deal." I could do this. I had loved planning parties for my children. That was why I had decided to move into party planning in the first place. I just let the mistakes I'd been making and Bitsy's intimidation tactics cram my head with doubts.

Well, no more. I would show Chaz exactly what I had, and then some. Okay, so that wasn't quite what I meant, but now it had me thinking of finding a pole and doing my own striptease. I shivered. *Focus, Zoe, focus.*

I had to find a way to focus or die trying.

"Come in, Mrs. Robinson, it's a pleasure to meet you." A petite older woman with a teased blond helmet of hair held the door as Troy and I entered and sat on a black leather couch.

"Thank you for seeing us on such short notice, Dr. Head-right." As I took in her red suit and squinty eyes, I found it hard to believe she could get anyone's head right, but Troy's guidance counselor had suggested her.

"Mr. Brimstone and I go way back." Dr. Headright slipped on a pair of glasses and read her notes. "If he says you need help, then you need help."

"Br-Brimstone?" An inkling of uneasiness filled me. I couldn't have heard her right. "I thought Mrs. Hurley called you?"

"She did. I am Mr. Brimstone's personal therapist, and he always schedules his own appointments with me. When she mentioned your name, I assumed he referred you to me."

"I meant help for my son, Troy, not me." These people were out of their minds. Even if I did need help, I wasn't about to listen to someone Brimstone went to. "I thought it odd at the time when Mrs. Hurley recommended someone two towns away."

"Well, I thought it odd you brought your son along for this type of therapy session. I don't normally work with teenagers, but I'm open to answering a few questions."

I glanced at the assortment of degrees decorating the wall above the overstuffed chair she sat in, and I nearly fell out of my seat. Her first name was Ruth? No way. This could *not* be happening to me. The funny thing was she even resembled the famous love doctor. Nervous giggles bubbled up inside me as if I'd swallowed a mouthful of dish soap. I had to tell her I didn't need help. I had to stop the madness. I had to find a way out of here.

Troy nudged me. "Mom."

Apparently, I had to answer her question. "I'm sorry what were you saying?"

She pulled out a pad of paper and a pen, then turned on the tape recorder on the coffee table between us, her eyes forming slits as she smiled at Troy. "I said, Mrs. Robinson, vhat seems to be zee prrroblem?" I knew she didn't have that accent, but my brain insisted on hearing it every time she spoke. I just couldn't get past the "Dr. Ruth infamous sex doctor" image in my mind.

"Excuse me." I covered my mouth and went into a coughing fit as I attempted to force the spin cycle going on inside me back to a nice delicate wash so these ridiculous bubbles of laughter could dissipate before I gave her a reason to think I really was nuts.

Troy fidgeted on the couch and kept shooting me worried glances.

"I'm sorry, I'm better now. Please continue, Doctor." My mind said to get the heck out of dodge while I still could, but my curiosity got the best of me.

"That's quite all right, dear. Most people experience some sort of nervous reaction when talking about intimacy."

Troy and I locked eyes, his brows skyrocketing while mine lowered. "I told you I'm not here for me, and I'm pretty sure Troy having trouble in school has nothing to do with intimacy of any kind."

Dr. Ruth's eyes squinted further, the crows feet at the corners sinking deep as she scribbled on her notepad. "Troy, dear, do you have any issues with intimacy?"

"Uh, nope, none." His fidgeting stopped, and he suddenly appeared a lot less nervous.

"As I thought. You are frrree to go." She swiped her hand through the air in a swift gesture.

I squirmed. "Hey, w-wait a minute. Troy's the one with the problem, not me." Why wasn't she listening?

"Troy, dear, do you have a problem?" She peered over the top of her glasses at him, communicating God knew what without saying a word.

"Nope, none." He smiled, this time not a hesitation or stutter in sight, obviously interpreting her just fine.

Dr. Ruth winked. "As I thought again. I repeat, you are frrree to go." There went that hand again in a good imitation of Zorro's grandmother.

"But, but..." What was happening here?

Clearly, she didn't believe me. Just because I was messing up catering orders, was blocked creatively, was snapping at my kids more than usual, and had progressed to a whole bag of Oreos and two glasses of Pinot Grigio a night did *not* mean I had a problem. I uncrossed and recrossed my legs.

Dr. Ruth's sharp gaze shot in my direction, then back down to her notepad. *Scribble, scribble, scribble.*

"Sorry, Mom, I'm following doctor's orders." Troy unfolded his long body from the couch, flipping up the collar on his golf shirt and hiking up his baggy cargo pants. "I'm gonna get some snacks and hang in the lounge."

I didn't care how many fancy credentials she had on her wall; I was not like Brimstone in any way. This appointment was made for me by mistake. I bolted to my feet, intending to follow Troy far, far away from Dr. Quack.

"Vait! You, my dear, are *not* frrrree to go."

"You might wanna stay, Mom. You have been kinda uptight lately." Troy slipped out the door and closed it in my face before I could say anything more.

The fruit of my womb was bailing on me? He at least could have tried to help me escape with him. Wait until the next time he wanted something. I'd suddenly be unavailable, seeking help for my many problems.

Scribble, scribble, scribble, came from behind me.

I was a grown woman. No one could force me to stay if I didn't want to. I reached for the door, but the sharp "Sit!" had me dropping my hand and doing as I was told.

"So, I repeat, Mrs. Robinson, Vhat seems to be zee prrroblem?"

"I-I don't have a problem, really. I'm happy being celibate." Now, where the heck did that come from?

"Aha!" *Scribble, scribble, scribble.*

I leaned forward a hair, curiosity and a bit of fear of the intimidating dynamo propelling me to ask, "Aha what?"

"You have a first-class case of denial."

"Over?"

"Your fear of intimacy, your guilt, your addiction to sex."

I couldn't hold them in any longer. Bubbles of laughter overflowed at that one. When I pulled myself together, I wiped my eyes and said, "I haven't had sex in two years. How can I possibly be addicted to it?"

"Just because you don't have sex, doesn't mean you don't crave it. You, my dear, are fairly oozing desire." She set down her pen and paper, then leaned in toward me, her eyes narrowing and, I swear, her helmet of hair growing bigger. She took off her glasses and cleaned the lenses with her shirt as she said, "Vibrating zee cakes, Peeping zee Toms, sexing zee phones...need I say more?"

Vibrators, and Toms, and phones...oh, my, my mind screamed.

I felt like Dorothy in the Wizard of Orgasm-Ville as I clicked my heels together three times thinking, *There's no place like home*, but my slippers weren't ruby and the good doctor sure as heck wasn't the good witch of the North.

She was the wicked witch of the West, drumming in my ear, "Forget home, Zere's no place like a g-spot, and I'm going to help you find your vay back!" She wasn't about to let me go home until she "fixed" me and my little "libido" too.

Apparently, I didn't have much say in the matter. Besides, Troy was right. I wasn't 'kinda' uptight, I had pretty much reached the point of busting my springs. Maybe this "session" was exactly what I needed to finally relieve my tension.

I sat back and gripped the arm of the couch, having a feeling this little tornado was about to take me on one wild ride, whether I wanted to go or not.

OKAY, so I'd pretty much died trying to find a way to focus. My attempt at using a vibrator had failed miserably. Working out my tension at the gym had only succeeded in adding more. My run-in with Chaz at the game had left me horny as hell.

But my therapy session with Dr. Ruth had pretty much sent me over the edge.

If I wasn't addicted to sex before, I sure as heck was now. She'd fixed my libido, all right. By making me focus on the cause of my tension, my libido was now in a state of unrelenting arousal.

I forced air into my lungs and dipped my roller in nude paint, then spread it on my living room wall in defiance. I wasn't going to change anything about me. If the people in this town didn't like me for who I was, then to hell with them. All I knew was if I didn't get some sleep soon, I would be a mess tomorrow. I was hoping working on my house would relax me. If it didn't, I didn't know what would.

I glanced at the clock. Midnight. *Ugh.*

I adjusted my t-shirt. It was a little tight and I didn't have a bra on, but no one would see me. It felt too good not having those thick straps cut into my shoulders. I never slept in a bra or underwear now that I lived alone. Max had been so old-fashioned; he'd frowned upon me being that free. After he left, I refused to wear them to bed again just to spite him. Over the years, it had become a habit. When I couldn't sleep earlier, I'd rolled out of bed and started painting in my pj's.

I adjusted my shorts and wiggled my bare toes on the ladder rungs to get the circulation going again. The hot-pink paint Morticia had used for my manicure and pedicure hadn't worn off, and neither had the black henna tattoo Harmony had painted on my ankle. Too bad there wasn't any Pinot Grigio or a single Oreo left. I adjusted my earbuds and turned up the volume on my cell as I continued to paint while softly singing along to good ole eighties music. I didn't want to wake up a house full of sleeping kids.

Ten minutes later, the hairs on the back of my neck stood up. The strangest sensation that I wasn't alone coursed through me. Probably Katy. When something touched the back of my leg, I glanced over my shoulder, then jerked, falling backwards off the ladder.

Straight into Chaz's arms.

My back slammed into his chest, and his hands came up instinctively and wrapped around me to break my fall. He landed on his back, with me plastered on top of him, and two fistfuls of my bare double Darlings. I'd knocked the lamp off the end table in my fall, and my cell went flying, followed quickly by my earbuds. The room had been reduced to near black, with only the light of the full moon slightly illuminating the living room.

Seconds ticked by while we both lay still, breathing heavily in the dark, with the sound of silence screaming between us. I inhaled the scent of his aftershave mixed with the musky smell of man after a late-night run as I tried to figure out how in God's name we had ended up in this position. He wore running shorts, but he'd removed his t-shirt and his skin was damp, his chest covered with just the right amount of blond hair to be sexy as hell.

That— along with him mouthing you left your door unlocked— was the image I'd seen just before I fell, and it would be permanently embedded in my brain. He started to speak, but I shushed him into frozen silence.

His hands remained on my breasts, and I didn't dare move for fear they would leave. Maybe I was dreaming. I was afraid to speak, because I knew I had to put a stop to this, and with sound came reality. With light came reality. Somehow in the dark silence, everything seemed okay. Chaz seemed to sense that because he remained still as well.

Right now, I wanted— no I *needed*— the dream.

Chaz started to move his hands, but I grabbed his wrists to keep them in place. The dream was exactly what I got as his hands squeezed gently, then stilled. Shivers rippled over my skin and tremors began down below. I moaned, and that was obviously all the consent Chaz obviously needed.

His fingers fanned over my nipples lightly, and I felt a stirring beneath my butt. I clenched my fanny, and Chaz let out a husky moan of his own. He slid one hand down my stomach, then hesitated, but it had been way too long for me. The last thing I wanted was hesitation.

I took his wrist and moved his hand down below the band of my shorts until he cupped me intimately. He groaned when he discovered I wasn't wearing underwear and caressed me over and over until I was writhing beneath his fingers. He slipped his finger deep inside the folds of my vagina, and I sucked in a breath, more than ready for Mount Saint Zoe to explode.

It had been so long. I'd had no idea how much I missed being held by a man, touched by a man, kissed by a man. I rolled over, my breasts squashed between us, and I could barely make out his features. His breath swept over my face and he started to say why he'd stopped by, so I pressed my lips to his. I couldn't let him talk, couldn't let myself think. I didn't care why he was there at the moment.

I just wanted to feel alive again.

He rolled over on top of me, cradling my face with his hands, and plunged his tongue deep, exploring my mouth and sending shock waves through my body. His kiss was as sexy as his voice. I wrapped my arms around him and ran them over every inch of his tapered back and firm buttocks. God, he felt so good. I'd forgotten the pleasure of touching a man, feeling the hard contours of his muscles, marveling over our differences, giving a man pleasure.

Don't think, just do it.

I slid my hand between our bodies and wrapped my fingers around his penis, stroking him long and slow. Once more he started to speak, and again I kissed him until he gave up. He seemed to understand exactly what I needed as he slipped off his shorts and pulled down my own. He lifted up the front of my t-shirt and took my nipple in his mouth, and I nearly came undone. I jammed my hands into his hair and tugged.

I couldn't take any more, I needed him now.

He slid up the length of me and kissed me as he entered me. My scream was lost in his mouth as I wrapped my legs around him, and quakes of pleasure washed over me. My hips moved in time with his. Minutes later, he joined me, urging me on until another eruption hit, molten lava burning up my insides at the same time he had an orgasm of his own. When we both quieted to nothing left but lovely little aftershocks, he rolled over and took me in his arms.

He stroked my back and held me until we could both breathe normally again.

The longer the silence lasted, the more my world came back into focus and the reality of what had happened settled over me. This wasn't a dream. This wasn't Max. This was Chaz. This was my house, and I'd just had sex with Chaz. Little Chuckie Anderson. And my children were right upstairs. So many emotions warred within me.

Oh, God, what had I done?

I pushed out of his arms and shoved down the front of my shirt, then yanked up my shorts. "You have to leave," I whispered.

"Zoe, I think we should talk about this." He pulled up his running shorts and sat up in the dark.

"Not now. The kids... oh, God, the kids. What if they heard?" I scrambled to my feet and wobbled on unsteady legs to the bottom of the stairs to listen, but I didn't hear a thing.

He slipped in behind me and touched my shoulder, but I flinched, so he dropped his hand. "It's okay, Zoe."

"No, it's not. It's not okay, Chaz, it's not." I started to pace.

He went to turn a light on.

"No," my voice hitched. "No lights. Just go, please." I started to shake.

I heard him sigh and saw his shoulders drop in the moon's silhouette through the living room window. I closed my eyes. The window. Please, dear God in heaven, don't have let anyone see us. I ran over to the window and searched the street. All was dark, even Mrs. Bee's house, thank God. I didn't need my mother calling tomorrow. I closed the blinds.

"Okay, Zoe, you win. I'll go, but don't think this is over. We *are* going to talk about this." He touched my cheek. "I won't let you shut me out again. Not now. Don't forget to lock your door this time. I saw your light on, and it was late, so I stopped to check on you. That's when I found your door unlocked. You really should be more careful in the future." And then he was gone.

I hadn't locked my door? That just goes to show how badly I needed that. Well, I had certainly gotten rid of my tension, but I was far from focused. I'd just added a tension of a whole new kind, and I had a feeling there was no going back.

I repeat... what had I done?

Chapter Ten

"The girl's body looks different. Lexi's posture is better than that." I scoffed, not sure I'd ever looked this closely at the images before, and I should have, instead of jumping to conclusions. "How can these people possibly still think she's the girl in these pictures?"

"I know, I'm just telling you the latest rumor buzzing about," Tiffany said.

"With today's technology, her face could have easily been photoshopped onto those pictures," Harmony added.

"People can do that?" Morticia asked.

Harmony quirked a brow. "Honey, there is a great big world full of things people can do. Maybe it's time you did more than read Gothic novels."

"At least I know how to read," Morticia muttered.

"Don't worry, Zoe. We'll find the real culprit soon." Tiffany patted my arm. "Let me guess, Morti. Tonight's theme has to be French." Tiff selected a slice of baguette bread and spread on some gourmet concoction. Taking a dainty nibble, she closed her eyes on a sigh. "Oh, how I love French food."

Tonight's girls' night was held at Morticia's house. I glanced around. Okay, so she lived in a small apartment, but it was part of a house. The massive old white colonial with the peeling paint and wraparound porch housed the funeral home and her father's apartment downstairs, with an empty apartment upstairs right next to Morti's.

It had been just the two of them for as long as I could remember, living alone in that big old house, but it worked for them. I couldn't imagine how her father would feel if Morti ever had a serious relationship.

"Not that I'm complaining, Morti, but why *do* you always pick a European theme?" Harmony ripped off a chunk of the bread and sank her teeth in, then took a chug of her Merlot, nothing dainty about her. When she set her sights on something, she went for it, full throttle. She wanted a companion, but she intimidated most people. And when she wasn't intimidating, her brothers stepped in to finish the job.

None of the girls knew how to help her.

Harmony couldn't seem to help herself. She'd been competing with seven older brothers over everything all her life and didn't know how to act any other way. She was an interesting, beautiful woman, but the men in Mayflower steered clear of her. She didn't just try to compete with them, she ran right over top of them, scaring most away.

"What's wrong with Europeans?" Morticia flushed, her dark eyes enormous and somehow guilty.

We all looked at each other. "Who said anything about people? Weren't we talking about food?" I sipped my Pinot, wondering what detour this conversation had just taken. With Morticia, you never knew.

"Food. That's what I meant. I love European food, that's all." Morticia got up from the modest white Formica table in her eat-in kitchen and carried out more quiche, crepes, and French cheese.

"It's your night, Morti. Anything you want to talk about?" I asked. Her father had been gone a lot lately. He said he was training Morticia to take over the business, but it seemed the more he was gone, the more reclusive she became. If we didn't drag her out, I don't think she would ever leave her house.

"Yeah, come on, babe. Something's up with you, so spill it." Harmony folded her arms over her chest and waited.

"Nope. Nothing's up. More wine?" Morticia asked, obviously done with that conversation. When Morti didn't want to talk about something, no amount of prodding could elicit a response from her.

"Well, I've got something to say. How come you never hung that print I got you for Christmas?" Tiffany glanced around at the empty white walls.

Morticia's pale face flushed flamingo pink. "It wasn't really my style." A sheepish smile tipped her lips.

"It was a Van Gogh." Tiffany held up one long manicured hand. "You don't get more stylish than that."

"Hey, yeah, where's the relaxing water fountain I got you for your birthday?" Harmony searched the end tables, but other than a plain lamp, there were only books. Lots and lots of books.

"Again, not really my thing." Morticia winced. "Sorry."

"There's nothing to be sorry about. Everyone has their own decorating style, and that's perfectly fine," I said. It looked like the only things she spent her money on were books, I thought as I glanced at the massive bookshelf covering one whole wall, amazed there wasn't a single empty spot. Knowing Morticia, she'd read every single one. Probably twice. Whatever made her happy, made me happy. Although, the lack of color would drive me crazy. "Do you ever get tired of the white walls?"

"No. White's pure. Peaceful. I like white, and I like to read. What's wrong with that?" She seemed more defensive than normal. I suspected something was bothering her, but she would tell us when she was ready.

"Not a thing, doll." Tiffany patted Morticia's arm, then lost her smile, her lips tilting down a hair. "I could use peaceful right about now."

"Yeah, why? What's up?" Harmony asked.

Tiffany sighed. "I didn't want to bring this up because it's not my night, but you know how close I am with my grandmother."

We all nodded.

"I mean, the woman raised me, for crying out loud. Well, her breast cancer is back."

"Oh, honey, I'm so sorry." I squeezed her hand, imagining the pain she must be going through. Max abandoning me suddenly had been hard enough to handle, but having someone you love suffer for months or years as you worried about them dying must be unbearable.

Tiffany sucked in a shaky breath, her normally smooth complexion red and blotchy. "I just can't believe my mother hasn't gone to see her. She's her only daughter."

"It doesn't surprise me." Morticia shook her head. "Anyone who can turn her back on her own child has something wrong with her."

"I know." Tiffany swiped a tear away. "But this is *her* mother. I just don't get how she can be so cold."

"Babe, you're more like a daughter than your mother ever was, and Grammy knows it." Harmony hugged Tiffany. "She knows you love her."

"Trust me; they know." Morticia sent her a sympathetic smile and nodded. "The departed always do."

"Still. What am I going to do when she's gone?" Tiffany blew her nose. "She's such a big part of this town and so strong. If it hadn't been for her wealth and power, I don't think anyone would have accepted what I do for a living. These people can be so damned old-fashioned. Regular prudes, I tell you."

"You underestimate how strong you are." I had seen Tiffany take on her share of Mayflower's citizens and come out on top. She was more like her grandmother than even she realized. "If anything happens to Grammy, you'll be fine. You'll pick your chin up and take one day at a time, just like the rest of us." I smiled at her, blinking my own tears away. "And you'll learn to let others help you." I winked, throwing her words from the ball-game back at her.

"You're right. I will." Tiffany laughed as she dried her face. "Speaking of getting help." She smiled the first genuine smile of the night. "Since we know you won't let a certain *something* help you, does that mean you've learned to let a certain *someone* help you these days?"

I'd put Snaky out of his misery once and for all, and Chaz had most definitely put me out of mine. I shivered, still feeling Mount Saint Zoe's aftershocks, and then remembered I had an audience.

"I... I...." I felt lightheaded. My face must have paled by the shocked expressions staring back at me. Damn, I walked right into that one. And damn Dr. Ruth and her stupid libido therapy.

"You didn't," Tiffany said in barely more than a whisper.

"Oh, hell yes, she did. Look at her face." Harmony laughed and ran over to check the *Scenes of Winter* calendar by Morticia's phone. "Ha! Pay up again, ladies."

"Harm, you promised you wouldn't use any of your psychic stuff for help anymore." Tiffany pulled a twenty out of her Coach purse.

Harmony lifted her hands. "Hey, I didn't use any help, I'm just damn good." She did a little jig back to the table.

"You're damned, period." Morticia went to her white coffin

cookie jar and pulled out a twenty. "You've won most of my mad money this month." She sighed. "Guess that Oliver King trilogy I want will have to wait until next month."

Harmony started with a comeback, but Tiffany tapped the table as if she were a judge with a gavel.

The women grew silent.

"Now that that's settled," Tiffany stared me down, "explanation please."

"There's nothing to explain," I tried.

Morticia quirked a brow, a small smile playing at the corners of her lips, but she didn't say anything.

"Oh, no you don't, doll." Tiffany wagged her finger. "We want details, don't we, ladies?"

"Every juicy little one, babe." Harmony passed around the tarts and settled in.

Who was I kidding? They weren't going anywhere until I talked, and if I was being honest, I needed to talk. What better way to figure out what to do than confide in my best friends. I charged full speed ahead and told them everything that had transpired after being blown into another world by crazy Dr. Ruth and her libido therapy session.

After we all got done laughing hysterically, Harmony said, "Let me get this straight. Chaz was out for a late-night run and stopped by, then you screwed his brains out?"

"Pretty much." I groaned.

"That must have been one hell of a therapy session." Morticia chuckled.

"You have no idea." I covered my face. "I didn't even know how Chaz got in last night. He'd tried to tell me, but I wouldn't let him talk. I wanted action not words, and he sure did comply. Then he called my cell five times today, and finally left a message when I wouldn't answer. He was there, and we did it. God, I can't explain it very well. You were the ones who told me to 'just do it,' and well, Dr. Headright gave me the urge to actually want to."

"I meant just do Snaky, but doing Chaz is even better. Only I can't believe you, of all people, forgot to lock your door." Tiffany looked amazed.

"I know. I'm telling you, I'm a mess." I closed my eyes. It sounded ridiculous now that I said it out loud. "He keeps calling, but I can't talk to him. I'm so embarrassed. Now that we've slept together, there's no way I can finish planning his parents' party."

"Don't be ridiculous. You have to plan his party. You can't afford not to." Tiffany frowned.

"How? I don't know if I can face him again. Ever."

"There's nothing to be embarrassed about," Harmony said squeezing my hand. "You're both adults. It was just sex."

"I told you I don't do 'just sex.'"

"So, how was the 'not just sex' then?" Morticia asked with a twinkle in her eye.

I rolled mine, but then grew serious. "It was the craziest thing. I couldn't get the image of him standing there barechested and sweaty, looking messy but so unbelievably sexy, out of my brain. Then I fell and everything went dark. Something inside me snapped, I guess. I never lose control like that, especially with my kids right upstairs. We didn't speak or see each other, we just felt." I bit my bottom lip to keep it from wobbling, then I met their eyes and forced down the huge lump in my throat. "It felt amazing," I said, and then I burst into tears.

"Oh, honey, then why are you crying?" Tiffany got up and hugged me, handing me a box of tissues.

"Because it's not supposed to feel amazing," I sobbed, looking at each of them, my heart breaking. "What if he's like Max," I whispered, then hiccupped. "I can't see Chaz again. I don't need a man." I wasn't sure who I was trying to convince more. Them or me. "I'll just have to find a different party to plan."

"I think Max discovered he's gay and ran off with his lover," Morticia said.

"I think Max was going through his mid-life crisis and ran off with another woman," Tiffany countered.

"I think Max is a jackass, and frankly, it doesn't matter," Harmony said. "Not every man is like Max, babe." Her jaw pulsed, and I could tell she was doing everything not to break down, too. "You're young and beautiful and full of life." She gulped the rest of her wine and slapped her hand on the table. "I think Max wins if you throw the rest of your life away out of fear."

"It's not like that."

"The hell it isn't. I'd give anything to have sex with a great guy. I don't care what you say, celibacy is not normal." Harmony got up and grabbed her keys. "You're crazy if you throw away this shot Chaz has given you. You'd better soak up every ounce of pleasure while you still can. I'd take a man any day over one of my little friends, but the damn cowards aren't man enough to take me on. Live, Zoe. Just live."

"Harm—"

She held up her hand. "I love you, but right now you're pissing me off. And I've gotta run. Don't throw away everything you've worked so hard for, out of fear. You don't know how lucky you are."

She left, and I sat there with my mouth wide open, not having a clue what to say. She didn't understand what it was like to spend that many years with a man you thought you'd grow old with and then have him decide he didn't want you. I didn't have a plan B, and I was scared to death to start over, to take another chance. I didn't want to be in a relationship.

"She's right, you know." Morticia got up and started

washing the dishes. "Maybe it's time to move on. Maybe it *can* be just sex."

"I have moved on, and I'm telling you I don't do just sex."

"Uh, I think you just did," Tiffany said.

Did I? I frowned.

Maybe I didn't have to be in a relationship. Was I capable of having an affair? I'd only been with one man ever until last night, but the reality was I was still young. I wasn't ready for marriage again, and I sure as hell wasn't ready for a mechanical lover, so maybe my girls had a point. Maybe an affair was the perfect solution. I felt less tense today, that was for darn sure.

A little thrill skittered through me. "Oh, my God, I'm actually thinking about it." I laughed.

"That's what I've been doing for years." Tiffany shrugged. "My husband didn't abandon me, I divorced his ass, but he scarred me just the same. I don't want a serious relationship any more than you do. But I'm also realistic enough to know most women hit their prime at our age." She started to clear the table. "Maybe it's time you were selfish and took what you wanted for a change."

"Harm's just more sensitive to the whole situation because no man will accept her for who she is, quirks and all," Morti added. "Harm had another date cancel on her just last night."

"I didn't know," I said softly.

"It's okay, Zoe. She understands you're going through a lot, and she wants to be there for you, it's just hard on her sometimes." Tiffany smiled with understanding eyes.

"You're right. I've been too self-absorbed lately. I love you ladies." I nodded once. "If I do this, I have to be in control. There will be rules that must be followed. If Chaz can't handle that, then the deal's off."

"Sounds like your mind's already made up." Morticia grinned.

"Doll, we're not the ones you have to convince," Tiffany wagged her brows, "so what are you waiting for?"

"Nothing, I guess." I grabbed my keys. "Oh, God, I can't believe I'm actually going to do this."

I left Morticia's apartment and headed to Chaz's house. Since Harmony had left early, our girls' night had ended at eight. Mrs. Bee always stayed until ten, so I had two hours to spare. Two hours. I shivered.

A lot could happen in two hours.

"Open your garage door," I said into my cell as I drove my minivan down Hope Lane. Chaz had a three-stall garage and only one car. There had to be room to hide my minivan in there somewhere.

"Zoe?" he asked. "I can barely hear you."

"Sorry," I whispered, looking left and right, but no one seemed to notice I'd cruised their street five times. Why in the world was I whispering? It wasn't like they could hear me. "Just open the door, please."

"Okay." One minute later, the garage door opened, and I pulled my vehicle inside.

Chaz stood in the doorway, wearing a pair of blue gym shorts and a white muscle shirt as he hit the button to close the door behind me. I sat there, taking in the long, toned length of him, and the strongest urge for a hot fudge sundae hit me hard. Ice cream and oozing hot fudge. Yum, yum.

Chaz was not helping my diet any.

Like people on any diet always said, I'd start being good on Monday. But right now, I was in the mood to be very, very bad. Tiffany was right. I did need this. Harmony was right. I deserved this, too. And Morticia was right. It felt damn good, and I hadn't even done anything this particular time.

But that didn't mean I didn't want to.

I got out of the car, and Chaz leveled me with those intense eyes. "Ready to talk now?" he asked, holding out his hand.

"Yeah, I think I'm finally ready." I tested out a tentative smile, still scared senseless, but I took his hand and let him lead me inside.

"Want a drink?" he asked, heading into the kitchen.

"Oh, I already had one earlier, and I'm driving. A drink's not what I'm here for."

His hand stilled, and then he finished mixing a vodka tonic. "If you don't mind, I think I could use one. Maybe a double."

"Not at all." I strolled into the living room and sank down onto the leather sofa. The first thing that hit me was the quiet. My house was never this quiet. How did he stand it? Then again, there was so much about him I didn't really know. That was okay, I reminded myself. This was just an affair.

Nothing serious.

He came in and flicked on the gas fireplace, then joined me on the couch but didn't say a word. He just stared at me, sipping his drink, making me squirm.

"You're not going to make this easy on me, are you?" I asked.

"I've asked you out, told you how I felt, and you've insisted we remain friends. I did my best to respect your wishes, then you make love with me but won't answer my calls. You're confusing as hell Zoe." He took another drink. "The ball's in your court. I don't know what to think anymore."

"What do you mean?" I stalled, trying to form coherent thoughts. God, I wanted this, I wanted *him*, but voicing my desires aloud took more courage than I had imagined.

"You know what I mean. Are we or aren't we friends?" He plunged his hand through his sandy locks, messing them up for once, his frustration evident. "What the hell do you want from me?"

I inhaled deep, then plunged ahead, blurting, "Sex. I just want sex from you."

His eyebrows shot sky high, and he choked on his drink. "I beg your pardon?"

"I know, I know." I got up to pace. "I lied when I said I wasn't attracted to you, but that was because I was afraid."

His eyes softened.

"I don't want a relationship, Chaz. All I know is I can't think straight when you're around. I need to focus on my work, but all I seem to focus on is screwing your brains out." Oh, my God, I couldn't believe I just said that. Now that I'd thrown it out there, I peeked at him to gauge his reaction.

A slow smile quirked the corner of his mouth. "I can live with baby steps." He downed the rest of his drink and set his glass on the table, then stood up.

My heart beat so fast and hard I thought I might be having a heart attack. "Wh-what are you doing?" I took a step back and rubbed my chest, beginning to think I needed help.

"Helping you focus." He took another step forward, and I suddenly remembered Chaz was a doctor.

"On what?" My back bumped into the wall, and I dropped my hand.

"On screwing my brains out, of course." He pinned me against the wall and kissed the side of my neck. Oh, yeah, the doctor was in the house, and I was more than ready to open my door. Only that was all I was ready for.

"Wait." I put my hands against his chest, and he stopped immediately.

"Zoe," he said on a groan.

"I have conditions."

He sighed. "That doesn't surprise me." He tipped his head back so he could see my face. "And they are?"

"No lights."

He narrowed his eyes. "Okay."

"No spending the night."

He seemed to think about that, and then he said, "I get that. Okay. Anything else?"

"Just one more thing." I cupped his face to make sure he understood I was serious. "No strings attached. This is just an affair, and no one can know about us."

He frowned. "Why?"

"Because I have my kids to think about. And this town doesn't like change. They already think I'm a Peeping Tom, with a daughter who takes sexy pictures, and I bake cakes with two-headed vibrators. They're not ready to see me as anything other than Mrs. Robinson, the Fire Chief's ex-wife. I don't need them to see me as Mrs. Robinson, the older woman with a younger lover. I also don't want anyone to think you only gave me this job because we're having sex."

His eyes darkened.

A shiver ran up my spine.

"*What* are we doing together?" He smiled slow and sweet, and his eyes dropped to my lips. "Say it again."

My breathing picked up, and I wet my lips. "We're having sex."

"I like the sound of that," he said just before his lips crushed against mine.

His tongue plunged deep, and his hands slid under my blouse and up my stomach to cup my breasts. I lifted one leg and wrapped it around him.

"D-Do you agree?" I asked, breaking away before I could no longer think at all.

"Huh?" he said, homing in on my mouth again.

He slid one hand down over my butt to cup me from behind. My eyes crossed. Lord in heaven, the girls were right. I needed this as much as I needed to breathe and eat. I needed him. I shook my head to clear it and raked my hands over his chest, thinking I would seriously die if he didn't say yes.

"D-Do you agree to my terms?"

"Well, I was thinking about a more open traditional movie and dinner dating existence, but I can live with secret sex in the dark if that's all you're ready for." His mouth swooped down over mine. He hoisted me high and hard against him, grinding into me intimately as he pinned me to the wall.

"Ch-Chaz," I gasped against his mouth.

"I know, baby, I know." He traced the contours of my face with his hands, and then he pulled me back and set me on the floor. He stared at me for a long, full, intense moment before he flicked off the lights and the fireplace and closed the blinds.

"Thank you," I said, pulling him down on the plush throw rug in front of the fireplace and claiming his mouth.

This time he stripped off all our clothes and took his time caressing every inch of me until I was writhing in ecstasy. Just before he entered me, he said, "We haven't really talked about it, but I wanted you to know I'm safe."

I gasped at the feel of him filling me, slowly, deeply. Leave it to Chaz to bring up something clinical in the heat of the moment, but he was a doctor first and a man second. "I-I figured. You being a doctor and all."

He pulled out, and slowly pushed back in as he fondled my nipples. "I read your chart when I was supposed to examine you, so I know you're safe, too," he said on a groan.

"I had my tubes tied," I managed. "So I can't get pregnant, either." My voice hitched as he picked up the tempo, and then licked my nipple with his tongue.

"So what you're saying is, we're free to be... free." He sucked hard, and I squealed.

"I guess so," I got out.

"Good." He picked up the tempo to a fevered pace and reached his hand down to caress the nub of my desire.

I screamed his name as an orgasm bigger than any I could ever remember blindsided me, lifting me up and slamming me down, again and again until I was left with nothing but sheer exhaustion. Mount Saint Zoe was thoroughly empty. He joined me, sliding his hands in my hair and kissing me deep as he stiffened against me shouting my name, then he took me in his arms and rolled over.

We lay there in silence until our breathing returned to normal, afraid to say a word.

I equated the force of my eruption every time we were together with the fact that it had been two years since I'd had sex. Not that Chaz could be responsible, because that would mean this was about more than just sex. And I refused to believe that was possible. I would have the same reaction to any man. It was just sex, and I was just horny. That was all. I glanced at the clock on the microwave in the kitchen, and my body trembled.

I still had an hour.

"You thinking what I'm thinking?" I asked, feeling more relaxed than I had in years.

"Are you thinking this?" he said, a smile in his voice as he kissed his way over my breasts and down my torso until he settled between my thighs and plunged his tongue deep.

I screamed, unable to answer, as Chaz proceeded to bring me to another mind-blowing orgasm. Now I knew why the man never played sports. He spent all his time learning about anatomy and physiology. No wonder he graduated at the top of his class. He was amazing.

And I was just getting started.

Chapter Eleven

"Bitsy." I nodded, wearing paint-splattered coveralls as I held a box of sheet rock screws and a bucket of spackle in the middle of Hal's Hardware store. I'd finished the living room and had moved on to knocking out the wall in my downstairs bathroom. It was amazing what you could learn to do through videos on the Internet.

"Zoe." She looked down her pointy nose at me, seeming completely out of place in her lavender suit and heels.

"I'd shake your hand, but as you can see, mine are full of supplies."

"That's quite all right." Her gaze traveled over me with disdain. "Really." She sniffed.

"And you're here because you want to fix...."

"Oh, darling, I don't 'fix' anything. I create, then hire others to fix."

"I see." Striving not to sink to her level, I forced a smile and glanced beyond her. "Mayor Edwards, it's good to see you. Still working on that deck for Mrs. Edwards?"

I hadn't expected to see the mayor, but I especially hadn't expected to see Bitsy. She didn't have any reason to be here.

Everyone knew she might look like Martha Stewart, and be able to plan a party like Martha Stewart, but Ms. Fixit, she was not. That could only mean one thing.

She was here to create trouble.

"Oh, dear heavens, no. I'm not exactly in the shape I used to be," he rubbed his protruding belly, his shiny bald head and plump apple cheeks gleaming, "but you know Eleanor. She thinks I can do anything." He chuckled, his shoulders bouncing and belly shaking his white linen suit. He didn't care that Memorial Day wasn't here yet, he always wore white. "I just go through the motions and then hire the job out when she visits her mother. I'm sure she's figured it out by now, but she never lets on, bless her sweet soul."

"Something tells me you're pretty handy when you put your mind to it. I've seen you in action with the town council. Very impressive." The mayor had always been a fair leader and nice person. Even if he'd heard the rumors, he wouldn't believe anything without proof.

He puffed up like an endearing puffer fish. "Why, thank you, Mrs. Robinson. I see you've been keeping busy yourself." He gestured to the supplies I carried.

"Oh, you know how it is. The house, the kids, work. It never ends." The minute I spoke, I wished I could snatch back those words.

Bitsy's eyes flashed, and she smiled an evil little smile, quickly adopting a concerned look. "I tried to tell her, but she won't listen." She plastered a phony, sympathetic look on her face and clicked her tongue. "Poor darling has worn herself out. Look at her. She's a mess. Why, Mrs. Bee said even her mother is worried sick, with all that's happened lately."

"Hmmm, yes, I had heard." Mayor Edwards frowned, the apples in his cheeks blossoming to the color of full-fledged cherries as he cleared his throat. "Maybe you shouldn't take on so much, Mrs. Robinson. Maybe—"

"I appreciate your concern, sir." I gritted my teeth but strove for calm, ignoring Bitsy and smiling with confidence at the mayor. "I'm fine, really. I have everything under control."

"That's good to hear, dear. Now that you don't have all those parties to worry about, I'm sure you're getting some much-needed rest." Bitsy fairly glowed as she beamed at Mayor Edwards.

"Well, done, Ms. Beaumont." The mayor nodded at Bitsy. "The buzz around town is you've landed yourself quite a few parties to plan."

More like stolen a few parties, I thought, but said, "I know, you poor, dear." I tsked and Bitsy's smile slipped. "You look a bit worn out yourself."

She tried to wrinkle her forehead, but the Botox wouldn't quite let her as she touched her short-cropped hair.

"But thank you so much for helping out with all those *little* parties." I fluttered my eyelashes innocently.

Bitsy's mouth fell open, but she snapped it shut and glared at me.

I turned to the mayor and smiled wide. "Now I have plenty of time to work on the prom and Dr. Anderson's retirement party for his parents."

The mayor's face lit up with genuine pleasure. "Ah, yes, Roz and Wally Anderson. Wonderful people. Just wonderful. You can bet I'll be there." He patted my shoulder. "Give them my best when you see them. Well, I'd better run before Mrs. Edwards calls Officer Pickles out to look for me. She does tend to hover on the dramatic side." He winked and turned to leave.

Before he reached the door, he said over his shoulder, "I'm impressed, Mrs. Robinson. That party will be almost as big as the Labor Day Bash. Keep up the good work." He waved as he left the store.

"Why you little—" Bitsy ground out until I cut her off.

"I told you this wasn't over." I lifted my chin a notch. "It doesn't have to be this way, Bitsy. There's room enough for both of us."

"You naive little fool. You represent change. I represent tradition. The two don't mix, darling. Everyone knows that. And when you fail, which you will, everyone will know you're out of your league. This town doesn't want change. You of all people should know that, *Mrs.* Robinson. What will the town think of their poor charity-case golden girl after that? Is it worth the price of finding out?" She stuck her nose in the air and strolled out of the store with an elegance and grace even I couldn't deny.

Charity case!

I ground my teeth, but could she be right? Was I doomed to fail? I straightened my shoulders, refusing to let her fill my head with doubts. This town might not like change, but one thing was certain. They needed change. Needed it as much as I did.

And I wasn't about to go down without a fight.

A week later, I strolled through the doors of Mayflower Family Physicians with one thing on my mind: getting up close and personal with Dr. Hunkorama.

"Mrs. Robinson, dear, so nice to see you. I hope everything's all right," Gerty Rogers said from the waiting room and adjusted her gaudy scarf over her typical dark drab garb. Big purple flowers over a red background, not at all like Gerty. She must have just come from Bertha's Beauty Parlor.

Bertha liked big. Big portions, big hair, and big flowers. I was surprised Gerty hadn't bothered to take it off. Maybe she was afraid of hurting Bertha's feelings, though she hadn't been worried about Lexi's or my feelings when she'd started that petition.

Whatever the reason, I made a mental note to cancel my next appointment.

Gabby Rogers poked her long nose out of the *Senior Citizen's Survival Guide* magazine and pinned me with wide owl eyes. "Why, sister and I didn't think we'd see you step foot in this office anytime soon, given what happened and all. Yes, indeed, I hope you're doing well." The resident busybodies put their heads together, tittering and clucking a mile a minute.

"I'm fine, sisters. And so's Lexi, in case you're interested."

"Well, good for her. You know, the petition has nothing to do with her, in particular. We're worried about *all* teens these days. The streets are not a safe place to be. Not safe, indeed." Gabby fanned her face.

"So, you're telling me you don't think Lexi is the girl in those pictures?" I crossed my arms and looked them each in the eye.

"Well, gracious, I would hope not, but one never knows who that floozy could be, does one? Not that we've looked at the pictures, mind you." Gerty smoothed her brown polyester pants which clashed with her bright floral scarf, and then hoisted her humongous purse onto her lap. Obviously, she hadn't taken my advice about getting a smaller bag. Probably the reason she was back to see the doctor again today. "Tell us, if you're okay, why are *you* here?" she asked.

Nosey old biddies. I had to tell them something because they lived to gossip. If I didn't give them a reason, they would make one up. "I'm here on business."

Gabby's eyes lit up. "Oh, my, what kind of business?"

"In case we should require your services," Gerty added.

"I wouldn't dream of keeping you uninformed. Should you

require my services, that is." I smothered a chuckle. "I'm planning the Andersons' retirement party."

"Ah, yes, I'd heard you were planning Roz and Wally's little shindig. Such wonderful people." Gerty flipped a page of the *How to Retire in Style* magazine on her lap, and a whiff of mothballs drifted to my nose. The lonely old spinsters had probably pulled those god-awful pants out of their long-forgotten hope chests. "They deserve the best, you know."

"Only the best." Gabby nodded. "Wonderful people."

"I agree." What was the point of this conversation, other than making me nervous now that we mentioned my planning abilities, which I'd already begun to doubt? I prayed Robin would call my name for my appointment with Chaz.

"Well, good, dear. I'm sure you'll plan a grand party." Gerty smiled.

"Grand, indeed." Gabby nodded harder.

"I'll do my best to come up with something unique. You can count on that."

"No, no, no. Unique is not the way to go." Gerty looked at Gabby and wrung her thin-skinned hands, the brown spots matching her pants.

"That is so right, sister." Gabby shook her gray head and a piece of hair slipped out of the bun at the nape of her neck. "Quite right. The Andersons have been a part of this town for a long time, you know. I think they might like something a little more...."

"Traditional," I said on a whisper, voicing my biggest fears aloud without intending to. Bitsy was right. This town didn't want change. And I certainly didn't want them saying I was going to ruin Chaz's party.

"Yes, traditional." Gerty beamed. "Good girl."

I straightened my spine. "I'll have to ask Chaz what he thinks since he knows his parents best."

"Oh, well..." Gabby sat there silent, for once at a loss for words.

"Take care, sisters." I bit my tongue on what I really wanted to say.

"Chaz will see you now, Mrs. Robinson." Robin hung up the phone at the front desk.

Thank God.

"Just follow Sarah. She'll take you to his office in the back."

"Good luck, dear." Gerty waved.

"I hope he likes your ideas." Gabby shrugged.

"I think Dr. Anderson will like what I have in mind." I smiled as I followed Sarah down the hall.

"Don't mind those busybodies. I'm sure Dr. Anderson will love whatever ideas you come up with."

"I hope so," I said. "Speaking of love, how are things going with your new man?"

"Amazing." Her face glowed.

"I'm so happy for you."

"Thanks, Zoe. I really hope you find the happiness you're looking for, too."

We reached Chaz's office. What I had in mind involved a party of two. Yes, I was there on business, but I couldn't quite help myself.

A zing shot through me at the thought of all the things I wanted to do with Chaz. Every day this week, we had made love in all sorts of wild and exciting places. Always with the lights off, or as many clothes on as possible, which somehow made it even more exciting.

We hadn't planned it that way, it just sort of happened. Ever since we'd slept together, I couldn't seem to get enough. It was as if Chaz had turned on a faucet inside me and forgot to shut it off. Desire flooded my system night and day. Tiffany was right; women our age were definitely in their prime. Or maybe it had been way too long since I'd had the attentions of a man showered upon me, and in more adventurous ways than I'd ever imagined possible. Either way, I couldn't stop thinking about sex with Chaz, and my volcano was having the longest eruption in history.

Who knew he'd turn out to be such a skilled lover?

Because our affair was secret, we'd had to jump at opportunities as they presented themselves. This was so out of character for me, which made it all the more thrilling. I'd lived out fantasies I didn't even realize I had: sex in an elevator, sex outside, sex in a public building. I couldn't wait to see what was next.

And I'd taken care of my underwear problem. I simply didn't wear any when I knew I was going to see Chaz. *Me*, with a dirty little secret. If I'd known how liberating that was, I'd have gone without underwear a lot sooner. I giggled. Maybe Dr. Headright had a point. I was addicted to zee sex.

Or at least addicted to having sex with Chaz. I grinned like an idiot.

Sarah stared at me with a slight smile and a perplexed look on her face as she knocked on Chaz's door. "Dr. Anderson, your twelve o'clock is here."

"Thank you, Sarah." Chaz looked up from his desk, and a slow smile oozed across his face, stretching those kissable lips wide. "Come in, Ms. Robinson, and shut the door behind you. We've got a lot to go over."

I watched Sarah walk away, and then I turned to Chaz and said, "I've been working hard for you, Doc." I licked my lips.

"Yeah?" His voice already sounded husky. "Got big plans, huh?"

"I have a feeling you're gonna love what I have in mind."

"I'm counting on it."

"Let me lay it all out for you." I stepped inside, shutting and locking the door behind me, preparing to do precisely that.

Indeed.

◦﹏

A COUPLE DAYS LATER, I stood backstage of the dance studio, filling in for Troy as a stagehand for the recital. He loved volunteering at Katy's dance school, but since he was failing science, I'd restricted him from helping out until he pulled his grades up.

When his replacement fell through at the last minute, the studio asked me to help out. How could I say no since I was the cause of them being short-handed? I adjusted Katy's tutu, preparing her for her big routine, when my cell rang. I checked the caller ID and groaned, only answering because the show hadn't started yet.

"Hi, Mom. How are you?"

"Oh, you know me. More aches and pains every day, but I'll live... or so they tell me, but you know doctors. Half of them are quacks, I tell you."

I ground my teeth. The Rogers sisters could be my mother. There wasn't a medical problem in existence she hadn't been tested for.

"Mom, I really don't have time to discuss your latest medical issues. Katy is about to go on."

"Well, for heaven's sake, that's why I called." She huffed as though I didn't have a clue. "Now, how's my precious granddaughter? Is she nervous?"

Katy did a pirouette, spinning on her ballet slippers, her brown ringlets tamed into a tight bun. "Hardly. She's so ready, she can't sit still. I'll take lots of pictures and text them to you first thing in the morning."

"Make it tonight. I can't wait. I wish I could be with you." She paused. "You know if you move—"

"Mother, you promised." I kissed Katy's head and waved her off to join the rest of the squirming dancers and frazzled instructors.

"I'm just saying...."

"Well, don't."

"Someone needs to say something. Goodness gracious, Mary Caputo told me all about Sister Mary Agnes fainting over your so-called 'mixer.' What must Father O'Dority think?" she asked, aghast. "And now they think you're a Peeping Tom? This can't be helping to clear Lexi's name. Any news on that end?"

I pinched the bridge of my nose in a vain attempt to ward off the inevitable headache. Every time I talked to my mother, I ended up with a migraine that lasted a whole day. I inhaled and exhaled slowly.

"I assured Officer Pickles I was only picking up trash. There is no Peeping Tom, just silly paranoid old biddies. As for the sexy pictures, we still don't know who is behind altering the images to look like Lexi, but we did manage to get the question-able website to take them down. That's something, at least. I just wish we could find out who the real girl is and who posted them. Troy is trying to ask around at school, but of course, no one is talking."

A long sigh filled the line, and I swear I could feel the heat over a thousand miles away. "At least Dr. Anderson was good enough to let you continue to plan his party," she went on, "but dear, the hours you're keeping are atrocious. Mrs. Bee said Dr. Anderson stops by at all hours of the day and night. Whenever do you sleep?"

"There's a lot of work involved with this job, but I'm really enjoying it." I hadn't lied. We were working when we were together, as well as playing, and I was loving every minute of it.

"Are you sure it's just work you're enjoying at that time of night? Because you know, they say sex is great for—"

"Mother, please. Chaz is a doctor. He has crazy hours, so we meet whenever we can. To work. That's all."

"I'm just saying, it wouldn't hurt you to—"

"Mom, stop. I've told you numerous times I don't want to discuss my love life with you, not that I have one." Good Lord. If she could tell something was up from that far away, then I was in big trouble.

"Mmmm-hmmm. Well, just don't wear yourself out, honey. I worry about you."

Obsessed about me was more like it. "Don't worry; I'm getting plenty of rest. I'm eating right, taking my vitamins, and I even exercise. I joined the gym. Listen, Mom, I've got to go." I rubbed my throbbing temple. "The dance recital is about to start."

"Okay, well tell my little princess her favorite grandmother — not that nitwit of a nana shmana from Alabama— told her to break a leg. And don't overdo it with Chaz, okay?"

My mother and my ex-mother-in-law had always had this ongoing rivalry when it came to grand-parenting, but it had escalated since Max had left. They blamed each other for his leaving us. I tried not to get involved whenever possible, but it was exhausting at best.

"I'll tell Katy you wished her luck, and don't worry about me. I'll be fine." Fine as soon as I got a hold of some Excedrin and a big ole glass of Pinot Grigio.

"If you say so, dear."

I hung up, rifled through my purse for some headache medicine, and tiptoed over to the edge of the stage to peek out at the audience. Dressed all in black, I tried to stay hidden as I held the stage curtain in my hand and scanned what I could see of the rows of Mayflower Citizens. Everyone was there.

Mayor Edwards preened as his wife, Eleanor, fussed over him. Principal Brimstone finger-combed his mop of hair over his bald spot, not looking happy in the least as Bitsy filled his ear with God only knew what. Probably still trying to convince him to give the prom job back to her. Mrs. Hurley and Dr. Headright had their heads pressed together—as much as you could press a helmet of hair— deep in conversation.

Behind them, Sarah and Robin chatted excitedly about something— probably Sarah's new "hot guy." Gerty and Gabby Rogers almost fell out of their seats, undoubtedly straining to hear the latest gossip. Mrs. Bee took up two seats, her hands flying a mile a minute as she talked to Vinny and Mary Caputo. The Morgans beamed over little Jimmy while Dr. Joy cooed and tickled his belly. Even Lolita flirted shamelessly with all seven of Harmony's brothers, while a red-faced Officer Pickles fumed in the row behind them. Poor guy didn't stand a chance.

I squinted. My girls weren't anywhere in sight. I recognized their coats, holding the seats in the front row, but where on earth were they? I opened my cell.

"What are you doing?" Tiffany asked from behind me.

I jumped. "You guys aren't supposed to be back here. It's crazy during a show, you know that." We were way off to the side, so hopefully, no one would get angry. "I didn't get a chance to call you earlier, but I have to help out, so don't worry about saving me a seat."

"Well, that sucks," Harmony said. "You have a hole in your crotch, you know."

I blinked. "What?"

"A rip" Morticia clarified, shaking her head at Harmony. "Your pants are ripped at the crotch."

I glanced down, and sure enough, my pants had a rip in such a bad spot. How had I not noticed the draft? I crossed my legs, panic seizing me. I knew this no underwear trend would come back to bite me in the butt, or in this case....

"You have to help me fix this."

"Go in the bathroom and tape them together— "

"Tape *what* together?" I croaked.

"Your pants, from the inside." Tiffany said, looking at me as though I were crazy. "No one will ever know."

I just stood there, relief flooding me. They didn't know my secret, how could they? I hadn't told anyone except Chaz, but I was paranoid the whole world would know just by looking at me, and now I ripped my pants right *there*, of all places.

"Well, go on, doll. We'll cover for you."

"Great idea." I grabbed a roll of duct tape from the supply closet, ducked into the bathroom to tape my pants together from the inside, then joined them by the stage again. "Thanks. Not the most comfortable solution, but it worked like a charm."

"I've got a few tricks left." Tiffany grinned.

"Where are Troy and Lexi?" I asked. Troy was supposed to be studying, but I hadn't wanted to leave him home alone.

"Troy's over by the exit sign, talking to his girlfriend," Harmony answered matter-of-factly.

My heart pinged at the thought of my baby growing up. "He doesn't have a girlfriend." I looked at the far corner of the room and laughed. "No, no. That's just his tutor, Molly."

Morticia's gaze followed mine. "That's his tutor?"

"Yeah, why?"

"Doll, what were you thinking?" Tiffany shook her head. "You really don't know much about the male species, do you?"

I frowned. They had to be crazy. My Troy wasn't into girls yet. He was way too serious for his own good.

"Yeah, look at the way he's standing with his chest all out," Harmony said. "And when did he start laughing like that?"

"I have no idea." I gaped, seeing Troy in a whole new light. "How could I have no idea? What kind of mother am I?"

"An awesome one," Morticia chimed in. "So, you've been distracted. Who could blame you?"

"I think we know why he can't focus on his schoolwork, now." Tiffany squinted as though to see better. "He's so tense. Aw, poor Troy. I think he needs—"

"A big ole smooch from his cutie patootie tutor."

"Harmony." I scowled at her.

"I didn't say he should." She snorted. "I just said that's what he needs. And it's only a kiss, for crying out loud. But if you don't want it to happen, then you need to find him a new tutor. She seems to be just as into him as he is her." She pointed to the pretty girl staring up at him with stars in her eyes.

"Ya think?" I let out a huff.

"For the record, that's what I was going to say." Tiffany frowned at Harmony. "Really, Harm, show some tact."

Harmony shrugged. "I was just kidding."

"Have you looked into a learning center?" Morticia asked.

"Yes, but I can't afford one. And before you even suggest it, I'm not asking my mother for help."

"What about a male tutor?" Morticia's dark eyes settled on me, looking so serious.

This was serious. If I didn't do something, Troy would fail for sure. After all he'd been through, he didn't need his friends to move on to the junior high, while he stayed behind in middle school.

"What about an adult tutor?" Tiffany tilted her blond head. "There has to be someone around who Troy feels comfortable with and who's smart enough."

"Maybe. I'll have to look into it."

The door in the back of the room creaked open, and in walked Chaz. I forgot to breathe for a moment. God, he looked so good. He'd tucked his peach polo shirt into charcoal-gray Dockers that clung to his backside, revealing an amazing butt. I shivered.

"Maybe you won't have to look far," Morticia said, her gaze zooming in on Chaz.

"Oh, I could never ask Chaz to tutor Troy. He's so busy. That would be overstepping my bounds."

"Honey, I think you've overstepped more than your bounds when it comes to him. There's not much that man wouldn't do for you," Tiffany said.

"Or *to* you." Harmony snorted.

"Would you be quiet?" My gaze darted around, and I didn't relax until I was sure no one had heard.

"I still don't see the need for secrecy, doll, but that's your call." Tiffany wagged her brows. "You're a hell of a lot less tense these days, that's for sure. Less uptight and more carefree, so keep doing whatever you're doing."

"Maybe it's because there's something I'm not doing." I bit my lip, feeling like a fool but needing to share this with someone.

"Yeah?" Morticia's Mona Lisa smile crept across her face. "What's that?"

"I'm not wearing any underwear," I whispered.

"Get out." Harmony's jaw fell open. "No wonder you freaked over the hole in your crotch."

"Rip in her pants," Morticia corrected. "Get it right, Harm. We all have holes in our crotches, for God's sake."

"Shhh." I looked around, feeling my cheeks warm. "I feel free and sexy not wearing underwear, except for right now with duct tape holding my pants together." I squirmed. "Oh, look, the show's starting." I shooed my best friends back to their seats. Later I planned to put on a show of my own, with an encore that was sure to shock Dr. Hunkorama a bit as well.

I risked another peek toward the back, and my gaze collided with Chaz's. How had he seen me? His intense eyes held me captive as he started walking my way, but he must have seen the panicked look on my face, because he stopped and his shoulders dropped ever so slightly, then he took my spot next to my girls in the front row instead of backstage with me.

I smiled a thank you.

His face softened, and he winked, sending the butterflies dancing in my stomach again. Just then, Bitsy walked over and crouched down beside Chaz. He bent his head low and listened intently, then got up and led the way out of the auditorium with Bitsy close on his heels. If he'd turned her down to plan his party, then what did they have left to talk about? She was up to something. I planned to get to the bottom of it, but right now, my daughter needed me.

I turned around to watch Katy dance, but a dance of a different kind caught my eye on the other side of the room. Looked like my other daughter needed me as well. Lexi and Scott were kissing in the corner in front of everyone, and Sister Mary Agnes and Father O'Dority were headed their way. What in the world was she thinking? I did not need this right now.

I groaned, motioning for Harmony to come here. "Can you fill in for me? Duty calls."

"Sure thing, babe." Harmony held the curtain for me. "Give 'em hell."

"You can count on it," I said, feeling as though *I* were in hell, being punished for having a life. I wasn't about to give up the best thing that had happened to me in two years, but one thing was certain.

Things were going to change.

Chapter Twelve

A couple days later, I sat with Morticia at a table by the window at Lolita's Place, listening to the hum of conversations and the clanking of silverware. I inhaled the delicious aromas of onion soups, pastrami sandwiches and Spanish rice, and my stomach growled.

Speaking of being hungry, I thought of Chaz. This was the exact table we'd sat at when he asked me to plan his parents' party. I couldn't help doing a quick sweep of the restaurant, hoping to see a glimpse of him in the growing lunch crowd. No such luck.

"How's Lexi?" Morticia asked.

"Mad as hell at me, same as always." I sighed. "She knows she's not supposed to hang out with this Scott kid, yet she defies me every chance she gets. I grounded her and took away her phone. Again. If he can't get to her, she won't have a choice but to listen to me. At least I hope that's how it will work out." I trailed my fingers through my curls, and then folded my hands on the table. "I don't know what to do anymore or how to get through to her."

"Don't worry." Morticia squeezed my wrist. "She'll come around."

"I hope so. I'm just so busy, it's getting harder to manage everything by myself. I know you guys and Mrs. Bee help out whenever you can, but lately, it's not enough."

"What about hiring a baby-sitter?"

"I haven't been able to find one, and with Lexi, I'd feel more comfortable with an adult. Chaz even offered to help." My eyes met hers. "He said he has a ton of little cousins he never gets to see, so if I ever wanted him to take the kids for ice cream or the movies, he'd be happy to."

"You should let him."

"I don't know." I shrugged. "I told him it wasn't necessary, but he said if I ever changed my mind, it was an open invite." I lifted my hands, palms up, then studied my best friend. "What about you? Anything going on?"

Her face looked pale; her dark hair pulled back tighter than usual in her constant bun.

"Nothing's going right." She toyed with her silverware, and her big eyes met mine. "I'm sick of my life. It's only been my father and me for so long, I can't stand it. I feel like I'm stuck in a rut, and I can't get out, you know? I'm not getting any younger. I'm starting to think I'll never get married or have a baby."

I nodded, smiling in sympathy. Here Morticia was dying for a change when change was the last thing I'd ever wanted, yet my life had changed in a huge way two years ago. It had taken me a long time to accept that Max was gone for good, so it seemed strange to have allowed Chaz into my life so quickly. I thought about that, rationalizing I was human, with human needs.

I'd needed some male companionship, that was all. Any man would have done, I just happened to know Chaz, so it had happened that much quicker. What we were doing was temporary, so it wasn't really a change. At least not a permanent one. Once this affair played out, I'd go right back to my old life. So why did I feel like I was trying to convince myself of this? I shook off that notion and focused on my friend.

"I say this in the most loving way. You have to put yourself out there for change to happen, Morti. You spend a lot of time alone. If it wasn't for us, you wouldn't have a social life at all." I took a sip of my iced tea.

She let out a frustrated breath. "I've tried to have a social life, but you know how I get when I'm around the living." She dropped her gaze to the table, now twisting her napkin with her pale hands. "Other than you guys, they freak me out."

"Okay, most people are freaked out by the *dead*, not the living." I chuckled.

"What can I say, the dead are good listeners. They don't talk back, so no awkward conversations there." She shrugged. "I have a life. I read and play around on the Internet. What's wrong with that?"

"You play games or join bookclubs. Nothing is wrong with that, but you've said you wanted a baby. A book or the Internet can't give you a baby. Look, there's nothing wrong with either, just don't let them consume your life. It's not good to be alone all the time. You're becoming a recluse." I squeezed the lemon into my tea and took another sip. "We all worry about you."

Finally, the waitress brought our food out, not quite meeting our eyes, and slipping away as quickly as possible. Even though we'd ordered the exact same thing, Morticia's portion was noticeably smaller than mine.

"Gee, I wonder why I'm a recluse." Morticia looked toward the kitchen, and my eyes followed suit.

Lolita stood in the open doorway with a satisfied smirk on her wrinkle-free, heart-shaped face, her cinnamon hair falling in waves over one perfectly toned shoulder. It amazed me how anyone could still look that good at forty.

Morticia smirked right back at her. "The woman hates me."

"I don't think she hates you. I think she's jealous." I mixed my dressing into my Caesar salad and took a bite.

"Of what, for God's sake? Look at her."

I glanced back by the door, but she'd disappeared into the kitchen. "That's the point. All she has is her looks, but you," I pointed my fork at Morticia, "you're so smart, and you have natural beauty."

"And you're too nice." She plopped a bite of her own salad into her mouth. After a moment, she said, "Lolita has never gotten over me winning her spot on the cheer squad. I never did understand why."

"Well, that's easy. She hates to lose at anything. By you winning her position, you gained popularity. Then when Eddy Heller asked you to the prom instead of her, she was crushed."

"But he only asked me as a joke. We never ended up going."

"Because you chickened out. He really did like you; you were just too insecure to believe it. But that doesn't matter. The point is he asked you and not her. In some strange, twisted way, she's been trying to outdo you ever since. You got a job at your dad's business, so she started her own. You donated books to the library, so she donated a new wing. And now whenever you so much as talk to a man, she makes you look weird until she wins him over, and then she sleeps with him."

"You'd think after twenty-two years, she'd grow up."

"Yeah, you'd think, but vicious cycles are hard to break. Someday there will be a man who won't fall under her spell, and who will see how amazing you really are."

"Yeah, well, I'm not holding my breath. It would have to take an outsider for that to happen."

"Hey, speaking of outsiders, who was the woman I saw your dad with the other day? I didn't recognize her."

Morticia's fork halted halfway to her lips. "What do you mean?"

"He didn't say anything?" I asked, but Morticia shook her head slowly. "Oh, well, maybe someone died." I smiled encouragingly, and then frowned at that thought. Good Lord, I was becoming as morbid as Morticia, but I knew this conversation was making her uncomfortable.

"We haven't had a funeral for anyone local in weeks, and for outsiders, in months. Besides, arrangements are normally made in the office at the funeral home. What, exactly, did you see?"

"Well, I saw your dad in here the other day having lunch with this young attractive blonde woman. They looked pretty serious, so maybe they really were talking about funeral arrangements, especially since she looked half his age. And let's face it; your dad hasn't had lunch with anyone except you since I've known him."

Morticia set her fork down as though she'd lost her appetite and took a long sip of her tea before she spoke. "So that's why Dad's been MIA lately. I can't get a guy to ask me out, yet my old man's banging a chick young enough to be his daughter. I need a drink."

"But you don't drink."

"Maybe it's time to start."

"Oh, honey, I'm sure it's not what you think. That girl is probably just planning ahead. Buying a plot for a parent, or something. I'm sure there's no banging of any kind going on." I tried to lighten the situation with humor, since Morticia looked really upset.

Morticia's lips tipped up slightly at the corners. "You been reading Harmony's tarot cards?"

"If only it were that easy to predict the future."

"I hear that." We clinked our glasses of iced tea. "As much as I want things in my life to change, that's not one of them. My dad hasn't dated anyone in almost forty years. Why now? And why hasn't he told me?"

"I don't know, honey, but you can't worry about something you can't control."

We finished our salads without talking, both needing the silence as we grappled with our own thoughts.

Change. A scary word.

Was my life about to change now that I'd allowed Chaz to become a part of it? My sex life had changed in a big way, but that was all. So far, other than my girls, no one knew about our affair. Chaz and I always met in secret, and only when my kids weren't around. I'd tried to keep them away from him as much as possible, because I didn't want them growing attached to him. As far as they knew, Chaz was their doctor and a client of mine, nothing more.

And that's the way I intended to keep it.

The problem was change didn't factor in our intentions. It happened whether we wanted it to or not, and there wasn't a darn thing we could do about it.

"You got an 'A', Troy. That's fantastic." I taped his science test to the refrigerator, pride bursting through me.

I'd told Molly we didn't need her services anymore, much to Troy's dismay, but I hadn't found a man willing to tutor him, either. Maybe he'd just needed the distraction to be gone, and he would be fine on his own. I got out the lemonade and poured a glass. Troy came over and snatched the test, pulling it down.

"Mom, you are not hanging this up. I'm not three, I'm thirteen." He flipped his blond hair to the side with a jerk of his head.

"You're a dork," Lexi said from the dining room table where she sat, working on her own homework.

"Lexi," I said, letting her know in no uncertain terms that her little comment was definitely 'look' worthy.

"He is not a dork. You are." Bobby jumped to Troy's defense, sword ready in hand.

"Thanks, little bro." Troy held out his fist. "Pound it." To which Bobby dropped his sword and smacked his fist against Troy's, wearing a huge grin.

"Lexi's not a dork. She's a princess. Right, Lexi?" Katy skipped to her sister's side, staring up at her with pure worship.

If Lexi shot her down, she'd be grounded for a year. Lexi was no fool. She glanced at me first, and then rolled her eyes.

When Katy's bottom lip wobbled, Lexi said, "Sure, squirt. Now go play so I can finish my letter to the queen."

"Yay, the queen, the queen. I'm going to draw a picture for the prince." Katy trotted off to get her paper and crayons.

"Yeah? Good luck with that one." Lexi shot me a scowl and went back to doing her homework.

I focused my attention on Troy. "I'm so proud of you, sweetheart. I won't hang your test up, but I'm not throwing it away, either." I slipped it on top of the refrigerator, out of sight, but there to remind him the next time he was having trouble.

"Good, because I wanted to show Chaz."

"Excuse me?" I choked on my lemonade. "Why show him, and since when did you start to call Dr. Anderson Chaz?"

"Since he asked me to."

"When?" My pulse skipped a beat.

"That time you were gone shopping and Mrs. Bee was busy, so you had him take us out for ice cream."

"Oh, that day." I clamped my teeth tight and spoke through

them. "I just didn't think he'd have you call him by his first name. So what did you guys do when you got back?"

"Studied. He helped me focus. I think I actually understand chemical and physical properties now. His explanations made a lot more sense than Molly's. Although I don't really remember what Molly said the last time she was here. You know, the time she wore that purple sweater." His blue eyes turned glassy.

Troy didn't remember what Molly said, yet he remembered what she wore. I bit back a groan, so not ready for this. And I'd only asked Chaz to give them ice cream, not science lessons, but how could I be mad after seeing the end result?

"Well, I'm glad he was able to help you."

"Hey, Mommy, know what?" Katy asked from behind me.

I turned around and smiled as I watched her plop down on the floor and open her portable dollhouse.

"Sweetie, you're playing with your Barbies again, that's great."

"Uh-huh, cuz I found out where the daddy goes when he's not at the doctor's office. See, right here by you in your big bed, so you don't have to sleep in the middle no more." She beamed.

"Uh... I... Oh, my." I glanced at her feet and latched onto another subject with a desperation I hadn't felt in weeks. "Honey, you know we don't wear our shoes in the house."

Her lip trembled, and she let out a wail. It took me ten minutes to calm her down. Once I did, she said, "Ch-Chaz taught me how to ties my shoes, and I just wanted to show you."

"He did, did he?" A small slice of sadness swept over me. This is what Max would have done, had he stuck around. He'd taught both boys how to tie their shoes, and now another man had taught his youngest daughter. Anger clogged my throat, but I managed to ask, "How long was he here, anyway?"

"That was the other time," Lexi said.

The lump momentarily forgotten, I narrowed my eyes.

"Which time was that again?" I hadn't realized how much I'd come to rely on Chaz. I'd been desperate for a sitter the first time, so I gave in and called him, and it had sort of snowballed since.

"You know, when he took us to the movie so you could go with Auntie Tiff, Auntie Harm, and Auntie Morti," Bobby said as he bounced by like a blond Tigger, fighting imaginary opponents with his sword. "He even mowed the lawn, Mommy, didn't you notice?" Bobby said as he bounced back the other way.

Spring had sprung quickly with warm temps. "I thought Troy did that."

"Nope. He told me to study. He took out the trash, too. I even had time to shoot hoops with my friends for a while."

"Really, now." I was thrilled to see Troy doing something fun for a change, but that didn't mean I wasn't angry at Chaz for stepping in and saving the day once again. Movies and mowing the lawn were two entirely different things.

"Yeah, and the next time he taught me how to hit the baseball. Didn't you notice I hit the ball every time in my game today?" Bobby looked at me with wounded eyes as though I hadn't paid attention.

"Of course, I noticed, honey." I hadn't, and now I felt guilty for being too distracted these days. Another thing I had Chaz to thank for. "You did a great job today. I also noticed what you did this morning," I changed the subject. "Taping all the toilet seats together?"

His guilty eyes met mine, but I had to give him an A for effort. "How did you know it was me?"

"Puh-lease," Lexi chimed in.

"You're kidding, right?" Troy added his two cents.

I just stood hands on my hips, foot tapping the floor, waiting.

"April fools?"

"Nice try, pal, it's a little late for April fools, don't you think?" I scooped a rebellious strand of hair off his forehead. "I nearly wet my pants before I got that tape undone."

"Well, that's not *my* fault. You shouldn't have waited so long to go potty." He shrugged my hand away and went back to sword fighting. "You always say don't hold it. Go when you gotta go."

He had a point. Still. "Well, I didn't think I'd have to spend time getting the lid up before going. Don't do that again. And speaking of going, go on up and take a shower, my dirty little devil. And Katy, march on up to my room. I'll be up to give you a bath in a second."

I didn't have to say a word to Troy about doing his homework. Now that he was doing better, I couldn't get him to stop. I marched into the dining room and crossed my arms under my chest. "Why didn't you tell me all the things Dr. Anderson has being doing to help out?"

"Why should I?" Lexi muttered. "You haven't listened to anything I've said lately, so why bother." Her amber eyes met mine. "What's with you and 'Chaz', anyway?"

I blinked a few times, my throat suddenly dry. "We're not discussing me, we're discussing you."

"No, we're not, Mom. I haven't done anything wrong. I stay in my little prison, do my homework, and watch my social life go down the drain." Her eyes never wavered. "Are *you* the one who's done something wrong?"

"Don't be ridiculous."

"Then what's the problem?"

"There isn't one, but I am your mother. I expect to hear about everything that goes on when it comes to my children. I know you think this is your prison and I'm your warden, but I'm trying to keep you from making a horrible mistake. Not to mention, clear your name. I love you, honey, and one day I hope you'll understand I'm doing this for your own good."

"Whatever." She scooped up her books and stormed up the stairs to her bedroom.

Change. That was the problem, I thought.

I didn't like change, I didn't need change, I didn't want change. Chaz was temporary, not permanent. I did not want my kids getting too attached to him, used to relying on him, but like it or not, that seemed to be happening all on its own. With attachment, inevitably came pain, and *that* was why I hated change. Just wait until I got my hands on him. I'd show him change, all right.

I had a good mind to change him from an alto to a soprano.

LATE THAT EVENING and several glasses of Pinot Grigio later, I locked up the house and headed upstairs to check on the kids. Chaz had called my cell several times, but I hadn't answered. I'd turned my phone on silent, not ready to talk to him just yet. I knew what he had on his mind, but I still had thoughts of making him sing soprano.

Not a good night for sex.

It was my own fault. I was the one who'd asked for his help, I just hadn't expected him to help quite that much. I tiptoed down the hall and checked on Bobby, who was sound asleep in the bottom bunk of his bunk beds, his sword still in hand. I slipped the sword out and covered him up, touching his cheek before I left.

Next, I peeked into Troy's room. He had sprawled out across his double bed, his textbook still resting on his chest. I picked it up and set it on his desk, covered him, and brushed a lock of hair off his forehead.

Further down the hall, I slipped into my Katy's room. She had her knees tucked up under her, with her butt sticking up in the air and her thumb in her mouth. The princess canopy above her bed draped down over her like a shroud. My heart melted. I covered her up and kissed her soft cheek.

The last door in the hall was the only one closed tight, the message clear. Keep out. No matter what Lexi did or how mad she got, I wasn't about to keep out. She needed me, she just didn't know it yet. I took a breath and opened the door, blinking against the darkness. I struggled to focus. My heart started thumping hard as I walked to the side of her bed.

Her *empty* bed.

"Oh, God," I whispered as I swept my hand across the covers. "Oh God, oh God, oh God." I searched the house, but couldn't find her anywhere, so I ran out to the kitchen and called Tiffany.

"What's the matter, Doll? I was just about to turn in."

"Sh-She's gone." I could barely get the words out.

"Who's gone?"

"Lexi. She's not in her bed." I paced back and forth, my breathing erratic. "Oh God, I have no idea how long she's been gone."

"Calm down, doll. Call her cell phone."

"I can't. I grounded her, remember? Why did I take her phone away? If anything happens to her, it's all my fault."

"Nothing is going to happen to her. Just stay where you are. I mean it, don't go anywhere without us. Call Mrs. Bee to come stay with the kids, while I round up the girls. We won't stop until we find her. It's going to be okay, Zoe, I promise."

"That's what everyone said when Max left, but he never came back, Tiffany. Oh God, what have I done?"

"Snap out of it, Zoe. Lexi needs you to be strong. I'll call the girls, and we'll be right there."

"Okay." A shaky breath hitched in my throat. "Okay."

I sat through the longest ten minutes of my life, and for once, Mrs. Bee didn't ask any questions. Finally, my girls arrived. Moments later, we climbed into Harmony's love bug and scoured the town.

"Where could she be?" I asked.

"I thought for sure she'd be with Scott." Harmony maneuvered the bug around the next left. "Did you see the look on his mother's face when we barged right past her and checked his bedroom?"

"Doll, did you see *his* face when we woke him up?" Tiffany laughed. "I don't think we have to worry about him hitting on Lexi anytime soon."

"Not after Zoe threatened to emasculate him if he came near her daughter again." Morticia chuckled. "I didn't know she had it in her."

"*She* is sitting right here," I said. "For the record, it was the wine talking, and I'd had emasculation on my mind long before we stormed into Scott's bedroom. Forget about that... *where* is my daughter?"

"We're just trying to take your mind off that, doll." Tiffany hugged me.

"I know." My voice hitched. "But nothing will take my mind off that until I find my baby. We've checked out all of the hotspots. Where the hell is she?" My cell phone rang again for the millionth time that evening after I'd taken it off silent. I didn't have to check the Caller ID to know who it was.

"Aren't you going to answer it?" Harmony glanced in the rear-view mirror.

"It's Chaz. He's been calling all evening, but I don't want to talk to him."

"You two have a fight?" Morticia craned her neck around from the front seat.

"Not exactly. You know how I took him up on his offer to help with the kids?" They nodded, and I continued. "Well, I'd had ice cream and movies in mind, not filling in as the man of the house."

"And that's bad because... " Harmony glanced over her shoulder at me and arched a brow.

"Because a big brother relationship they can handle, but a temporary father... not so much. I didn't want my kids getting too close to him, but I think it's too late. They adore him, even Lexi, which surprises me because I didn't think she adored anyone these days."

The women all stared at each other, then Tiffany said, "Call me crazy, but do you think Lexi would have gone to see Chaz?"

Could it be that simple? Could I have been that stupid not to see it? "I don't know. I guess it's possible. He has called more tonight than ever. I just thought he must be really horny or wondering why I'd blown him off."

"Did he leave a message on your answering machine?" Morticia asked.

"I, um, sort of turned it off." I had a home phone still, but I never used it.

"And your cell's voicemail?" Harmony asked.

"Well, I... I erased all messages without listening to them, okay? What can I say, I was angry."

I felt like such an idiot. If she'd been with Chaz all this time and I'd worried myself sick out of sheer stubbornness, well, it would serve me right. At this point, I didn't care. I wanted her safe.

"Call him, Zoe," Tiffany said.

"Okay." I dialed Chaz's number and held my breath.

He answered on the first ring. "Where the hell have you been? I've been calling all evening, Zoe. Lexi is here."

I started to cry.

His tone softened. "She's okay, sweetheart."

"I'll be right there." I hung up.

Five minutes later, I was at his house, my girls waiting in the driveway.

Chaz stood in the doorway, looking so solid, so dependable and safe, I wanted to crawl into his arms and have him make it all better. He waved to my best friends as he let me inside and opened his arms. I flew against him and sobbed, and he kissed the top of my head.

"You didn't have to come over," he said.

"Yes, I did. I was so scared I'd lost her forever. I won't be able to sleep until I see her. Where is she?" I leaned back, and he wiped my tears away with his thumbs.

"She was running away, but she didn't get far, when something possessed her to come to my house. I'm just glad she did. She's sound asleep in one of my guest rooms. Good thing I had an air mattress since I still haven't furnished those."

He took my hand and led the way upstairs, and then we quietly peeked inside the room. I stifled another sob as I stroked her brown curls softly and kissed the crown of her head. Only once I was sure she was really here and safe, did I let him lead me back downstairs.

Chaz said, "I think you should let her stay. She had quite a breakthrough tonight, and she's pretty exhausted."

"B-Breakthrough?" I hiccupped.

"Yeah. Turns out she doesn't want a boyfriend; she just wants some male attention. She cried on my shoulder for hours as she talked about how much she missed her dad."

"She cried? Oh, my God," I breathed. "She hasn't cried in two years. I've tried to talk to her, the girls have tried, even her therapist. How did you—"

"I don't know. Maybe because I'm a guy? Was her therapist a woman?"

I felt my eyes widen. "Yes. How stupid of me not to see that."

So, this was what had been going on with Lexi. She had needed a man to talk to. I was relieved, but it wouldn't help prove she wasn't the one in the pictures. If anything, it would only make her look worse. She couldn't talk to me, so she was reaching out to the men in Mayflower. First her principal and now Chaz.

"Well, there you go. And you're far from stupid, Zoe, you were just trying to make her comfortable. Safe. I think she needed a father figure to talk to. We've been talking all week, and I guess she felt comfortable with me."

"About that. We need to talk, but not tonight." Again, how could I be mad about his infiltrating my life after an outcome like getting through to Lexi?

"I figured you'd want to talk, but just so you know, I didn't plan to become such a big part of their lives." His eyes met mine, his sincerity as clear as day. "It sort of happened, and well, I liked it. They're great kids."

"They are great kids who can probably handle more than I'm giving them credit for." I took a deep breath. "You can spend time with them, and even... help them, but I still don't want them to know we're anything more than friends. Because we're not. It's just sex, okay?"

He stared at me long and hard. "Sure. Whatever you say." He poured me two fingers of bourbon and said, "Drink. Then go home and sleep. I know she scared you, Zoe, but go easy on her tomorrow, okay?"

"Done." I tossed back the liquid and winced as it burned a path down my throat, landing in my stomach and warming my whole body. "I'm so glad she's safe." I kissed him lightly on the lips. "Thanks, Chaz."

"Anytime, sweetheart. I'd do anything for you; don't you

know that by now?" His voice held a teasing note, but his eyes were dead serious.

I smiled and turned to leave before the bourbon made me say something I'd regret. Like what I wanted him to do for me and to me for the rest of.... I repeat, change never brought anything but trouble. And I'd had about all the trouble I could handle for one night.

He touched my arm to stop me. "Wait. There's something more you should know."

"What now?" I groaned as I faced him once more.

"This came about an hour after Lexi got here. Who knows how many others are out there." Chaz held up an eight by ten collage print of the sexy pictures people claimed were Lexi, his face a mixture of sympathy and anger.

"Oh, my God," I whispered. "They're going to think Lexi did this, aren't they?"

"Tell them she never left home."

"Are you kidding? Mrs. Bee can't keep her mouth closed, and I'm sure poor Scott will need therapy after tonight. Besides, Harmony's love bug isn't exactly discreet. I'm sure people saw us driving around town this late." I'd made such a mess of things, this time I had no qualms about looking to Chaz for help. "What am I going to do?"

"Tell them she was here all night. I won't tell anyone I received a copy. If she was with me when the pictures were delivered, there's no way she could be responsible," he said simply, but we both knew what that meant.

"Chaz. I— I can't."

"More like you won't because everyone will know something more than party planning is going on between us if your daughter ran to me for help."

"There has to be another way." I started pacing, racking my brain for something, anything other than telling the town about our affair, but I kept coming up blank. My shoulders slumped, and I fought back tears as I looked up at Chaz. "My daughter is more important than my career or my reputation. I'll do it."

Chaz stared at me for a long moment, his eyes boring into mine as though he could see straight into my soul. A brief flash of something— sadness maybe, but I couldn't be sure— flashed in his hazel eyes seconds before he shook his head.

"Wait. I think I've got a plan."

Chapter Thirteen

"People, one at a time please," Mayor Edwards spoke into the microphone from the front of city hall auditorium. The town council members sat on either side of him at the long table, and all of Mayflower filled the audience, including most of the teenagers. When the rumble of conversation echoing off the walls quieted, the mayor pointed his finger. "Go ahead, Ms. Rogers."

Gerty made her way up to the table and pulled out a stack of papers from her enormous purse, setting them in front of the town council. The petition, no doubt. "As you can see, most of our fine citizens agree something must be done. Our young folk have spun out of control, I tell you. Out of control."

Gabby appeared by Gerty's side. "Out of control, indeed, sister. Why, I found several copies of those pictures floating around town just this morning." Her pale wrinkled hand smoothed over her gray bun, then fluttered to her typically drab bosom. "If these children," she turned around and her gaze landed on Lexi, who stood defiant but trembling beside me, "were forced to stay indoors under their parents' supervision after dark, then we'd all be better off."

A grumble of protest came from the corner of the room where all the teenagers sat. Well, most of them, anyway. Lexi wasn't invited to join them, hence her defiant posture, poor baby. She didn't deserve any of this, and I'd had enough.

"Seems to me it's not just the children who need to stay in after dark." Bitsy glared at me, and all eyes followed.

"I saw Mrs. Robinson and her strange friends," Lolita jerked her chin toward Morticia who sat between Tiffany and Harmony, "tearing up the streets in that tacky junk mobile in the middle of the night."

"At least I *have* some junk in my trunk," Harmony muttered.

"Apparently, she doesn't have any taste either, doll. I saw that dress on a clearance rack in Boston. It has last season written all over it." Tiffany looked down her nose at Lolita's feet. "Don't get me started on her shoes."

"Well, I never—" Lolita started.

"That's not what I heard." Morticia high-fived Harmony, her Mona Lisa smile in place. Don't mess with my girls, because taking on one meant taking on all.

"Ladies, please," Mayor Edwards interjected. "Back to the matter at hand." He motioned to Mrs. Hurley to speak.

"Well, I have to say the rumor that Lexi ran away concerns me, especially with all the problems Mrs. Robinson has been having lately. Is it true?" Mrs. Hurley asked.

Scribble, scribble, scribble.

My gaze darted to the woman beside her, and there was no mistaking that blond helmet of hair. Dr. Headright was writing furiously in that blasted notebook. I couldn't believe she had ventured two whole towns and clear across the swan pond, but she had vowed not to quit until she helped me.

Apparently, I was the only one whose head she hadn't got right.

"Well, I did see Mrs. Bee walk over to her house. She usually watches the children when Zoe steps out. She must have been looking for her daughter, who was obviously up to no good putting pictures in people's mailboxes." Bitsy pounced on Mrs. Hurley's question as she adopted a phony concerned look, but when her eyes met mine, the corners of her lips tipped up a smidgen.

"I was borrowing a cup of sugar," Mrs. Bee snapped.

"Darling, since when do you bake?" Bitsy blinked at Mrs. Bee, who flushed the same shade as her favorite dessert: peach cobbler.

"At least I try," Mrs. Bee snapped. "You don't know everything." Her eyes met mine in apology, but I shot her a little wink and a grateful smile.

Gerty chose that moment to chime in. "I say it's time to vote on the matter."

"I second," Gabby parroted.

"If you don't mind, I'd like to say something." I focused on the parents, and the room grew quiet. "Yes, Lexi ran away, but she was upset. Understandably so, considering what she's going through. She came back home after she thought about what she was doing, right, Mrs. Bee?"

Mrs. Bee's face beamed. "That's right. She sure did because she's a good girl." She glared at Bitsy. "Always has been."

I put my arm around Lexi's shoulders and gave her a squeeze. "I know my daughter, and I trust her. If she says she isn't the girl in the pictures, then I believe her. She doesn't deserve to be treated like this, just as none of your children would." I looked at the other teenagers in the room, who couldn't quite meet my eyes. "You do realize if this petition goes through, the prom and all that goes with it is off since it does take place outside of your parents' houses, and it is after dark."

Several teenage faces registered surprise as though none of

them had considered this. A loud protest reverberated throughout the room. I glanced at the back door, but still no Chaz. I needed the last piece of the puzzle to seal the vote, but I was afraid he wasn't going to make it in time.

"The prom can happen during the day, and I can plan it, for that matter," Bitsy said.

"Well, now, let's not be hasty." Brimstone stepped in, meeting my eyes with a slight nod, reiterating 'what happens on the boulevard, stays on the boulevard'.

Bitsy turned her focus off me for a change as she gaped at Brimstone.

He ignored her and continued, "The kids have worked hard and deserve to have a prom. A real prom. And Ms. Robinson has earned the right to plan it." He turned his intimidating stare on all the parents. "One that happens at night with limos and dinners and after parties, same as we all had when we were kids. You only get one senior prom, folks. Is this how you want your children's memories to be?"

"Maybe Lexi should be the only one who doesn't get to go since she's the one who started all this," a teenage girl piped up from the back.

"Who's that?" I whispered to Lexi.

"Scott's ex-girlfriend. She hates me because she thinks I stole Scott from her. I swear, I didn't know they were still going out when, you know, that thing after school happened," Lexi whispered back as she dropped her chin to the floor.

I squeezed her shoulder again. "If my daughter doesn't go, then I don't plan the prom. Simple as that."

Lexi's head snapped up, and her lips parted. "You would do that for me?"

"Yeah." I stared hard into her eyes, trying to express all we never seemed to be able to convey through words. "I would do anything for you."

"Well, I think—" Bitsy started.

"I couldn't agree more, Bitsy. No one should be judged before we have all the facts," Chaz said as he marched through the doors with Scott in tow. "Isn't that what you were just telling me earlier today?"

Bitsy stiffened but backed off immediately.

I frowned.

"Scott here has something he would like to say, don't you, son?" Chaz patted Scott's back.

Scott cleared his throat, looking nervous and guilty. "I, um, I ran into Dr. Anderson yesterday, and well, he saw some pictures of mine and thought I needed to come clean."

"Go on, you're doing great, son," Chaz prodded.

"I mean... oh, man, it's not my fault, it's all hers." He pointed his finger to his ex-girlfriend in the back. "She's the one who made me post those pictures of Lexi on the Internet, just because she was jealous I dumped her."

"You jerk!" the girl screeched. "You didn't dump me, you cheated on me. I can't believe you told. You only agreed to post those stupid pictures so I wouldn't tell everyone you have crabs. Lucky for her she didn't sleep with you, you pig."

A gasp rang out in the auditorium.

"That's enough, Michelle." The girl's mother grabbed her arm and pulled her toward the exit, saying, "You can forget about the prom, young lady."

"Who cares?" the girl screeched. "Everyone got to see I'm much prettier than her, anyway, since *I'm* the one in the pictures."

Her mother cried out and yanked her through the door, leaving a stunned and quiet crowd behind.

Scott turned to Lexi, his face red and head hanging low. "I'm sorry, Lex. I never meant to hurt you."

Lexi refused to look at him. I rubbed her back, and she lifted her head high, not uttering a single word, but her trembling had vanished along with the town's doubt concerning her innocence. Oh, sweet vindication. I'd never been more proud of her.

Scott's mother grabbed his arm and hustled him out, muttering, "You should have thought of that before you embarrassed me in front of the entire town. Crabs? How am I ever going to live this down?"

"Well, people, while I think a curfew is important, I don't think lowering it to a ridiculous hour is warranted. I say two bad apples shouldn't spoil things for the whole bunch. It's time to put this matter of lowering the curfew to a vote. All those in favor say aye," the mayor said.

I held my head as high as Lexi's and scanned the crowd. Everyone sat in stunned silence.

"All those opposed say nay."

People snapped out of their shock, and a chorus of "Nay's" rang out, reminding me of a herd of bleating goats.

"Then I think it's safe to say, this meeting is adjourned." The mayor nodded once. "It looks like the prom is still on."

The room broke out in cheers, but I only had two words I needed to say. My eyes met Chaz's, and I mouthed, "Thank you." He just winked, but I knew exactly what that meant. I could do my own personal cheer for him later. I do believe I had to second that, seeing as how I had a rather large set of pom poms I was more than ready to shake.

Meeting adjourned. *Hear, hear.*

ONCE A YEAR, on the anniversary of Tiffany's divorce, we held our girls' night in the local Irish pub instead of her house. Paul McGinnis used to be the owner, but he'd sold the pub to his nephew, Matt, this past year. Since they were a big Irish family, with strong traditions and roots, they had kept the business in the family for generations, making very few changes along the way.

The place was quaint and cozy with sturdy wooden tables, a fireplace in one corner, Irish band in the other, and beers from around the world. When the music played, the entire bar joined in to sing. I imagined this was exactly what a real pub would look like in Ireland.

"Sex suits you," Harmony said.

"Excuse me?" I choked on my wine.

"She's right." Morticia shrugged. "You look happy. Relaxed."

"I think even Dr. Headright would give you a clean bill of health right now." Tiffany smiled.

"You really think so?"

I thought about all the wonderful things Chaz had brought to my life. Troy was doing so much better in school, Bobby and Katy were more energetic than ever, and Lexi had done a complete turnaround. She actually smiled the other day, and she hadn't gotten in trouble in over a week. Chaz had even taught her how to drive.

"I guess I am happy. The kids have grown so close to Chaz, but that's okay because they know he's just a friend."

"Right." Harmony coughed into her fist.

"Well, he is. A friend with benefits, that's all. Like you guys said, it's just sex."

"Thought you didn't do just sex." Morticia smirked.

"Well, I've learned to. Even when this," I struggled with the word, "*affair* plays itself out, we'll still be friends."

Tiffany eyed the other women. "Sure you will, doll."

"So where is 'Mr. Just Friends' anyway?" Morticia asked.

"Hanging with my kids."

"Right." Harmony snorted.

"What? They like spending time together, and it's more convenient for, um, later." I cleared my throat, desperate to change the subject. "So Tiffany, it's your night. Anything you want to talk about?"

She took a sip of her martini. "Had a fight with my mother again."

"You actually talked to her?" I asked.

"Yeah, and it wasn't pretty."

"Holy shit, you're kidding." Harmony gaped.

"What's it been, like five years?" Morticia asked.

"More like eight. Talked to my sister, Tabitha, too. She doesn't get why I won't go see our mom. Then again, she's the twin they kept. Our parents are still golden in her eyes." Tiffany sighed. "My mother still won't go see Grammy because of the fight they had years ago, even though the woman is on her deathbed."

"You're gonna hate me for saying this, but they don't get along, either." Harmony did a shot and chased it with a beer. "Put yourself in her shoes. You barely talk to your mother." Meeting Tiffany's gaze head on, she asked, "Would you go see her even if she was on her deathbed?"

Tiffany scowled and opened her mouth, then let out a huff. "Hell, I don't know." She tossed back a mouthful of her martini in true Harmony fashion, but then dabbed the corners of her mouth with her napkin in true Tiffany style. "On another lovely note, my bastard ex keeps calling, demanding more money. Apparently, his back is so bad, he's permanently disabled."

"More like a permanent deadbeat," Morticia muttered.

"Ain't that the truth. Speaking of dead 'beats,' what's up with this music?" Harmony turned to the Irish band in the corner. "Yo, laddy, you got anything peppier in that fiddle?"

The big, blond Irishman frowned. He had to be related to

Matt McGinnis because he looked just like him, I thought as I studied him.

"Forgive my friend." Tiffany smiled sweetly. "We're having a celebration."

The cute blond winked, then moved from the slow rendition of *Danny Boy*, into a lively jig.

"Atta boy." Harmony raised her beer in salute, but the man ignored her. Same as all the other men in the bar. "Goddamn men. Who the hell needs them?" She shook her red, spiky head of hair and focused on us. "To another year of freedom, babe."

"To another year of happiness," I added.

"To us," Morticia chimed in.

"I'll drink to all of those." Tiffany clinked her martini to Harmony's dark beer, Morticia's Diet Cola, and my Pinot Grigio.

"I heard there was a celebration," said a deep voice. Matt McGinnis stood there, looking like a curly-haired blond giant with sparkling blue eyes focused solely on Tiffany as he held a tray of drinks in his huge hands. "These are on the house." His smile spread across his rugged face, his dimples sinking deep.

Tiffany blushed. Tiffany *never* blushed.

"Why, thank you, doll. That's so sweet of you."

"My pleasure. So, what are you celebrating?"

"My divorce."

His blond brow crept higher, and his smile slipped a little, but then he winked. "Okay, then." He glanced at the customers waiting for refills at the bar. "Looks like the new guy needs me. Have a good one, lass."

Tiffany watched him saunter away, her gaze fixed on his muscular glutes, and she looked as though she was about to swoon. "He's not the only one who needs you, doll." She faced us. "Did you see that ass? And those hands. My God think what those hands could do." She shivered.

"Oh, yeah, baby. Very nice." Harmony took a swig of her beer, and clunked the mug on the table when she was done.

"Did you see New Guy?" Morticia focused on the young dark-haired man behind the bar, looking frazzled as he tried to keep up with all the women swarming him. "Matt McGinnis is a smart man. New Guy is sure to bring in a ton of business."

"Oh, wow, look at that." I pointed at Sarah sitting on the last barstool and smiling up at New Guy with pure adoration. "New Guy is Sarah's guy. Check out that smile."

"You can tell all that just from her smile?" Harmony studied Sarah.

"And from what she's told me. The proof is right there."

New Guy poured another drink for Sarah and stroked her cheek before he went back to running around like a chicken with its head cut off. Meanwhile, Matt McGinnis looked right at home, moving around the bar with ease and an unmistakable grace for such a big guy.

"Good for her. They look so cute together," Tiffany said, but her eyes were still focused on Matt, his booming laugh and adorable dimples lifting everyone's spirits. Her smile deepened. "Thanks, girls. This is just what I needed."

"Hear hear," I said, but all I could think about was what I needed.

A certain sandy-haired doctor with hazel eyes and a whiskey-smooth voice, who was tucking my kids into bed and waiting to give me another enlightening lesson in anatomy and physiology. I'd never done that well in school, but I was a straight 'A' student in this class. Probably because I'd never wanted to learn anything more in my life, and hot for the teacher didn't begin to describe what I felt for Chaz.

~

"Let me stay," Chaz said a couple nights later as he turned on the small reading lamp on the end table by my queen-sized bed.

I gasped and ducked under the covers. "Chaz, the light."

"Relax, Zoe, I can't see anything." I poked my head out, and he tucked a strand of hair behind my ear, the heat from his eyes boring into me, holding me captive. "Not that I don't want to. Hell, I've felt and tasted every inch of you. I think I have a pretty good idea what you look like already, and I'm liking the mental picture a hell of a lot." He slowly pulled down the covers.

I bit my bottom lip and shook my head, then gripped the blanket, tucking the edges securely over my Double Darlings as I sat up and scootched back against the headboard. I couldn't give in. If I did, there would be no turning back. As much as I liked Chaz, I liked my independence more. At least I think I did. I frowned.

"No." I shook my head harder. "You promised. We need to stick to the rules. No seeing me, no spending the night, and no one can know."

He plunged a hand through his sandy locks and sat up, the covers falling to his waist. I sucked in a breath in awe over the sheer beauty of him, his musky scent mixing with his aftershave, sending goosebumps over my flesh. I could get drunk breathing him in.

My eyes feasted on the sight of him.

Smooth taut skin covered firm muscles, and golden blond hair sprinkled his chest in a fine layer that tapered to a thin line and disappeared beneath the covers. He was gorgeous, which firmed my resolve not to let him see me.

Cellulite, stretch marks, and loose skin were a far cry from gorgeous.

"Why can't I stay just for tonight?" He slid his foot under the covers and hooked a leg under mine. "Lexi and Troy are at sleepovers, and Bobby and Katy are staying with Harmony, having a wild time, I'm sure. Nobody will know." He reached out and took my hand in his, toying with my fingers.

"You forget how nosy Mrs. Bee is, and Bitsy keeps close tabs on how long your car is in the driveway. People *will* know, Chaz." I threaded my fingers through his, enjoying touching him, being with him.

"Why is that such a bad thing?" He tilted his head to the side.

His gaze burned hotter as it swept over my bare shoulders and covered my breasts, my nipples visible through the sheet. I watched him trail his fingertips over my nipples, and my breath caught.

"It's not that it's bad, i-it's just not something I want to d-deal with." I moaned and shifted out of his reach so I could think straight.

"Everyone will think you only hired me because I slept with you. I want to be seen and heard. I want to be taken seriously, be known as Zoe, not the town doc's lover. We just cleared Lexi's name. I do not need to be linked to a new scandal. Besides, they still think of me as the poor abandoned wife of their fire chief and probably always will."

Chaz looked me in the eyes and just listened.

No wonder my kids loved him. I smoothed a hand over the covers and looked down at my lap. "You know, I still can't believe Max did that to us... to me. After all these years. How could he throw it all away? How could he let his children down like that?"

My eyes locked on Chaz's, knowing the pain in my chest would never completely go away, but somehow Chaz eased that pain.

"I'll never forget waking up to a note on his pillow. I gave up so much to dedicate my life to taking care of him and raising our children, yet all I was worth was a note. And they deserve a hell of lot more than postcards and presents from him. If only I had a chance to tell him what I thought."

Chaz cupped my cheek with his palm. "I see you, and I hear you, Zoe. You're an amazing woman and he's a fool, Zoe. It wasn't your fault. You can't blame yourself."

I turned my face into his hand and kissed his palm. "I know, and I don't. I just feel like a failure sometimes. Other than the beautiful children I gave birth to, my marriage was such a waste, but it did open my eyes. I realized just how strong I am and that I am important. In order to take care of my kids, I had to learn to take care of me."

I tried to think of a way to make him understand why I never wanted to get married again, not that he was asking, but I didn't want him to get any ideas.

"When Max was around, I didn't have anything of my own, you know. I took care of him, and I took care of the kids, always putting myself last. Don't get me wrong, I was happy because I didn't know what I was missing. But now." I nodded. "For the first time in my life, I feel empowered. It feels wonderful to do something just for me."

"You deserve to put yourself first for once."

"I know it sounds selfish, but I can't lose sight of that ever again. It might be silly, but I don't want to choose a side of the bed. I want to sleep right smack dab in the middle and be free to do so."

He chuckled. "That's not silly. I happen to like the middle myself." He winked. "And you're not being selfish. I think it's admirable. I'm not asking you to give up anything, Zoe." He rubbed his jaw. "Believe me, all the women I've met in the past wanted to be taken care of. Your strength and independence are wonderful qualities you should never give up for anyone. My ex-fiancée—"

"You were engaged?" Why that mattered was beyond me, but my stomach twisted into knots at the thought of Chaz marrying someone else.

I knew what we had would end, but I didn't want to picture him with another woman, even though that was a distinct possibility. He was four years younger than me and had never been married. It stood to reason he would want that one day.

Children. My heart flipped.

I know we said we were both safe— free to be free— but he might change his mind and want children someday. I couldn't have any more children, not that I would ever need to, I reminded myself. I just couldn't think about another woman giving birth to Chaz's baby right now.

"Zoe, did you hear me?"

"Huh? Sorry. I was thinking."

"About?"

"Nothing important." I ran my fingers through the hair on his chest. "You were saying?"

He shrugged. "Well, I said I was engaged, but not for long. Victoria didn't do a thing. She expected me to take care of her and fulfill her every whim. She only liked the prestige of marrying a doctor. When she landed an even-bigger doctor, she dumped me. It hurt when it happened, but now I realize I'm better off for it."

"That's terrible. I'm sorry you had to go through that."

He trailed his hand down my arm and locked his fingers with mine. "She was a far cry from the woman you've become. I love that you could give a rat's ass about the whole doctor status. All you see is the Dorkmeister. I can't believe I'm going to say this, but I'm actually glad you see me as the Dorkmeister, because that means what's between us is real."

"I'm not denying it's real, it just can't be—"

He swooped down and claimed my lips for a searing kiss,

stealing my breath and curling my toes. When he broke away for air, both of us were breathing heavy.

"You admitted it's real, and that's a start." He skimmed his fingers over my breasts and began to pull down the covers again. "One more for the road?" His breath was hot against my neck as he licked my skin.

I stilled his hand with mine. "Th— The lights."

He kissed the tip of my nose. "One of these days you're going to let me see you," his whiskey voice sent shivers through me as he whispered in my ear, "and then you'll finally believe how beautiful you are to me."

"One of these days," I managed, "but not today." I kissed him hard. "Now hit the lights, Doc, and let me show you just how beautiful *you* are to *me*."

"Okay, honey, take a left up here at the light," I said, trying not to panic as Lexi jerked the minivan to a stop at the corner. Mrs. Bee was watching the other kids so Lexi could practice without any distractions.

"Sorry, Mom. You barely have to touch Chaz's brakes, but I feel like I have to stomp on these." She winced.

Things were slowly getting better between us. She still confided a lot more in Chaz than she did in me, but at least we weren't fighting anymore. I never should have doubted her. She wasn't so angry, either, especially since everyone wanted to be her friend again. And we hadn't had a phone call from Principal Brimstone in a while. That was progress in my book.

"It's okay. We just need to get you out more in the minivan since that's the car you'll be driving when you get your license."

"Yay, me."

"I know a minivan isn't the coolest car, but we can't afford your own car right now."

"I know." She shrugged and actually smiled a little. "It could be worse. Mia's mom drives a rusted old station wagon." Mia had been the one true friend to Lexi, and Lexi wasn't likely to ever forget it. One thing was certain, she chose her friends a lot more carefully now. Best friends were hard to come by, and when you found one, you held onto them.

I was blessed to have three.

"Look what you'd have to drive if Aunt Harmony was your mom."

"Are you kidding me? The tie-dyed love bug rocks. Maybe she'll sell it to me someday."

"Maybe." We looked at each other and grinned, and we both said, "Nah."

Twenty minutes, two three-point turns, and four parallel parks later, we pulled in our driveway. "I'm so proud of you, honey."

She looked down at her lap, then up at me, her eyes glistening. "Thanks, Mom, and... I'm sorry."

I stroked her long curls. "For what?"

"Everything."

I opened my arms and she slipped inside, burying her head against my shoulder. I didn't need to ask what she meant. I already knew. "You're welcome. I love you, you know."

She pulled away. "I know. Me, too." She smiled as she slid out of the van. "Wait until I tell Mia I parallel-parked and got it right the first time. She'll be so jealous."

She jogged into the house, looking lighter and happier than I'd seen her in a long time. I had a certain handsome doctor to thank for that. Warmth spread through me as I thought, life was finally good again.

Until my cell phone rang.

I willed myself not to cringe. "Hi, Mom."

"Hi, dear. I'm getting so excited to see you guys, I can't stand it."

"See us. What do you mean?"

"Why, Easter, of course. It's two weeks away, you know."

"Two weeks?" How could I have forgotten Easter? Shows how distracted we all were, because the kids hadn't even mentioned it.

"You are coming, aren't you?"

"I-I don't know. I really can't afford it right now." Not to mention, I most definitely didn't want to be away from Chaz.

"But you have to. We'll pay your way. You simply must come to Florida. I won't take no for an answer."

"It's not only the money, Mom. The Andersons' retirement party is coming up fast, and I still have so much to do." The last thing I needed was her hounding me all week to drop everything and move to Florida.

"But, dear, the children—"

"Will see you this summer when you come to stay for a month."

"Well, I guess if you're too busy to come spend time with your own mother..."

"You know that's not it. You have your other grandkids, you know."

"Whom I see all the time because they live here, so they are going away to see their other grandparents." She sniffed. "I can take a hint. No one wants to spend time with me anymore."

I rubbed my throbbing temples. "Mom, my kids have other grandparents, too."

"Who monopolize all their time."

"They do not. They live in Alabama, for Pete's sake. Every holiday the Robinsons want us to go to Alabama, and you want us to go to Florida. It's a fight I'm not up to at the moment. I've decided to stay home for Easter." There, I'd said it. I held my breath, waiting for the backlash, but silence filled the line. "Mother?"

"I'm here, I just... oh, look at the time. I've got to go, dear. Give my love to the kids. Talk to you soon." She hung up. Mother never hung up first.

What the hell did that mean?

I climbed out of the car and rounded up the kids from Mrs. Bee's house, then strode inside to make dinner. The little red light on my answering machine blinked. My heart sped up at the thought of Chaz calling, but he never called the house phone. When I pushed the button, I couldn't believe my ears.

"Zoe, honey child, your mama just called me. What's this I hear about you not going anywhere for Easter?" My ex-mother-in-law paused. "I understand why you don't want to go to Florida, but you just have to bring the little munchkins down yonder to see us. I'll simply die if'n y'all don't come."

We weren't the only ones Max had abandoned, and he was her only child, so that pretty much left me and my children to pick up the slack. A full-time job I wasn't up to dealing with at the moment.

This was just like my mother to stir up trouble.

I said I wasn't up to a fight, so she started one anyway. I didn't want to go to Alabama any more than I wanted to go to Florida. Listening to a born and bred New Englander adopt such a phony thick southern accent in such a short amount of time was more than I could stomach for a week. This just reaffirmed my decision to stay home.

And nothing or no one was going to change my mind.

Chapter Fourteen

After church on Palm Sunday, I cleaned the house, folded the laundry, made dinner, did the dishes, put Katy and Bobby to bed, but couldn't stop staring at the phone in my bedroom.

Neither my mother nor my ex-mother-in-law had called all week, and Easter was only a week away. This wasn't like either of them. If they weren't fighting with me, then who on earth were they fighting with?

The doorbell rang.

"I got it," Lexi called from downstairs.

I tore my gaze away from the phone and fluffed my hair in the mirror above my dresser. Chaz was due to come over any minute so we could work on his party, and much later after Lexi and Troy went to sleep, we'd work on a few other things. I smiled, getting tingly all over at the mere thought of what 'other things' entailed.

"Ohmigod, I can't believe it." Lexi's startled voice carried all the way upstairs.

I flew down the staircase with Bobby's bat in my hand, only to trip on the last step and fall flat on my face. Lifting my head and brushing the hair out of my eyes, I stared at two sets of heels before me. It couldn't be. I couldn't look higher for fear of what I would find.

"Whoa, no way. Grandma Fitzpatrick *and* Nana Robinson both? What are you guys doing here?"

I groaned, banging my head against the floor three times for good measure. Now I knew whom they'd been fighting with all week. Each other.

"Mom, what are you doing?" Lexi whispered, squatting down to my level.

Putting myself out of my misery, I thought, but said, "Checking for dust bunnies." I slowly got to my feet. "Mom, Lil. What a nice surprise." I gritted my teeth.

"Oh, just call me Lilabelle, honeybunch." My ex-mother-in-law traipsed through the front door, her poofy floral dress with the wide belt cinched at the waist bouncing as she rolled her enormous luggage inside.

I blinked. I'd always called her Lil. What was with the new name? I squinted. Was that a hoop skirt beneath her dress?

"Oh, for God's sake, Lil, since when have you become a belle? You aren't fooling anyone with that accent or that silly straw hat." My mother, Andrea Fitzgerald, marched through the door with her head held high as she smoothed her starched skirt and matching mauve jacket. "Be a darling and get my luggage, dear," she said to Troy, who looked at me but obliged.

"Why, whatever are you talking about?" Lilabelle said, blinking her eyes rapidly. Good Lord, those false eyelashes were twice as long as the real deal and whirled about at a speed that made my head spin.

"Your accent's not the only thing that's phony." My mother huffed. "You don't turn seventy and suddenly sprout a pair of C cups."

"You're just jealous because I'm still perky, and you're, well, not." My mother-in-law pulled her shoulders back tighter.

"At least I look my age. You can't even close your eyes they're pulled back so tight, and those lashes are god-awful." My mother squinted. "What are they, diamond tipped?"

"Well, at least I don't look like my old hound dog, Rex, anymore. Droopy lids and no lashes to speak of." She reached out and lifted my mother's eyelid with her fingertip. "Hmmm, exactly as I thought."

My mother swatted her hand away. "What planet do you hail from, Lil?"

"...abelle, sugar. Lilabelle. And I'm just saying Medicare will pay eighty percent to have your eyelids raised if you pass their peripheral vision test, is all. It'll take ten years off, or so I'm told." Flutter, flutter, flutter went her lashes as she flashed her pearly whites, and I wondered briefly if Medicare had paid for her tooth whitening as well.

"Ten years isn't the only thing that quack took off. Your eyebrows are all but gone. I don't need my eyelids or anything else raised, so you can keep your hands to yourself, you twit." My mother focused her attention on me, raising her brows high and keeping them there.

I hated to admit it, but Lil was right. Mom could give good ole hound dog Rex a run for his money these days, and I looked a lot like Mom. Not a good sign. I shook away that disturbing thought and focused on where I stood, and who stood before me.

"Mom, Lilabelle. What are you doing here?"

"Why, I'm spending Easter with you. This way you can save your money, and you can get your little party-planning work done while I spend time with my grandkids." My mother looked down her nose at my mother-in-law. "I don't know what *she's* doing here."

"Oh, posh, you stuck up old biddy. You knew all about my coming here. Hell, we've been fighting about it all week." A bit of that New England attitude crept into Lil's voice, then she took a cleansing breath and continued sugary sweet. "Why, I mean, I didn't want y'all to be lonely, given it's a holiday and all. I flew all the way up yonder to take care of my grandbabies, so their mama could get her work done. Don't worry, Zoe, you won't even know I'm around."

"Because you won't be around." My mother turned to me and demanded, "Choose, Zoe. I can't stay in this house with that meddling woman another minute." She lifted her nose even higher, if that were possible, and smoothed her short, sleek gray strands. Like she hadn't meddled right along with Lil.

"Yes, honeychild, you really should choose whom you want to help you out this week. Think of the children, sweetcakes." She batted those lashes again, looking ridiculous with that enormous hat slightly off center over her loose, bottle-blond waves. All she needed was a price tag, and she'd be Minnie Pearl's long-lost cousin— who looked ten years younger, apparently.

I wanted to tell them both to leave, but I couldn't. As much as they didn't get along and as much as they both interfered with my life, I knew they loved my children and me. So, I crossed my arms and stared them both in the eye.

"Ladies, you created this situation, so now you can deal with it. You're staying."

"Who," they both said in unison, sounding and looking like a pair of owls with their wide, startled eyes and puckered oh-shaped lips.

I smiled, thoroughly enjoying this moment. "Both of you."

They began to argue, but I held up a hand and repeated, "*Both* of you."

My mother gasped. "You can't seriously—"

"I can."

Lilabelle stammered, "You don't actually—"

"I do."

The argument ensued, but I cut them off again.

"The children, ladies." I gestured toward Lexi and Troy who sat riveted to the scene before them. "Think of the children." I winked at the kids, and they giggled. "Mom, you can have Lexi's room. She can take the couch. Okay with you, Lex?"

"Sure."

"Why, I wouldn't dream of putting Lexi out. A girl her age needs her space. I'll simply take your room."

Figured; she had no qualms about putting *me* out. "Not a chance, Mother."

"Well, there's really not room for both of us to stay." My mother hated not getting her way, and I savored every minute of my small victory.

"I like sleeping down here, Gram." Lexi smiled at me, obviously enjoying this as much as I was. "My room doesn't have a TV. This does."

"Attagirl." I winked at her. "And Lilabelle, you can take Troy's room. He can sleep in Bobby's other bunk."

"Oh, he's a growin' boy. I couldn't put the little dumpling out. Andrea is right, there's no room for the both of us."

"I don't mind. Bunk beds are cool." He grinned wide, and then flashed his nicely-toned brows at me.

"That's my boy." I blew him a kiss. "So, it's settled, then."

"Nothing's settled, but obviously, we don't have a say in the matter." My mother snatched her suitcase and huffed up the stairs, managing to look dignified despite her irritation.

"For once, I agree with you, Andrea." Lilabelle grabbed her suitcase and swayed up the stairs as though she were performing live on Dancing with the Stars.

"At least you agree on something. That's a start," I called after them and laughed as I heard both doors slam shut.

Maybe next time, they'd learn to respect my wishes.

I STOOD BACK and watched the scene unfold before me with utter weariness. I'd had to cancel with Chaz the night they'd arrived, and everything had gone downhill since. I was exhausted. Mrs. Bee washed the dishes, while Andrea and Lilabelle fought over who would get to dry the next plate. This had been going on all week. They fought over what we would have for dinner, who would cook, who would clean, who would help the kids.

All under the pretense of letting me get some work done.

Ha! That was a joke. I hadn't gotten anything done all week, let alone work. So much for spending time with Chaz. These women were smart, so I'd made excuse after excuse as to why I couldn't see Chaz. Now, I was horny as well as exhausted.

"Enough!" I closed the Anderson folder and slammed my pen down on the dining room table, my head pounding. "I mean it, ladies, I can't take any more."

"Well, that was rude," my mother said.

"I'll say," Lilabelle agreed.

They only ever agreed when I was yelling at the both of them.

"Maybe I should go." Mrs. Bee wiped her hands on her apron.

"I'm sorry, but I'd like to have a word with these," I wanted to say meddling monsters, but I bit my tongue, "these two *wonderful* women alone." My stiff smile hurt my cheeks.

"Zoe Robinson, you can't ask someone to leave your house." My mother leveled me with a disapproving look, but I was used to that look. I'd seen it most of my life.

"No, you most certainly cannot, honeypie." Lilabelle batted those ghastly lashes.

Rainbows of light reflected off the diamonds like an eighties strobe light stuck on high, until one lash slipped off and landed on her cheek, thank God. I was so dizzy I couldn't see straight. She swiped it away like it was a bug, and the eyelash flew off, leaving her looking oddly lopsided.

I jerked myself out of the mesmerized state my bizarre creature of an ex-mother-in-law had put me in, and then responded to her comment. "I can, and I did," I said, then turned my attention to Mrs. Bee. "Would you mind?"

"Not at all, sweetie." She patted my shoulder, then weeble-wobbled to the door. "How'd you ladies like to go to bingo tomorrow?" She winked at me over her shoulder.

"Oh, no, I couldn't possibly. Easter Sunday's the next day, and we have so much to do," my mother said.

"No, we don't. I ordered all the food," I added quickly. I hadn't, but I sure would now. Anything to get rid of them for a couple hours.

"You did what? Why, my word, how will that look? A party planner having her own holiday dinner catered. Oh, the scandal of it all." Lilabelle fanned her face as though the vapors had set in.

"It will look exactly like it is, that I'm busy— which I am— and that I wasn't expecting company— which I wasn't." I glanced at Mrs. Bee and smiled my gratitude. Hallelujah, a night alone. Better yet, a night with Chaz. "They'll be over at seven."

She nodded and hurried out the door before the women could protest further. Now, if only I could get rid of them this afternoon, I just might stand a chance of keeping my sanity.

Someone knocked.

Both women started arguing over who would answer the door, but I snapped, "I got it." Then I left them in the kitchen.

"Harmony, thank God." The girls all knew how horrible this week had been, because I'd called and complained at least once a day. I frowned. "I thought you had a lunch date this afternoon?"

"Another cancellation, go figure."

"I'm sorry." I hugged her.

"Don't be. The guy was another one of my mother's blind date freakazoids. Not my type." She shuddered. "Besides, now I get to be your savior, babe." She winked and sailed past me as though she were on a zip-line that ended in my kitchen. "What's up, mamas?"

"Well, I... hello, Harmony, you're looking rather," my mother's gaze swept over Harmony's spiky red hair and tattoos, "colorful these days."

"I try my best." Harmony grinned.

"Gracious me, does that hurt, butterbean?" Lilabelle reached out and touched the tiny little diamond in Harmony's nose.

"Nah. Looks to me like that hurts more. What'd you do, pluck all the lashes out of one eye?" Harmony leaned closer to study Lilabelle's face. "Oh, never mind. You're just missing a set of those fake thingies you got on."

"Oh, my word." Lilabelle flopped down on all fours in a flurry of skirts as she scoured the floor, looking for her missing lashes.

"Get a hold of yourself, Lil." My mother rolled her eyes. "You look like an animal."

"A non-droopy animal to you," Lil grumbled. "And for the last time, it's Lilabelle."

"Looks like I came at the right time," Harmony said.

"For what?" My mother puckered her forehead, looking

wary. She should be when it came to Harmony. One never knew what crazy idea she had up her sleeve.

"Yes, for what, sweetings?" Lil peeked up from beneath the bangs that had fallen in front of her eyes.

"For your rubdowns." Harmony's grin looked downright devilish.

"I beg your pardon?" My mother gaped.

Lilabelle gasped. "R-Rub *what* did you say?"

I nailed Harmony with 'the look,' but she just held up her hands. "What?" She loved to shock people every chance she got, so I took a stab at what I suspected she meant.

"Your massage. My guess is Tiffany scheduled you both for a full-body massage today."

"Exactly what I said." Harmony smirked.

"Not," I responded, but she just laughed.

My mother was already shaking her head. "Oh, well, I don't think—"

"Don't think, Andrea. You look so stressed." Harmony stood behind my mother and massaged her shoulders. "Your shoulders are awful tight."

My mother nailed me with a pointed look and mouthed, "Is she... you know?"

"No," I mouthed back, and who cared if she was.

My mother didn't look as though she believed me in the least. She might have moved away, but she still thrived on small-town gossip, same as the rest of Mayflower's citizens. She must have heard about all of Harmony's dates canceling lately and how desperate her mother had become to make Harmony more feminine.

Poor Harm couldn't win.

"Well, I, for one, haven't had a full-body anything in far too long," Lilabelle said with a flushed face as she found her missing eyelash and stared at her reflection in the toaster to press it back on. "There. Right as rain." She faced Harmony. "I'm game." She leaned in. "Do they have a male masseuse?"

"As a matter of fact, they do." Harmony grinned.

"I'm not letting anyone 'rub me down,' especially a man." My mother eyed Harmony warily, adding, "Or a woman."

"That doesn't surprise me." Lilabelle giggled like a school-girl. "Someone like her just can't handle a rubdown like we real women can. Isn't that so, Harmony?"

"I don't know," she turned to my mother. "Is that so, Andrea?" The challenge blazed within her green cat eyes.

And the gauntlet had been thrown.

My mother snatched up her purse, lifted her nose in the air, and marched to the door. After a moment, she turned to the women and said, "Are you coming or what?"

Harmony laughed. "Let's rock and roll, ladies."

"Shotgun!" Lilabelle sprinted ahead of my mother, who threw up her hands and stormed after her, high heels clicking an angry staccato across the floor all the way.

Alone at last.

"THEY'RE GONE," I said into the phone.

"For how long?" Chaz asked.

"About an hour and a half, I figure. Please tell me you can slip away. The kids are at school, and I'm alone."

"My afternoon's pretty open today. Let me finish up with this last patient, and I'll tell the staff something came up." He chuckled. "Hell, it won't be a lie. Something's been up for about a week now."

"I think I might have the perfect cure." I giggled for the first time in a week and felt the stress begin to melt away. "Hurry."

"I'm on my way."

After I hung up, I turned on some soft music, put a bottle of wine on ice, and whipped up a cheese and cracker tray. Then I sprinted up to my bedroom, changed into a burgundy silk camisole with a short black skirt, and smoothed cucumber melon body lotion on my bare legs and feet.

I pulled my hair out of its ponytail and fluffed my curls just as the doorbell rang. Adding a quick spritz of body splash, I dashed downstairs to answer the door with a huge smile on my face, my heart fluttering faster than a hummingbird's wings. Or Lilabelle's lashes. Take your pick.

"Well, I can't say I'm as happy to see you as you obviously are to see me."

My smile dissolved like Jell-o in hot water. "Bitsy, what are you doing here?"

"I'm here to see Andrea, not that it's any of your business."

I stopped breathing as shockwaves coursed through me. "Um, it's my house, and she's my mother. I'd say that makes it my business."

"I'll only be a minute. May I come in?" Her stiff smile looked as though it killed her to be civil.

"I'm working."

She leaned to the side and scanned the kitchen, taking in the music, the chilling wine, and the cheese and cracker plate. Her gaze roamed over my attire and her pencil drawn blond brow twitched. "Just *what* exactly are you working on?"

"The Anderson party, not that it's any of *your* business."

"Interesting planning technique."

"I like to put myself in the party mood when sampling the goods."

The deep rumble of a sports car purred as it turned into my driveway, and the driver cut the engine. I didn't have to look to know who was here.

Bitsy glanced at the driver, then back at me, her arched

brow climbing even higher, if that were possible. "Well, I won't keep you from your 'sampling.'" She grinned an evil little grin. "Just give these macaroons to your mother, please. And let her know the recipe she asked for is inside."

My jaw hit the front steps, and Bitsy's smile turned smug. "My mother asked you for one of your recipes?"

"What can I say? Your mother has good taste, and she simply adored my macaroons when we had tea the other day."

I went into a major coughing fit and nearly swallowed my tongue. "You had tea with my mother?" I choked out after I could finally breathe again.

Her smile turned Cheshire cattish. "Like I said, your mother has good taste." Her gaze swept over me once again. "You must take after your father."

My grip tightened on the plate of macaroons. "Why, you—"

"Ladies." Chaz joined us on the steps.

"Dr. Anderson." Bitsy nodded in a regal way like a queen. Queen of the snobs, maybe. "Don't you have office hours today?"

"I had a light afternoon, so I cut out early to run some errands." He smiled in a pleasant way.

"And seeing *Mrs.* Robinson was one of those errands?" Bitsy said, reminding me yet again of my place in the eyes of this town. No matter how hard I tried to establish myself as Zoe the party planner, the town never seemed to notice.

"As a matter of fact, seeing Zoe was the first errand on my list." Chaz's smile remained fixed in place. "If you don't mind, Ms. Beaumont, Zoe and I have much to go over. Or did you need to speak to me more about that matter we discussed earlier today?"

Alarm flashed in Bitsy's eyes, and she pursed her lips. "No, no. I think we covered everything we needed to. By all means, don't let me stand in the way of your errands."

"Oh, don't worry, you won't," I couldn't resist adding, but part of me wondered what they'd talked about earlier.

"Good day, Dr. Anderson." Bitsy spun on her heel and marched away with her nose held high.

I watched until she disappeared back into her house, and then I turned toward Chaz. I was going to question him about Bitsy, but when my eyes met his, the desire I saw blazing within floored me.

"Ms. Robinson, I have a couple things I'd like to go over," Chaz said as his gaze ran over my Double Darlings.

I shivered in anticipation. "Then by all means, don't let me stand in your way." I giggled.

"Oh, don't worry, you won't." He chuckled right along with me as he backed me into my house, shutting the door behind him before he leaned down to kiss me.

"B-But I have goods I want you to sample," I said, avoiding his lips while I could still think straight. I did have some actual work I had to do since the mamas had me way behind schedule.

"That's music to my ears." His lips trailed down my neck as his skilled hand cupped my breast.

"The w-wine. Sample the wine for the party."

"I'm sure whatever you choose will be perfect." He slid his hands over my bottom and pressed me against his arousal as he nipped my earlobe.

I sighed. "Works for me." Then I yanked his dress shirt out of his Dockers and ran my hands over his back.

He pulled away enough to look at me, his breathing as heavy as mine, his smile coming slow and sweet. "I missed you, Zoe Robinson."

I smiled back. "I miss you, too, Dorkmeister."

He chuckled, and his smile dissolved as he stared into my eyes. His eyes burned as he swooped down to devour my mouth.

Alone at last, I thought again, and lost myself in his kiss until voices penetrated my brain.

"It's your fault," said a familiar voice outside the front door.

"Well, I don't rightly know what you're talking about," said another familiar voice.

I tore myself away from Chaz and smoothed my hair, mouthing, "I'm sorry," ready to make a couple of meddling mamas sorry they'd ever come to visit me.

He sighed long and deep, tucking in his shirt.

"If you ask me, it's both your faults." Morticia opened the door and halted when she saw Chaz. Her gaze shot to me, and her lips parted. "Oh, boy. Harmony had to bail, so I got stuck babysitting." She smirked. "Not fun. Having tea at a fashion show with Harm's mom would have been less painful than hanging out with yours."

"Babysitting? Honestly, Morticia." My mother huffed and stepped through the door, fixing the lapels of her jacket. "It's not my fault that twit caused such a scene."

"You're the one who caused the scene because Maxim chose to rub me down over you, darlin'." Lilabelle strolled in and took off her floppy hat.

"He didn't choose you; you forced yourself on the man like a dog in heat. You scared the hell out of him is my guess. Why, I wouldn't be surprised if he's never the same."

"Me, now that's just silly. You, dearest, are the one who threatened to unman the poor soul if he didn't rub you first."

"Gee, I wonder why he chose not to massage either of you." Morticia grunted. "You could have chosen another masseuse, you know."

"After she wasted half our time, there was no point." My mother huffed.

Morticia looked at me and shrugged an apology.

Lilabelle blinked as though just noticing Chaz. "Why,

sweetings, who's your darling little friend?" She thrust out her hand.

Chaz chuckled and held her fingers so he could kiss the back of her hand. "Dr. Anderson, ma'am."

Her lashes sped into overdrive. "Oh, my. You don't happen to give rubdowns, do you?"

My mother rolled her eyes. "Good Lord in heaven, you really are a twit. For God's sake, Lil, he's a doctor." She turned a perfectly poised smile on Chaz. "Delighted to make your acquaintance, Dr. Anderson." She glanced at me and did a double-take, alarm registering on her face. "Zoe, dear, whatever's the matter? You're so flushed. Why, I think you might be feverish. Dr. Anderson would you examine my daughter at once? I think she might be sick."

Oh, I was sick, all right. Of them! Why'd he have to be late after getting held up with his last patient? And why'd they have to go ruin everything by coming back early? My eyes locked with Chaz's. His smile blossomed all the way to his knowing hazel eyes, and my face flamed even hotter.

"I'm fine, Mom. Just frustrated you're here. Cha— Dr. Anderson— and I were sampling the goods, I mean, wine for the party."

"Ooh, I love wine." Lilabelle clapped her hands and sashayed over to the kitchen, grabbing another wine glass and pouring herself a drink. "Why, this is divine. I always said you have wonderful taste, honeypie."

"Hardly," my mother spat. "After all, she did marry your son." She strolled over to nibble on some cheese and crackers. "He always did take after you."

Lilabelle ignored her. "My goodness gracious me. Chuckie Anderson, you sure did grow up fine." She smoothed her cumbersome hoopskirt and fluttered those ridiculous sparkling lashes again.

"Yes, how are Wally and Roz these days, anyway?" My mother smiled fondly. "I always liked them. Such fine people." Her scowl shot to Lilabelle, and she smiled back at Chaz.

"They're doing well. I'll tell them you said hello."

"Why don't you invite—"

"Look at the time," I said and grabbed Chaz's arm to glance at his watch. "Dr. Anderson has to go."

"I do?" He quirked the corner of his lip.

I scowled. "Yes, you do. That thing. Remember?" I knew how he felt about keeping our affair a secret, and if he so much as one word to the mamas, he could kiss it all goodbye.

He sighed and looked at his watch. "It was nice seeing you both again. I do have to get going."

"What about the sampling? You don't know what you're missing; it's simply divine." Lilabelle took another sip of wine.

Chaz's eyes never left mine. "I'm sure you're right, but I'll have to take a rain check. Something came up." He winced and shifted his stance.

"Right. Another time. Now, say goodbye to the nice ladies." I yanked his arm and led him to the door.

"Bye-bye, ladies. I'm sure I'll see you again soon," he called over his shoulder.

"Not if I can help it," I muttered under my breath and pulled him all the way out the door, closing it behind me and leaning back with a huff. I shut my eyes for a moment and groaned, then opened them only to see Bitsy sitting on her front porch, watching us with a knowing smug look.

Across the street, Mrs. Bee smiled out her kitchen window as she dried her dishes. I smiled back, feeling powerless. I hated this, hated having others dictate how I acted and what I said, but that didn't mean I was ready to come forward with anything.

Chaz reached out to take my hand, but I stepped aside. "Don't. People will see."

"I don't care, Zoe. This sneaking around is ridiculous." He shoved his hands in his pockets.

"I know, I'm frustrated, too. But once they leave, things will be back to normal."

"There's nothing 'normal' about our situation." He started walking to his car, and I followed. "I'm going home to take a cold shower. Let me know when you can see me for longer than five minutes."

"Tomorrow night."

He climbed in his beamer and stared at me out the window. "What's tomorrow night?"

"Bingo."

"You want to play bingo?"

"No, I don't want to play bingo. Mrs. Bee is taking the mamas to play bingo. They leave at seven, so be here by seven-fifteen. The girls will have the kids."

He sat for a long moment, not saying anything. For a brief second, I thought he might say no. "Okay," he finally agreed, then shoved his car in gear and drove away without another word.

He didn't look back.

I knew just how he felt because I felt the same way, but it wasn't my fault. I looked at my house. It was *their* fault. The mamas were screwing up everything, while I wasn't screwing anything. If I didn't get rid of them soon and have some alone time with Chaz, there would be hell to pay.

Chapter Fifteen

The next afternoon, I managed to slip away on the pretense of needing a few things from the party supply store and picking up our Easter dinner for the next day. The mamas were still mad I was "buying" our dinner. They had offered to cook but couldn't agree on what to have or who would fix it.

Like I would let my mother cook after the Bitsy macaroon incident. No way would I take a chance on Bitsy's recipes feeding my family. I'd put my foot down. It was my house, and I was the hostess. I could have Easter dinner however I wanted, so I'd ordered all the food and was supposed to pick it up this afternoon.

Then the mamas fought over who would watch the kids, so I divided them up. Troy and Lexi were self-sufficient. I gave Katy to my mother and Bobby to Lilabelle. I would only be gone for an hour.

How much could happen in one hour, right?

First, I had a little pit stop to make. I bit my lip and searched the street to make sure no one would see me go into Nancy's Negligees. When no one was looking, I darted inside and gasped, then turned back toward the door.

"Zoe? What on earth are you doing here?" Bitsy said from behind me, as though I couldn't afford to shop in the high-class store. It was expensive, so I was sure Bitsy bought all her bras and underwear there.

I turned around and pasted on a phony smile. "I, um, I... I'm here for Lexi."

"I'm surprised Lexi shops here. She's awful young for such fine things. Aren't you worried about spoiling her?"

Who was she to give me advice? Like she knew anything at all about having kids. "Well, I didn't have time to go to Victoria's Secret in the mall, and she desperately needed new underwear today."

Bitsy frowned. "Really, now. She didn't have a single clean pair of underwear?" Her disbelieving stare swept clear down her ski slope of a nose and landed in my direction, as though to prove she was the better competitor and my skills had come up lacking.

Well, I wasn't about to settle for a silver medal. "Yeah, really," I said, jerking my head back several times and attempting to look down my nose at her. She was too tall. I undoubtedly looked more like a novice than a gold medalist, so I gave up. "Desperate times call for desperate measures."

I'd wanted to buy something special to wear to surprise Chaz tonight when the mamas went to bingo to make up for yesterday afternoon. I'd never worn lingerie in front of him before, but I was now comfortable enough to give him that small concession. Not that I would take it off, but at least it was sexy and semi-transparent. Looks like that wasn't going to happen today.

"Well, I shop here all the time. Let me help you." She led me to a sale rack in the back and asked, "What size is she?"

"I've got it, but thanks."

"Certainly." Bitsy stayed by my side under the pretense of

shopping when we both knew she didn't do sale racks. She just wanted to see what I was really up to. I ended up buying an extra small pair of bikini underwear with a 32C matching bra. Like I could fit into those any more than I could afford to blow a hundred bucks on one matching bra and panty set.

Lexi would be thrilled.

Chaz, not so much.

I paid for my garments, with Bitsy watching the entire time, and then I headed to the store to pick up my non-homemade Easter dinner. The only things I'd made from scratch were the pies, two of which I dropped off at Truman's house. He hadn't even asked for any this week, but I wanted to surprise him with chocolate and cherry ones.

It was Easter, after all, but Truman never took anyone up on an invitation for dinner because that was when his wife had died, the poor man. I'd heard the Rogers sisters were bringing him a plate, so between that and the pies, he should be taken care of.

Exactly one hour after I left, I arrived home, feeling as though I hadn't accomplished a thing except becoming more frustrated. Three more hours, and at least I'd get to spend some time with Chaz. I stored Easter dinner in the refrigerator in the garage. All I had to do was reheat it after church tomorrow. Easiest Easter I'd ever prepared and worth every penny. Come Monday morning, the mamas would be gone.

I walked out of the garage and ran into Lester with his gap-toothed smile. I had no idea who he was spending Easter with, but I drew the line at how much I was willing to give. Besides, I think I'd given up enough by putting up with the mamas for a week, thank you very much.

I headed in the other direction. What on earth was Pete's Plumbing doing in front of my house? I opened the front door and Pete walked out, nodded hello to me, waved to Lester, then got in his truck and drove away. Something was up, and I had a sinking feeling I didn't want to know. Sure enough, as I stepped inside, I stared in utter disbelief.

"That apple tasted yucky, so I threw it in the toilet, but it didn't flush. Now I'm all messy with poo-poo water," Katy wailed, dripping nasty water all over my hard wood floors.

Poo-poo water? I turned to my mother, my mouth agape. "Mom?"

"What, it's not my fault. I was peeling potatoes for potato salad, and she must have snuck one when I wasn't looking. She took a bite, realized it wasn't an apple, then threw it in the toilet. Uncooked potatoes don't dissolve. Did you know that? I had to have Pete the plumber come over, and even he couldn't fix it. You should have seen it. He had to pull the whole toilet off and take it out to his truck. What a mess." My mother shook her head. "You really should teach her never to throw anything in the toilet." She stared at me as though all this were my fault.

"I didn't throw anything else in, Grandma. When I had to goes real bad and you sent me to the upstairs potty, I threw my toilet paper right in the trash. It was really stinky. Blech." She plugged her nose and stuck out her tongue.

"Oh, heavens me. No wonder that bathroom still smells." My mother waved her arms, windmilling through the air as she flapped her way upstairs to empty the smelly trashcan.

There was an image that wouldn't leave my brain anytime soon.

"What did I do now, Mommy?" Katy's bottom lip trembled.

"Nothing, sweetie. This isn't your fault. Just remember poo-poo toilet paper goes in with the poo-poo water, but nothing else, okay?"

"Okay."

"Lexi, will you give your sister a bath so I can check in with your other grandmother?"

She unfolded her curled-up frame from the couch and motioned for Katy to go ahead of her, not about to touch anything 'poo-poo' related, even her sister. Couldn't say I blamed her. "Sure, but you aren't going to be any happier with Nana Robinson."

I dreaded finding out what other disasters had occurred while I was gone. I would expect this behavior from kids, but the mamas were adults who'd raised children of their own. "I'm afraid to ask."

"She's in the kitchen but watch your step. It's slippery."

I entered the kitchen and jumped out of the way as Bobby zoomed through mounds of bubbles across the kitchen floor on his skateboard. "Bobby, what do you think you're doing?" I said.

"Snowboarding, Mommy. Isn't it cool?"

"You know better than to skateboard in the house, and where did all those bubbles come from?"

"Oh, honeychild, it's not my fault, I sway-yer." The more frazzled her nerves, the heavier her accent.

Of course, it wasn't her fault, I thought. Neither mama could admit she was wrong, that's why their arguments went on forever. I was sure this was going to be my fault as well.

"You really should teach that boy the difference between dish detergent and dish soap. I think you can guess which one he put in the dishwasher." She patted down the front of her enormous hoop skirt. "Why, my dress will never be the same."

"Neither will my floor," I muttered. "Bobby, get that thing out of my kitchen and get me the mop."

"I'm afraid dinner is ruined, seeing as how there are bubbles simply everywhere. We'll just have to skip bingo tonight and help you clean this up."

"No!" I screeched.

Lilabelle stared at me as though I'd lost my mind, and my lashes blinked as fast as hers for once.

"I mean, I would hate for that to happen. Mrs. Bee is counting on your company, and we wouldn't want to break her little ole heart, now would we?"

"Well, I suppose not."

"Good. Bobby take a shower, and Troy order a pizza, please. Chop chop, boys, we have lots to do in very little time."

They'd go to bingo or to an early grave, and I'd gladly do the time. At this point, jail would be preferable to enduring one minute more of misery from the mamas.

Three hours later, I'd cleaned up the mess, fed my family pizza, shoved the mamas off on Mrs. Bee ten minutes early, dropped my kids off with my best friends, and donned another skirt and tank top. Chaz was running late but due any minute, so when the doorbell rang at 7:30 sharp, butterflies danced in my stomach.

I opened the door with a huge smile on my face, but the smile died instantly.

My life was a living circus.

Mrs. Bee stood there scowling, looking just as lumpy, but not half as sweet. No amount of cobbler would fix this. "I'm sorry, honey, but they disrupted the whole bingo night, arguing over who had what card." She shook her head. "First time in twenty years bingo was cancelled." She frowned at both women and said, "You two should be ashamed of yourselves."

I couldn't believe it. I couldn't move, could only stare at them at a loss for what to say. This could *not* be happening again. At this point, I was afraid I really would be arrested for putting them in an early grave.

"Well, I—"

I held up my hand to silence my mother. "Don't say a word."

"But she—"

I glared at my ex-mother-in-law. "You either, Lil."

"Abelle," she whispered, then clamped her lips tight at my scowl.

I walked upstairs, unable to even look at them, and called the girls to bring the kids home. I had to call Chaz and intercept him before he got here— yeah, that was fun— then pretend I wasn't miserable for the rest of the evening.

My biggest headache yet pounded behind my temples to the beat of *kill them, kill them, kill them*. Better yet, I decided to stay in my room where everyone would be safe and keep chanting the only thing that kept me from doing bodily harm.

One. More. Day.

ALL OF MAYFLOWER'S citizens packed the pews of Sacred Heart Church on Easter morning.

Tiffany sat right up front by her grandmother, who looked regal despite her illness. Her mother and twin sister, Tabitha, were nowhere in sight, but that wasn't unusual. God forbid anything happened to Granny Eisenhower. Tiffany would be all alone.

In the next pew, Morticia sat behind her father and the young blonde woman I'd seen him with at Lolita's place, fuming. Turns out Morti was right, and I was wrong. He was dating the much younger woman and happier than I had ever seen him, but I was still shocked he'd found someone before Morticia.

Judging by the stony look on her face, so was she.

And then there was Harmony. Poor thing. She sat wedged between all seven of her brothers on one side, and her parents on the other. I bit back a giggle but not quite enough. Harmony shot me a glare over her shoulder. A full-fledged laugh slipped out of me. Her makeup shone bright, and her hair fell soft and flowy, no spikes in sight.

I mouthed, "Sorry," and she rolled her eyes, jerking her head in her mother's direction.

Obviously, she'd given her mother an Easter present because she'd even worn a dress. I hadn't seen Harmony in a dress since pictures of her from kindergarten. Why, she'd even gone to the prom stag and had worn a tuxedo to boot. That should have been a clue there was nothing girly about Harmony, but her mother continued to hold out hope.

A crackling noise beside me brought my attention to my youngest. "Katy Ann Robinson, you know you don't bring toys to church," I whispered as I snatched the Barbie microphone she had hidden behind her back in the pew during the Easter morning service.

"But, Mommy, you said to bring something to occupy me," Katy wailed, using the folds of her dandelion-yellow sundress to wipe her tears.

Several eyes darted our way, and Lexi slid down low with a moan, while Bobby giggled, and Troy nudged him to be quiet. My mother scowled at me, shooting an apologetic smile to the Caputos in the pew in front of us and the Morgans behind us while I attempted to console a blubbering Katy.

"I meant something to draw with, honey, not sing with." I stuffed the microphone in my oversized handbag right next to my cell phone, and I pulled out a pad of paper and pen.

"But we sing in church all the time." She sniffled and hiccupped, taking the offered replacements.

"I know, but we don't want to hurt God's ears, now do we?"

She shook her head, her brown ringlets flopping about, dress now tear-stained and wrinkled. "Nope, cuz then he might need a hearing Band-Aid like Papa John wears, right Nana Lillybells?"

"It's Papa Johnboy now, honeybunch." Lilabelle winked.

Gerty and Gabby Rogers ducked to keep Lilabelle's floppy hat from hitting them as she swung her head around to the rhythm of the church organ. Truman sat on the other side of the Rogers' sisters, grinning wide at Lil and snapping his fingers to the beat, while the sisters tsked and swatted his arm down.

"Stop that flopping about, Lil, this isn't a discothèque," my mother hissed. "Papa Johnboy? Just wait until Robert gets a load of this," she muttered.

"Robert who?" Lilabelle batted her fake lashes again, in a vain attempt at ignorance. "Why, do you mean that dear old husband of yours, Bobbie Jo?"

"No, I most certainly do not. His name is Robert Joseph. You'd do well to remember that. And who you calling old? Robert's not as old as your 'Johnboy.'"

"Would you two stop fighting, for God's sake?" I snapped and received a startled look from Eleanor Edwards accompanied by a frown from the mayor. I smiled sheepishly and made the sign of the cross.

Father O'Dority went on with the homily about Jesus dying and forgiving us for our sins. I risked a peek at my mother and ex-mother-in-law, neither of whom could see the error of their ways. They felt perfectly justified meddling in my life. Forgiveness? Hard to do when I had a table full of work, and I hadn't spent a single moment alone with Chaz.

One more day, I thought again.

Forget forgiveness. I pressed my palms together and prayed for God to grant me the patience of a saint. Then I asked for a sign if he heard me.

A loud buzzing reverberated throughout the church, startling everyone as it echoed off the stained-glass windows and the rafters above. I jumped, bumping my purse with my hip, and the sound buzzed louder. It wasn't a sign, it was... dear God in heaven.

Katy's microphone must still be on.

"Everybody stay seated, no need to panic," I said over the loud buzzing and growing hum of speculation.

I opened my purse and dipped my hand inside, and all eyes locked on me, accusation blazing within. I giggled nervously and said, "Katy's Barbie microphone must be pressed up against my—"

"No!" The parishioners chorused in unison, sounding like an off-key choir.

"—cell phone," I finished as I pulled my vibrating cell phone out of my purse and shut it off to a collective sigh of relief. They were never going to let me live down the vibrating Snaky mixer.

I'd told Principal Brimstone to call so I could fill him in about the prom details; I just hadn't expected a call during church. Figured; he didn't attend. Lexi was practically under the pew now, Katy was drawing two-headed Snakys, Bobby's giggles were full-out laughs, and Troy's elbow looked ready to fall off from jabbing him.

"Sorry, Father, please continue," I said, feeling the fire in my cheeks.

The mayor frowned, Bitsy gloated, my mother's scowl couldn't get any deeper, and Lilabelle's eyelashes flapped faster than a bumblebee on crack.

Father O'Dority shot me a pointed look as he said, "Let us pray," and Sister Mary Agnes fingered her rosary beads, looking as though she needed more smelling salts.

There weren't enough prayers in the universe to fix my problems.

My gaze found Chaz, and he smiled at me with sympathy and shot me a wink full of promise. Oh, yeah. Prayers weren't what I needed at all. I needed time alone with Dr. Hunkorama, and I needed the mamas to be gone. I repeat.

One. More. Day.

"WELL, Mrs. Robinson, I have to say you've outdone yourself. I don't think I've ever seen a prom decorated quite the same way. Where did you come up with the whole feather theme? It's brilliant." Principal Brimstone scanned the school gymnasium.

"That was the point. To be unique. Every prom I've ever seen has streamers and satin draped everywhere and balloons galore. I thought with our resident swans looking so graceful floating on Freedom Lake, why not do the prom in a swan theme?"

"Well, it worked. The kids love it."

"Thanks." He walked away to join Chaz at the punch table, since Chaz was one of the chaperones.

I surveyed my work with pride. Ice blue velvet carpet, black satin draped walls, silver stars hanging from the ceiling. I'd even added white fluffy clouds and a huge silver disco ball to represent the moon. And of course, soft white feathers everywhere. They all looked like graceful, elegant swans dancing across Freedom Lake under the light of a full moon with a million stars twinkling in the sky.

As much as this town said they didn't want change, the parents couldn't have been happier when their children sent them excited pictures. I'd received several text messages congratulating me on the prom theme, and then many had scheduled parties with me.

I walked over to the snack table and made sure nothing needed refilling, when out of the corner of my eye, I saw Bitsy. She was talking to Chaz, gesturing wildly with her hands. Chaz nodded but didn't say a word. She caught me looking, shrugged, and hurried toward the door.

I marched over and intercepted Bitsy as she tried to slither back out. "Bitsy, fancy meeting you here. Problems in party-planning land?"

"Certainly not. I had to firm up a few minor details for Suzy's sweet-sixteen party next week, nothing more."

"Minor details that required you to meet Maria tonight, of all nights?"

"Well, why not?"

"Maria Caputo is in the coatroom, not by Dr. Anderson."

"What I talk to Dr. Anderson about is none of your business, and I already talked to Maria in the back."

"Right." I crossed my arms and tapped my foot.

She looked at her manicure, then threw her hands up in the air. "Oh, all right, I'll admit I was a bit curious to see what you came up with."

"And...?"

"And it's a bit gaudy for my taste, but it suits you perfectly."

"Thank you. From you, I'll take that as a compliment."

She grunted. "You would." She swiped a non-existent piece of lint off her skirt. "Oh, there's the mayor. I simply must speak to him. Some of us have work to do." With that, she stuck her nose in the air and strolled over to Mayor Edwards, waving her arms like a loon.

I turned to the dance floor to check on Lexi. She'd begged me to let her go to the dance with Tommy Jones, Harmony's nephew. I'd agreed because I didn't want to do anything to ruin her newfound social acceptance. Besides, I knew Harmony's oldest brother Hank would kill him if he made one wrong move. I scanned the room until I spotted Lexi, but she wasn't dancing with Tommy. Chaz swirled her around the floor, and she stared up at him, her eyes full of adoration, and her smile wider than

I'd seen it in years. I was sure he made her feel like a princess; he had that way about him.

My heart swelled with tenderness, and a lump formed in my throat. She looked like an angel in her pink satin gown with rhinestones studded down the back and her hair swept high in an elegant up do. My little girl was growing up, and I so wasn't ready. Tommy cut in, and Chaz bowed slightly, then handed Lexi off and turned in my direction.

I wiped a tear away from the corner of my eye as his gaze locked on mine. He crooked his finger for me to join him on the dance floor. I slowly made my way over, drinking in the sight of him. He'd gone all out. Black tuxedo with a white cummerbund, while I'd stuck with the swan theme, wearing a white form-fitting gown.

"You look beautiful," he whispered in my ear, and I slipped into his arms.

"So do you," I whispered back.

He spun me around, and I laughed, for once not caring what anyone thought. There were mostly students with only a few chaperones, and all we were doing was dancing. Still, this was as close as I was prepared to go in bringing our affair out in the open. Most people assumed we were close friends and business associates.

By the time the dance ended, people had already started to clear out. I stepped away, but Chaz lingered in holding my hand for a moment, then let go as he said, "Tonight at my place?"

"You can count on it, Doc." I smiled.

The last two weeks had been heaven. After the mamas left, we'd spent every possible minute together to make up for lost time. I didn't want to be away from him, and when I was, all I did was think about him. Part of me was concerned my feelings for him had grown so quickly. Another part rationalized it was all a part of the fantasy I was fulfilling.

I'd never regretted getting married so young, but I had always wondered what college and affairs and one-night stands might have been like. My gaze ran over Chaz's backside. He'd removed his tuxedo jacket, taken off his cummerbund, and loosened his tie. He sure filled out a pair of pants nicely.

"Mrs. Robinson," Mayor Edwards spoke from behind me.

I whirled around, trying not to look guilty. "Mayor Edwards, how are you? You're looking quite dapper tonight."

He puffed up like the Stay-Puft Marshmallow Man in his white tux with tails and top hat. "Why, thank you. My dear sweet Eleanor picked this out, and I do aim to make her happy."

"Well, she did a fine job." I nodded.

"I must say you did a splendid job yourself with this shindig. Most impressive, young lady. Most impressive."

"Thank you. If you like this, you're going to love what I have planned for the Andersons' retirement party." I winked.

"I can hardly wait." He rubbed his protruding belly. "Well, mustn't keep the Missus waiting."

"Give Eleanor my best." I smiled.

"Will do." He waddled away.

My gaze wandered back to Chaz, but he had already gone. Probably a good thing he didn't linger to say goodbye. Most everyone had left by now, and all that remained was the clean-up crew. Johnny must have given Lexi a ride home, but I wasn't worried. Harmony was waiting at my house for a full report.

My chat with the mayor made me realize I'd have to tread more carefully when it came to Chaz. I wasn't ready to give him up yet, but I couldn't let anything stand in my way of getting this town to realize I had something important to give. I wasn't just the fire chief's jilted ex, I was Zoe the person, and I had a hell of a lot to offer.

Chapter Sixteen

"You did great tonight," Chaz said as he grabbed a bottle of wine, two glasses and my hand. We headed upstairs to his bedroom.

"Thanks," I said. "I think the kids really liked it, and the mayor seemed impressed. I'm still worried because Bitsy is good at what she does. What if she wins?"

"She is good, but you're different." He set the wine on his dresser, then opened the bottle and poured us a couple glasses.

"Gee, thanks." I accepted the glass he handed me and took a hefty sip.

"I mean different in a good way. You offer this town something unique. It's refreshing." He tucked a curl behind my ear and smiled.

"Well, you might think so, but you've lived away." I paced the room, wearing a path in the plush chocolate carpet. "The diehard locals are the ones who will sway the mayor one way or the other. If I can pull off your party and impress them, I might have a shot. But I don't know...."

"Hey." He caught my hand and pulled me in front of him.

"You will. I have faith." His eyes were so sincere and his smile so tender, I melted.

"Why are you this good to me?" I asked in barely more than a whisper.

He stared at me for a long moment, the green of his eyes blurring into the brown. "Because you're good *for* me." He leaned forward and kissed me softly on the lips.

"You're good for me, too." I cupped his cheek, and he turned his face into my palm and kissed it.

He made me feel like I could do anything, *be* anything. But mostly, he made me happy. I wished for a moment I could give him more, but I was afraid. Although, there was one thing I could give him.

My heart started to pound over the mere thought of what I was about to do. I stepped back and set my wineglass on the end table by the bed, then wiped my sweaty palms on my dress. Biting my bottom lip, I unbuttoned the front of my gown. Chaz reached for the light switch, but I said, "Wait."

His hand hovered only inches away. "For what?"

"This." I unfastened the last button, letting the silky material slide off my shoulders and fall to the floor, leaving me nearly naked as I stood before him.

Chaz's lips parted, eyes widened, and he stared at me. He blinked. "Zoe, sweetheart, you don't have to."

"I know." I smiled slowly. "I want to." And I did. As nervous as I was, as insecure as I felt, I wanted this. I wanted him in ways I never thought possible.

He swallowed, his Adam's apple bobbed, and his eyes dropped to my Double Darlings and glazed over. I reached behind my back and unhooked my bra. Now it was my turn to swallow hard as I peeled the front away from my breasts, their weight causing them to sag a bit. I kept my gaze on the floor, afraid to look. Would he be disappointed? Age and babies had dimmed the glory of what they once were.

He slipped his finger beneath my chin and tipped my face up. "My, God, you're breathtaking." His mouth swooped down over mine, and he crushed my chest to his, devouring my mouth. When he broke away for air, he whispered, "Thank you."

I didn't know what to say. My heart burst over all he'd given me. He made me feel free and alive and... beautiful. For the first time in a long time, I felt comfortable in my own skin. For that, I would always be grateful.

In response, I slipped my hands beneath his shirt and pushed it up his hard, amazing body and over his head, then tossed it aside. I ran my nails through his chest hair and over his nipples, eliciting a groan from him. He trailed his hands up my torso, then over my breasts and let his fingers tease my nipples.

"Chaz." I tipped my head back, and he bent down to take my nipple into his mouth. "Oh, God, I'm gonna lose it."

"Not yet," he whispered. "I'm just getting started." He swept me off my feet and laid me down on the bed, the light of the lamp on the end table illuminating the bed fully.

Part of me wanted to ask him to turn the lights back off because he hadn't seen the rest of me. The stretch marks and c-section scar I wouldn't be able to hide once my nylons were off. But I wouldn't ask him to dim the lights. I'd come this far for a reason. I trusted Chaz. I knew he would never hurt me, not intentionally at least. So, I lay still as he rolled my nylons over my hips and down my legs.

"Have I told you how much I love this 'no underwear trend' you've adopted?" He stroked his hand down my stomach until he cupped me intimately.

"A-At least ten times." I gasped when he slid a finger inside.

"I also told you one day I'd get to show you how beautiful you are to me." He kissed his way from my breasts down my stomach, following the path his fingers had taken, leaving me breathless in his wake.

When I could no longer stand it, I said, "Ch-Chaz. Please."

He entered me in one swift movement, and I gasped over the feel of him filling me, completing me. He was right, we were good together. We fit. He picked up the tempo, and I matched him stroke for stroke, until we erupted together and fell limp and exhausted, totally spent in each other's arms. Mount St. Zoe would never be dormant again, and I was just fine with that.

Seconds turned to minutes, slowly creeping by until our breathing turned to normal. "I don't want to sneak around anymore, Zoe."

I stopped stroking his chest and looked up at him. "Chaz, we talked about this. You agreed to these terms."

"Yes because that's what you needed at the time. You've grown, Zoe. We've grown together. What we have is too special to hide it. I want the entire town to know how I feel about you. Zoe, I—"

"You're out of your mind, is what you are." I pulled away and sat up, tucking the sheets over my breasts. Why was he doing this? We had a good thing going, and he was changing the rules. "You know how I feel about this. The kids—"

"Adore me, as I do them." He tried to take my hand, but I scooted away.

"Adore you as a family friend, not a potential father. What about when it's over? It will crush them."

"Who says it has to end?"

I ignored that, unable to even consider the possibility. This affair was temporary. It had always been temporary. I thought he knew that. "The town," I said, grasping for something. Anything. "What will they think of me dating a younger man? They will never understand."

"They will come around when they see how much we care

about each other, and that we're good for each other. You said so yourself. Beside, you're not that much older than me. Four years is nothing after high school."

"We're good for each other as separate entities, not as a couple. I told you; I want to make something on my own. I want to be Zoe, not the doctor's lover. I don't want to lose me ever again."

"Who says you have to?"

My eyes locked on his. "I was married for twenty years, you never were. I'm just being realistic."

"You're just being foolish." His frustration was evident in his tone and on his face as he added, "Your thinking is old fashioned and irrational."

I gasped. "How dare you?"

He sighed and raised his hand in resignation. "You're right. I'm sorry. I was out of line."

"You're damn right you were." I scooted off the bed and scrambled back into my clothes.

"Zoe, I said I was sorry, okay. Where are you going?"

"To sort out my foolish old fashioned, 'irrational' thoughts. I need time to think, and I can't do that with you pressuring me to tell everyone about us. You knew how I felt going into this, so I don't get why you would want to ruin a good thing."

"Because I want more, dammit." He plunged his hand through his sandy hair, and a muscle in his jaw bulged. "You're right. I knew how you felt from the start; I just didn't anticipate my feelings would grow this strong for you."

I stopped and stared at him, my heart hurting for him and for me. "Neither did I." I sighed. "And you do deserve more, but I'm not sure I can give you more."

"I want it all, Zoe. I think if you search your heart, you'll see you do, too. Tonight proved that to me more than ever." His brow pinched together as he looked at me. "I don't know if I can do this anymore."

Was this the end? A sharp pain shot through my chest, nearly bringing me to my knees. My breath stuck in my throat at the thought my time with Chaz was over.

"I knew this day would come, but I wasn't prepared for how much it would hurt." A soft sob slipped out.

"It doesn't have to be like this." His eyes filled with all the anguish he felt, and I almost gave in. Something inside me couldn't.

"Yeah, it does," I said on a shaky breath. "I'll see you next week at the party. If I need anything before then, I'll give you a call, okay?"

He nodded once, curtly, his Adam's apple working overtime. "Take care of yourself, Zoe."

"You too," I whispered, and fled as tears streamed down my cheeks. Why couldn't I give in? Everything about Chaz was amazing and wonderful and perfect. The problem wasn't with him, it was with me.

And I had no clue how to fix it.

"It's over. I can't believe it's over." I blew my nose and started crying again as I sat at Tiffany's ceramic and glass kitchen table. I'd called an emergency girls' night, and we'd all agreed to meet at Tiffany's so prying little ears wouldn't hear. "Isn't champagne for celebrations?" I asked, taking a sip.

"Sorry, doll, this meeting was last minute." Tiffany shrugged a dainty silk-clad shoulder. "It's all I had in the fridge." She spread some caviar on a cracker and nibbled on the corner.

"Let me guess. Leftovers from another hot date with some random rich businessman" Harmony popped a caviar cracker in her mouth and chased it with a gulp of her champagne, then wiped her hand on her jeans, her dress long gone and hair all stiff and spiky once again.

Tiffany winked, nibbling on her own caviar cracker and sipping more champagne.

Morticia took a swig of her Diet Cola, curling up in a chair, all nice and comfy looking in her sweats. "Don't know how you guys eat that crap."

"It's called having good taste, not tasting good, doll." Tiffany finished her cracker and dabbed her mouth with an embroidered cloth napkin as her gaze ran over both of their outfits.

"Hey, jeans beat the hell out of some frou-frou dress any day, that's for damn sure." Harmony popped another cracker in her mouth and tossed back the rest of her drink.

"How is your mother, anyway?" Tiffany asked.

"Backing off, finally. But only after I threatened to sell my shop and move out of town."

"Moving out of town sounds good to me. I wouldn't have to watch my father drool over a woman young enough to be my sister." Morticia made a make-me-puke gesture, and then stuffed a cracker in her mouth.

"Well, he's happy at least. You have to want that, doll."

"I guess." Morticia admitted but didn't look all that sincere.

I tapped the table to the tune of *Show me the way to go home. I'm tired and I wanna go to bed. Had several drinks a couple minutes ago, and they went right to my head*, as I said, "Well, I'm not happy. I'm a little sappy, but I sure as hell am *not* happy."

I hiccupped, feeling a buzz from the champagne that had gradually replaced the urge to cry with a nice warm fuzzy feeling. Warm and fuzzy but now slightly annoyed. I frowned, my annoyance quickly turning to anger.

"He called me foolish and irrational. *Me*, irrational. I'm about the most rational person out there."

"When it comes to your work and your kids, yes," Tiffany agreed. "But when it comes to men, not so much."

"Here, here. I'll raise my glass to that," Harmony chimed in, glancing at her glass, her auburn brows knitting. "My empty glass." She got up, snagged the champagne bottle from the ice bucket, and refilled all our glasses, then tossed Morticia another Diet Cola.

"Gotta admit, Tiffany has a point." Morticia winced at my look. "Sorry, but it's true."

"How so?"

"Oh, let me see, your vow of celibacy for one," Tiffany said. "Completely irrational."

"True." Harmony winked at Tiffany.

I huffed. "That was not irrational. I know plenty of celibate people."

"Name one," Tiffany asked.

"I can name two." I couldn't quite meet their eyes. "Father O'Dority and Sister Mary Agnes."

Harmony rolled her eyes, then hopped up and down in her seat. "Oh, oh. I got one. How about being afraid to go into Adult World and not willing to use a freaking vibrator?"

"That was *not* irrational, that was smart. It had two heads and it spit for God's sake. Morticia stared me straight in the eye. "Here's one for you. Thinking you, of all people, could have an affair and walk away unchanged."

The truth of her statement hit me hard. I should have known better. Maybe I had, but I hadn't been strong enough to resist. My defenses kicked in as I flung my hand toward all of them. "It's your fault. You all told me to just have sex."

"But you didn't just have sex, you turned what you had with Chaz into an affair," Tiffany said. "You are not an affair kind of woman, Zoe. You married your high school sweetheart, for Pete's sake."

"Who abandoned me to go find himself. Why couldn't he have been a normal man and had an affair with another woman to solve his midlife crisis? Or, hell, I could even accept an affair with another man? But no, my husband had to go and lose his mind. Who quits their job and goes backpacking across the country looking for some epiphany?"

"Max Robinson, that's who," Tiffany said.

"So, what am I supposed to do about Chaz now?" I asked, totally defeated and knowing they were right. What Chaz and I had was so much more than just sex.

"Go for it." Harmony shrugged. "Why not? I mean, it could lead to something amazing. What are you afraid of, anyway?"

"I don't know. A lot of things, I guess. I don't want to lose myself again, and you know how stubborn this town is. And fickle. One minute I brought the plague down on them as the vibrating-cake-mixing, Peeping-Tom mother of the local strip-per, and the next I'm the town's charity case. They either won't accept me dating Chaz, or they will totally accept it, and I will be known as an extension of him, same as I was with Max. I've worked too hard for that to happen. Besides, he and Bitsy have been spending a lot of time together. I think they might be having an affair."

"No way. I've seen the way he looks at you," Harmony said. "I'm sure whatever he and Bitsy are talking about has nothing to do with love and romance."

"We're talking about Bitsy, not Lester," Morticia pointed out. "It's more likely she's having an anxiety attack because you're whooping her butt. Have you noticed she looks a mess lately?"

"I'm with them. Stop worrying about Bitsy. She's obviously going through something, and a romance with Chaz isn't it. I think the real root of your problem is you're afraid Chaz is going to change his mind like Max did, so you won't let him in." Tiffany covered my hand with her own.

"I know it's stupid, and it probably is irrational, but I can't help it. He's younger. Never been married. Doesn't have any kids of his own." I met each of their eyes. "What if he wants more than I can give? I can't go through falling in love and having the person leave again."

"We get it, babe." Harmony put her hand on top of Tiffany's.

"No matter what you decide, we're here for you." Morticia covered Harmony's hand with hers. "Same as always." She slapped the table, sealing the deal.

"Thanks guys. I don't know what I would do without you." The question was, what was I going to do without Chaz?

Like it or not, I was about to find out.

"Thank you," Chaz said, not quite meeting my eyes.

We stood by the buffet food table under the enormous tent in Chaz's backyard. Each flap of the tent sported hand-painted destinations where the train stopped, and the food consisted of meals from Roz and Wally's favorite restaurants they frequented along those stops.

"You're welcome," I said. "Everyone seems to be having a good time, and your parents were thrilled with the theme."

Chaz kept his gaze on his parents as they formed a dancing train with Wally in the front as the engineer, the townspeople in the middle as all the various cars, and Roz in the back as the caboose. They hopped and wiggled their way across the makeshift dance floor, following the painted train track pattern while laughing and singing all the way.

"The party favors sure were a hit," he added, and chuckled. They all wore train hats and blew on wooden train whistles to the beat of the music.

"I'm just glad it didn't rain." I hated making small talk. We hadn't seen each other all week, hadn't even spoken until I'd arrived this morning to set up. Even then, we'd managed to avoid each other by staying busy.

"Chaz, I...." I didn't know what to say.

His gaze met mine, and a flash of pain registered for a brief moment before he masked it and smiled slightly. "It's okay, Zoe."

"No, it's not." My heart tightened painfully in my chest. "I never meant to hurt you." My voice hitched.

He took my hand and squeezed, and warmth spread throughout my entire body. "I know."

"I miss you," I whispered. "C-Can't we go back to what we had?"

He gave my hand one final squeeze, then let go. "I'm sorry. I can't." His sizzling hazel eyes bore into mine. "I want more."

Every part of me wanted to tell him I could give him more, but I couldn't. I couldn't lose me, I couldn't lose him, and I couldn't lose the mayor's bid. The risk was too great. I tried to speak, but couldn't, so I shook my head instead.

"Why?" He stared at me, looking lost and helpless and... agonized. I'd managed to hurt him again, no matter how hard I tried not to. He had no idea how much I cared about him.

"I... I...." I still couldn't get the words out.

"I get it. You don't care about me as much as I thought you did. Because if you did, you'd never be able to let what we had end like this." His mouth formed a hard line.

"Chaz, you know that's not true."

He glanced over by the podium we'd set up in front of all

the tables. A man clanked his glass to quiet the audience and ask everyone to take their seats.

"I've got to go. It looks like the railroad employers are ready for me." Chaz walked away without another word, his back straight and shoulders stiff.

I pressed my lips together, feeling my heart break into a million pieces as I watched Chaz take his place beside the head of the railroad. I couldn't believe our relationship had come to this. My friends were right. I didn't do just sex. I should have known I could never have an affair and not grow attached. Chaz had been willing to wait for me; however, he hadn't realized the extent of my fears. No matter what I said, he would never understand. I didn't fully understand. I just knew something inside wouldn't let me take that next step.

The head of the railroad called Roz and Wally up to the podium, gave a speech about what wonderful employees they had been and how much they would be missed. Then they presented them with matching watches and a beautiful plaque. Wally and Roz shook the hand of their former employer and hugged Chaz hard, then gave a thank you speech, stating their appreciation.

"And last, but not least, I'd like to thank Zoe Robinson for planning such a wonderful party," Wally said, meeting my stunned gaze from afar.

"Zoe, would you come join us, dear?" Roz asked, with a glowing smile.

I blinked a couple times and stood there with my mouth agape. How was I supposed to go up there in front of the entire town and not fall apart when I was dying inside?

"Don't be shy, dear." Roz held out her hand. "You deserve this. Doesn't she, Chaz?"

Chaz barely looked at me. "Absolutely. Mrs. Robinson

worked hard. She deserves everything that's coming to her." A muscle in his jaw bulged.

I could tell his hurt had turned to anger. That was the first time he'd called me Mrs. anything. I wanted to take him in my arms and tell him everything would be okay, but it wouldn't be okay, because I couldn't give him what he needed.

I took a shaky breath, pasted on a stiff smile, and made my way over to the podium. I tried to stand between Roz and Wally, but she wasn't having any of that. She squeezed me right between her and Chaz. The length of my side pressed against him, and he stiffened.

"Roz and I wanted to express our gratitude, Zoe. The amount of thought you put into planning a party that was absolutely perfect for us, right down to the last detail, is greatly appreciated, and a lot more than many anticipated."

His gaze swept over the crowd and several guilty eyes skirted away.

"This is more than just a party to us. You've given us a memory we will never forget."

He reached over and folded me into a bear hug, and I held on tight as the ache in my throat became unbearable. My parents weren't here, and right now, he was the next best thing to hugging my dad.

Here I was, forty years old, yet all I wanted was to hug my dad.

I stepped back, but Roz swooped in and wrapped her arms around me, smelling of sugar cookies. I thought of my mother. As much as she drove me nuts, she was always there for me, telling me it would be okay. I hugged Roz back, a sniffle slipping out. I pulled away, swiping my eyes, and she tilted her head, her brows knitting together in concern.

"Are you all right, dear?" she asked.

"I-I'm fine," I croaked, and my breath hitched again.

Chaz tapped me on the shoulder, and I turned around in surprise. He handed me a dozen red roses, keeping his eyes on the flowers as he said, "These are for you, Ms. Robinson. Thank you for... everything."

"Y-You're welcome," I barely got out, wanting desperately to get this over with so I could escape to fall apart.

Chaz must have heard the anguish in my voice, because his gaze locked on mine. I pressed my wobbling lips together and struggled not to cry, but a single tear slipped down over my cheek.

Chaz cursed under his breath, his mouth swooping down to cover mine.

Gasps rang out through the crowd, and I pulled away in stunned surprise.

I looked out at a frowning mayor and a smirking Bitsy, and felt my stomach drop out from under me. Gerty and Gabby Rogers were whispering, their heads pressed close together. Truman looked around, confused since he couldn't see more than two feet in front of him. Lester looked even more twisted, standing there gaping at me with his goofy grin. The Caputos were talking to the Morgans, and Mrs. Hurley yammered on to Principal Brimstone, who reached in his pocket and pulled out his phone, probably to call Dr. Headright and tell her I wasn't cured after all.

My best friends just stood there with their mouths agape, and my kids looked confused. Father O'Dority shook his head, and Sister Mary Agnes fanned her face as though she were about to faint again. And Mrs. Bee had already opened her cell phone. I knew exactly whom she was calling, and anger replaced my surprise.

"How could you?" I turned on Chaz.

"Zoe, I'm sorry." Chaz tried to take my hand, but I stepped away. "I only meant to console you, but I couldn't help myself."

"You knew how much this job meant to me, what was at stake." I started to shake. "You've undone every ounce of credibility I had. I hope you're happy."

"I love you, Zoe. I couldn't stand to see you hurting. Can't you see I would do anything for you? Dammit, I want to spend the rest of my life with you. Why is that so hard for you to accept? I hadn't planned to tell you like this, but now that it's out there, you can't deny what we feel for each other. I know you're scared, but we're good for each other, and you know it. I know you love me, too, Zoe. Look me in the eye and tell me you don't love me. Put me out of my misery and marry me, Zoe. What do you say?"

The crowd gasped again, and the hum of conversation grew to a dull roar.

I scanned the crowd one last time, and then looked at Chaz. "I can't believe you did this to me. Marry you?" My voice hitched. "I don't want to marry you. In fact, I never want to see you again." I burst into tears and ran out to my car. I had to get home. The girls would take care of my kids.

Right now, I needed to be alone.

Chapter Seventeen

Six days, two hours and ten minutes later, I curled up in an old recliner. Wearing faded sweatpants and a sweatshirt, I sipped a cup of chamomile tea. I'd always hated this ugly chair, but right now I was in the mood to surround myself with misery.

Chaz had called several times, but I wouldn't talk to him. Then he just gave up.

According to the rumor mill, he'd gone from being hurt to flat-out pissed over me humiliating him in front of the entire town. Ha! He should talk. What about me? He kissed me in front of everyone, taking away from my moment. The focus was no longer on all the hard work I had done. People would think I'd slept with him to land the job. I couldn't believe he'd asked me to marry him. He knew I would say no, yet he'd asked anyway. What had he expected me to say?

I hadn't left my house, either, for fear of running into the citizens of Mayflower and seeing the judgment on their faces. I didn't want to talk to anyone. My best friends tried to tell me the rumors around town were all in my favor, but I was afraid no one would take me seriously now.

I was sure the mayor would give Bitsy the Labor Day Bash.

Tomorrow was the Memorial Day picnic at the gazebo in the center of town, and the mayor was scheduled to make his big announcement, but that wasn't what bothered me the most. Chaz said he loved me and wanted to spend the rest of his life with me.

And I'd said I never wanted to see him again.

Thinking about it had the contents of my lunch churning in my stomach, demanding to be set free. Up until that moment, a small part of me had hoped I could convince Chaz to pick up where we'd left off, but he'd changed the rules. Love wasn't temporary. Neither was marriage. The thought that we were really over for good this time was killing me. He loved me, but I didn't believe he could be truly happy with me.

Not enough to take that kind of risk, anyway.

"Can I get you anything, Mom?" Troy asked, looking more serious than he had in months.

"I'm okay."

"You sure? If you said no to marrying Chaz because of us, you didn't have to," he rushed on. "Chaz is cool. We all agree. We wouldn't mind at all."

"My saying no had nothing to do with you guys, okay? I'm sorry. I know you really like Chaz, and you know he's still here for you whenever you need him, but I can't marry him." I wrapped my arms tighter around my ratty old clothes. "For a lot of reasons."

"Oh." He glanced at the ugly recliner, and then down at the floor. "Well, let me know if you need anything."

Here I was worried about Chaz disappointing them, yet now I was the bad guy. As much as I wanted to blame Chaz, I knew this was all about me and my issues. "I'm fine, honey. Don't worry about me, okay?" I smiled, and he nodded but left the room still wearing that worried look on his face.

"I don't have to go to the mall with Mia. I can stay home if you want." Lexi sat on the footstool by my feet, fingering the fringe of her miniskirt, not quite meeting my eyes. She wasn't any happier with me than Troy was, but they both seemed to sense my vulnerability.

"Yes, you do. I want you to go. You've been so good lately; you deserve to go."

She leveled me with a motherly look I wasn't expecting. "You know, it's okay to talk about your feelings and let someone in."

Those were the exact words I'd fed to her time and again with no success. Chaz had been the only one to break through to her. Ironic, since he was the only man to ever break through my defenses, too.

I hugged her. "When did you grow up on me?"

She stared at me long and hard. "When I met Chaz." She dropped her gaze back to her lap, looking like a troubled teen once again. She was as lost without him as I was.

"Hey, you." I tilted her chin up. "Like I told your brother, I'm fine. Go have fun."

Her shoulders slumped slightly, and she nodded, but she didn't look any more excited than Troy did as she left the room.

Bobby walked in next without a single bounce, a handful of dandelions clutched in his dirty fingers, and handed them to me. He silently kissed my cheek and looked down at his socks as he scuffed the carpet with his toe. He'd removed his shoes without me having to ask? Something was definitely up with him.

"Hey, what's wrong? You're not bouncing."

He shrugged. "Not much to bounce about anymore." Now that I thought about it, he hadn't bounced since Chaz stopped coming around.

"Where's your sword? I'll even let you use my armor if you want."

"Nah. Don't wanna." He walked out of the room without another word.

I held up okay until my little Katy walked in, carrying a box of tissues, and climbed into my lap. Snuggling down against me, she asked, "Why you so sad, Mommy? Is it cuz Dr. Chaz made you cry? I miss him."

"I'm just tired, sweetie. And I miss him, too."

"My eyes don't get red and puffy like Kermit the Frog's when I'm tired." She gave me a hug. At least she hadn't called me Miss Piggy. "I'll let you sleep, Mommy. You must be *really* tired." She hopped off my lap and went up to her room to play.

Good Lord, I had to snap out of my depression for the sake of my kids, but I didn't know how. I felt empty and alone inside. I looked at the phone on the end table beside me and cringed, but I picked it up and dialed before I could change my mind. Then, feeling like I was in the middle of a Judy Blume book with me as Margaret and Mom as God, I said, "Hi, Mom, it's me, Zoe."

"I know who it is; I'm just surprised you called me. Given the way you shipped me off after Easter and the fact that you've barely spoken to me since, I didn't expect you to make the first move."

Okay, I so wasn't Margaret, and she sure as heck wasn't God. What had I been thinking, calling her for advice? It was just that sometimes a girl needed her mother, darn it, no matter who that mother was. My kids had reminded me of that today.

"I guess I needed to hear your voice," I admitted, too drained to argue with her.

She paused, for once not keeping the argument going. "I heard what happened, dear." Her voice was soft and comforting through the line.

"I thought you might have," I said, remembering Mrs. Bee on her cell phone. "I'm just surprised you didn't call first."

She sighed. "I really am trying to take what you said to heart and stay out of your life."

I sniffed, then blew my nose. "I don't want you to stay out of my life, Mom; I just want you to respect my wishes."

"Do you even know your wishes, Zoe? What do you want? I mean it. Think about it. What do you really want?"

I couldn't remember the last time she had asked what I wanted. Hell, I couldn't remember the last time anyone had asked what I wanted, not even Chaz. He'd asked what I wanted from him, but not what I wanted for myself. Me. Zoe. Just Zoe. Not Mrs. Anyone. My whole life had been spent taking care of others. I never made the time to take care of myself.

"I don't know, anymore. I thought I knew what I wanted, but I didn't think it would hurt this much."

Guilt had played a huge role in my holding back from Chaz. I'd made vows to Max, and even though he didn't honor his, I still felt those vows. Twenty years was a long time to be committed to a person, and two years was the blink of an eye when it came to ending that commitment.

"I think you were right. Maybe I should move to Florida."

"No."

"No?" I blinked and wiped my eyes. My mother had just gotten her way, finally, after all the arguments and all this time. And she was saying no?

"That's right, no. You might not know what you want, but I saw the way Chaz looked at you. Whether you want to acknowledge it or not, I saw the way you looked at him, too."

"It was that obvious?"

"Honey, you can't hide feelings like that no matter how hard you try."

"But the town—"

"The town is not blind. If they can't see it's time for you to move on, then that's their problem."

"It's not just the town that's holding me back." I played with the hem of my old sweatshirt. "What if I take a chance and Chaz rejects me, too? Do you have any idea what that feels like?" My voice broke. "Like someone rips out your soul until there's nothing left but a shell. I can't go through that again, Mom, I just can't." I sobbed, letting the tears fall freely for the first time in a long time. It felt good to cry, freeing somehow, like I'd needed to let go of some of the pain before there was room for hope.

"I know you're scared, but honey, you can't predict what's going to happen in life. By never taking a risk, are you ever really living? You could be cheating yourself out of something amazing. I'm going to tell you something I never told anyone. Do you remember crazy Aunt LuLu?"

"The one with all the cats who names her plants?" I said on a hiccup, and then sniffed.

"That's the one. Well, she wasn't in love with Uncle Bernie when she married him, you know."

"Haven't they been married for like fifty years?"

"They sure have, and she loves him with all her heart now. But years ago, she was madly in love with another man."

"What happened?" I sat up straighter and dried my eyes.

"Well, he was the love of her life, and she was positive she would never love another man like him. His name was Andrew, and he went to school with her. He was friends with your Uncle Bernie, but she and Bernie weren't dating at that time. She spent the whole summer with Andrew, and then he went in the army. After he left, she found out she was pregnant. She tried to contact him, but by the time her letter made it through, he had already fallen in love with a woman in Vietnam and married her."

"Oh, my God, you mean Bernie junior isn't really a junior? But he looks just like his dad."

"No, no. Bernie junior's every bit a junior. LuLu knew your uncle had a crush on her all through high school, but back then, she'd only had eyes for Andrew. When Bernie found out she was pregnant, he offered to marry her. In those days, you didn't raise babies out of wedlock, so she agreed, though she didn't love him. She was eight months pregnant when she went into labor and delivered a preemie stillbirth, the poor dear. Bernie stayed by her side and held her hand the whole time. He had grown to love that baby as much as she did, even though it wasn't his own. With the last trace of Andrew gone, she realized she'd fallen in love with your uncle."

"Wow, I don't know what to say."

"My point is, if crazy Aunt LuLu hadn't taken a risk by marrying Uncle Bernie, she never would have found a love more powerful than anything she'd ever felt for Andrew. It didn't discount what she felt for Andrew, it simply meant she had room for more than one love in her heart. Some things are worth taking a chance on, Zoe. Stop thinking with your head, and listen to your heart, or you'll wind up like Bitsy. Bitter and lonely, without so much as even a cat for a companion."

Who would have thought being a crazy old cat lady would be a desirable thing? Suddenly, I felt lighter than I had in years, as though a heavy weight had been lifted. "Thanks, Mom." I felt the bond between us grow stronger than I'd ever imagined possible.

"I love you, honey. I just want to see you happy. That's all I've ever wanted."

"I know."

"Good, then stop wallowing in those ugly old clothes and get out of that house."

"How did you—"

"I know you better than you know yourself, child."

That was probably true, but still. "Mother...."

"Oh, all right. Mrs. Bee said you haven't left your house all week except to get the paper. Kiss my grandbabies and tell them their *favorite* grandmother will see them in a month."

She hung up, and I smiled for the first time in a week. I still didn't know what I was going to do, I just knew I was going to face the town and the mayor tomorrow with my head held high, and my heart open to new possibilities.

I glanced down at my ratty clothes and my chipped nail polish, and then ran a hand through my tangled hair. Catching my reflection in the mirror on the wall, I groaned. I looked like Broomhilda, for God's sake. No wonder my kids were so concerned. I marched up the stairs full of determination and a renewed confidence I welcomed.

So much to do, so little time.

"Pay up again, ladies. I knew she'd come," Harmony said as I weaved my way through the buzzing crowd at Mayflower Park to join them in front of the gazebo.

Blue sky, warm temperatures, and a slight breeze made for a perfect Memorial Day celebration. Harmony brought my attention back to her as she held out her hand and winked, wiggling her fingers at the other girls.

"Damn. Don't get me wrong, I'm glad you're here," Morticia directed her comment at me. "I just hate being broke." She glared at Harmony, and then slapped a twenty in her hand.

"Sorry," Tiffany said to me. "After our last conversation, I didn't think you'd come." She paid Harmony, and then straightened the strap on my floral sundress. "You'll do fine, just look them in the eye and smile. And don't worry about the kids. We've got you covered."

The kids went to stand by my best friends, and I fixed my

shoe. I'd added a pair of cute strappy sandals and opted to go without nylons, but I was wearing underwear this time. A brand new pair in *my* size from Nancy's Negligees I'd bought for just this occasion. I'd even left my hair down in long curly strands, rather than my old business suit and French twist.

It was past time I started showing this town the real me.

Bitsy stood up in the gazebo beside the mayor in her starched suit and perfectly styled, over-sprayed hair. Although she looked tired, and she'd put on weight. Looks like the stress of this competition had gotten to her, too. Well, I was through trying to be something I wasn't. She was classical, and I was contemporary. It was time the town chose whether to move forward or stay in the past.

I hadn't made eye contact with anyone, afraid of what I might see, and I'd tuned out the whispers coming from the throng of people who'd gathered in the park. Now that the Memorial Day Parade was finished, the mayor was ready to make his announcement about who he chose to plan the Labor Day Bash.

"My stomach's a bundle of knots," I said to the girls, too nervous to join the mayor just yet.

"Just picture them naked." Harmony chuckled.

Morticia smacked her. "Stop it."

"What?" Harmony rubbed her arm. "Just keeping it real."

"You're making her more nervous, is what." Tiffany frowned at her, and then looked at me. "What's the worst that can happen? The mayor won't choose you. So, you'll go back to catering instead of party planning. The point is, you'll survive. Now quit worrying, doll. Buck up and show them what you're made of."

Mayor Edwards spotted me and motioned for me to join him.

"This is it. Wish me luck." I took a deep breath and joined

the mayor up in the gazebo, then looked out at the crowd and nearly swooned.

There were so many people. All of Mayflower had to be there. Now more than ever I wanted to win. This would catapult my business into an instant success, and everything I'd worked so hard for would finally be mine. Everyone I knew would have to see me for me, not as an extension of anyone else.

The mayor started to speak. My palms began to sweat, and I could feel the pulse beat in my neck. "Citizens of Mayflower, I must say, this town is blessed to have two wonderful party planners at our disposal. Ms. Beaumont provides us with a timeless elegance and class no one can deny."

The crowd cheered, and my mouth grew dry, my shoulders slumping slightly.

"And Mrs. Robinson, here, provides us with a fresh unique style filled with fun."

The crowd cheered even louder, and I inhaled sharply, my lips parting in surprise.

"Both of these women are needed equally, I do believe. And since I simply couldn't decide, unbeknownst to these women, I held a poll and let the town choose."

Bitsy gasped, and I just stood there, gaping like a trout out of water, unable to breathe.

"The time has come to announce who will plan this year's first annual Labor Day Bash." The mayor pulled an official-looking envelope out of his suit coat pocket. "And the winner is," he opened the envelope and smiled wide, "Mrs. Robinson."

The crowd roared with unmistakable approval and acceptance, but... oh, my God... they weren't chanting Mrs. Robinson. They were saying Zoe over and over. Just Zoe. It was the sweetest sound I'd ever heard. A smile burst over my face, and tears sprang to my eyes. I turned to shake Bitsy's hand, but she was already gone.

"Well done, Zoe. Well done." Mayor Edwards held out his hand, and I shook it, trying not to let him see me tremble.

"Thank you, Mayor Edwards. I won't let you down."

"I'm sure you won't." He patted my shoulder. "Now, I've got to find the Missus. She baked my favorite for the picnic, and I want to make sure I get a piece before it's all gone. Or before Truman gets a hold of it." He rubbed his belly. "There's nothing quite like razzleberry pie."

I stayed in the gazebo for twenty minutes, shaking hands with all the citizens of Mayflower, hearing over and over how they loved what I'd done with the prom and the Anderson's party. Mouse droppings, nude paintings, vibrating cake mixers and sexy pictures were all but forgotten.

Gerty and Gabby even claimed they'd known all along that such a sweet girl like Lexi couldn't possibly have been the girl in the pictures, and they were glad that Mayflower could finally get back to normal. Everyone tactfully refrained from mentioning either Max or Chaz's names, but hinted in more ways than one they were glad I was moving on.

Is that what I was doing? Moving on? I guess it was.

Coping with Max's abandonment had been hard enough, but moving on was scary as hell. Yet, ever since breaking down over the phone with my mother, I felt as though my heart had room for someone else. I might not have closure with Max, but I was open to letting Chaz in. I waited ten minutes longer, but the one person I'd wanted to see most had failed to show up. I was thrilled I'd won, but it felt empty without Chaz to share it with. Empty without him, period. I sucked in a sharp breath as the truth hit me hard.

Oh, my God, I was in love with him.

My knees buckled, and I had to grab onto the railing to steady myself. Once all my doubts and fears had been resolved, the extent of my feelings for Chaz were plain as day. He was

270

right. I loved him with all my being, and I wanted nothing more than to spend the rest of my life with him, too.

Elation filled me.

I was scared senseless, but I felt lighter admitting it to myself. I loved him, but I was afraid to show it because I might lose him. An overwhelming sense of loss replaced my elation when I realized, ironically, it looked as though I'd done just that. I forced determination and hope back into my heart.

I hadn't been able to do anything when Max left, but Chaz leaving was a loss I refused to accept. This was a loss I could get back, and come hell or high water, that was exactly what I was going to do. My mother was right. Some things in life were worth taking a chance on, and Chaz was one of them.

The question was how did I win him back?

"DID you hear that Bitsy put her house on the market? She's moving." I poured each of the girls a glass of champagne and passed the buckets of Chinese food around the antique harvest table in my dining room.

"I figured she would. She can't accept that you beat her, and she's too hardheaded to admit the town could use both of you." Harmony shrugged and dug into her kung pao chicken.

"I heard she's pregnant," Morticia said.

My jaw dropped. "So that's why she looked tired and had gained weight."

"And that's why she was constantly talking to Chaz. Guess she wasn't hitting on him after all, doll."

"Wow. No wonder he was so secretive about it. He couldn't say anything even if he wanted to. Poor Bitsy. All alone with a baby on the way. I actually feel sorry for her," I said.

"I can't imagine what man could possibly be the father."

Harmony shook her head. "Her moving means more business for you. How is business, anyway?"

"Great, actually. News spread to the neighboring towns. I've received so many calls to book parties this past week; I'm going to have to hire an assistant." I laughed.

"Careful what you wish for, right?" Morticia took a bite of Sweet and Sour Pork. "Can't believe you ordered take-out. Isn't that Tiffany's department?"

"Hey, I never claimed to be talented in the kitchen." Tiffany winked and fingered the pearls at her neck. "Let's just say my talents lie elsewhere."

"Nothing wrong with take-out once in a while, and I wasn't going to cook my own celebration dinner," I said.

Tiffany frowned. "But we already celebrated your win a week ago."

"Yeah, hunkburgers and horndogs. My kind of night." Harmony snorted.

"Hello. That was the party after the party at McGinny's Pub." Morticia rolled her dark eyes. "Did you forget about dinner at Lolita's Place?"

"Why would you want to remember your portions were half the size of mine? I focused on the fonder memories of the evening, aka, hunkburgers and horndogs." Harmony grinned wide.

"Why would you want to remember the hunks and horns who wouldn't give you the time of day, no matter how many times you goosed their cabooses?" Morticia spiked a brow.

Tap tap tap went Tiffany's hand on the table. "I wish you'd both forget the whole conversation. I'm dying to know what we're celebrating." She nibbled on an egg roll, and all eyes settled on me.

"I've decided to take the next step."

"Did I just hear you right?" Morticia asked.

"I think she needs meds, stat," Harmony said.

"I don't need meds, but I do need a doctor. I just didn't realize how much. I'm talking about Chaz." I paused as three pairs of eyes gaped at me. "I'm going to tell Chaz I love him. And I'm going to say yes to his marriage proposal."

"Holy crapola." Harmony sat back, dropping her fork.

"What she said." Morticia sat there, holding a fortune cookie halfway to her mouth, staring.

"Well, good for you, doll. I say it's about time." Tiffany frowned at the other two. "Close your traps, ladies, we all knew she was falling for him. This shouldn't come as a surprise. And I do believe that makes me the winner of *this* bet. Um, how does it go?" She shot a gloating grin at Harmony and held out her manicured hand. "Oh, that's right. Pay up, girls."

"It's ladies," Morticia grumbled.

"Girls, ladies... it's all the same to me. Now, fork it over." Tiffany wiggled her fingers, the blue in her ring sparkling as bright as her twinkling eyes.

"Yeah, yeah." Harmony fished a twenty out of her jeans and handed it to Tiffany. "All I have to say is losing sucks."

"I'll drink to that." Morticia downed the rest of her Diet Cola and handed a twenty to Tiffany.

"And winning feels oh, so fine." Tiffany poured us each another glass of champagne and popped the top to another Diet Cola for Morticia. "Now we definitely have to celebrate."

Harmony smirked and turned her attention to me. "I'm happy for you, Zoe, but after the way you left Chaz standing on the podium with his own Snaky in his hand, I thought you really meant no."

"I can't believe I said no." I dropped my face into my hands. "I didn't realize I loved him until I won the bid and looked out in the audience for the one person I wanted to share my success with the most." I glanced up at them. "But he wasn't there, and I was too afraid to go after him." I stared off, remembering, and the same sense of loss consumed me. "I felt empty. My life is empty without him, and my kids have missed him so much. He probably hates me now." I met each of their eyes. "I've lost him for good, haven't I?"

"Not necessarily." Tiffany eyed the other women. "We all know the way to a man's heart is through his stomach, and who's a better cook than you, right?"

"I guess, but how am I supposed to cook for him if he won't even talk to me?"

"I'm sure we'll think of something," Morticia said.

"I already have." Harmony winked.

Lord only knew what that meant.

Chapter Eighteen

What the hell was this? I wondered as I opened my mailbox and pulled out a postcard. A picture of the square in downtown Mayflower. Why would someone send me a postcard of Mayflower? I flipped it over, but all it said was:

I found myself.

A wave of shock rocketed through me. It couldn't be, could it? I sat in stunned silence, no name necessary for me to know exactly who had sent me this card. Max. Only this postcard wasn't from some random state he'd just visited. This one was from where we met, where we married, where we raised a family, where he left me... where it had all began. What did he mean, he found himself?

My God, he was coming home.

Did he honestly think he could come back and pick up where we left off? As much as I hated him, I realized a part of me had never moved on because I'd secretly wished he'd someday do just that. Realize he made a mistake and say he wanted to be a family again. Had Chaz not re-entered my life, I might have taken Max back, despite all the heartache he'd caused me.

Being a single mom was hard, but everything was different now.

I was independent and strong and— I smiled— in love. I had changed so much since Max left and, in a way, I owed him. He'd forced me to find myself as well, and I liked what I'd discovered. I liked being my own person, not an extension of him.

No, I didn't need or want Max in my life again, and I sure as hell didn't want him messing up his children's lives. He'd given up all rights to them when he gave me full custody and left us to fend for ourselves. The phone rang, and I ran into the house to answer it. I glanced at the caller ID. Speak of the devil. I never did get closure, but it looked as though I would finally have the chance.

"Hello, Max," I said, not feeling any of the emotions I thought I would. No anger, no sadness, no anxiety... just calm. I had no doubts. What had seemed so important to me for two long years suddenly seemed trivial. I knew exactly what I had to do, and it didn't involve wasting my energy on Max.

"Hello, Zoe. Before you say anything, let me just say I'm so sorry. I was wrong to leave, especially in the way that I did, but one good thing came out of it. I found myself. I finally found exactly what I want. The grass is not always greener on the other side, and it took leaving to realize what I lost. I want to come home to you and the kids. I want us to be a family again."

I waited, but the only emotion that ran through me was pity for him. He gave up four amazing kids and a pretty damn good wife. "You're about two years too late, Max. All I want is for you to stay out of our lives. We have all moved on without you, and the kids are finally in a good place now. I won't let you mess that up the next time you have another crisis. This is not your home, we are not your family, and this is not going to happen. So do me a favor and go find someone who cares."

"But—" He sounded absolutely floored. Had he really

thought I'd just be waiting here for him to come back? Based on my past behavior, that was exactly what he'd thought.

"No buts, Max. If you come back, I'll make your life miserable. You can count on that. You made your choice two years ago, now I'm making mine. Take care, Max. I really do wish you the best. Goodbye." I hung up, feeling rejuvenated, then set off to get the one thing I wanted more than anything else. The one person I knew would never leave me or my kids. The one person who had made all the difference in the world.

Dr. Chaz Anderson.

OKAY, so I wasn't quite a crazy cat lady, but I had to be nuts to be doing what I was about to do. Max hadn't bothered me again, but I still didn't have what I wanted. Chaz wouldn't answer my calls, and I needed to talk to him. Tell him how I felt. My kids were all on board, and the entire town had insisted on getting involved. They might love to gossip and meddle, but they accepted me for who I was and wanted to see me happy again.

Darkness surrounded me, and claustrophobia threatened to set in. Beads of sweat popped out on my forehead, yet the party hadn't even started. I could hear the band tune their instruments, and people shuffling about, putting the finishing touches on all the details I had planned.

The excited hum of conversation buzzed as tables were adjusted and folding chairs scraped across the cement floor. My mouth watered at the smell of barbecue chicken and fried clams. The whole town had pitched in, and all was set.

Nothing more to do but wait for the guest of honor to arrive.

What seemed like hours passed by, when in reality, it had to have been about ten minutes. "Dim the lights," someone said. "Quiet. He's coming," someone else said.

I heard a squeak as the doors to the fire hall opened, and then Chaz said, "Lexi, I'm here, honey, are you okay?"

"Surprise," everyone yelled.

They must have flicked on the lights because Chaz said, "What the hell? Where's Lexi? Is she hurt?"

"Happy birthday, sweetheart," Roz said. "Lexi is fine. See, she's right over there."

Silence filled the fire hall. Not a good sign.

"You tricked me? I thought we agreed you weren't going to throw a party for me, Mom."

"She didn't," Wally said.

"Then who did?"

I popped out of the broom closet, throwing my arms wide as I yelled, "I did. Happy birthday, Chaz."

He looked at Lexi and arched a sandy brow.

"Sorry, but I do need you. We all do." Lexi put her arm around Katy, and Troy put his hand on Bobby's shoulder.

"Yeah, who's gonna fix my boo-boos?" Katy stuck out that big bottom lip of hers.

"I'll still be here for all of you; just like I told you when I saw you last. You know that." He glared at me as though to say *I can't believe you played the kid card*, and I smiled sheepishly. What could I say? I was desperate. Then he set his jaw, just as I'd feared he would, and he turned around, heading for the door.

It was now or never, and I knew what I had to do. Only, I hadn't expected the food table to be set up in front of the closet. I couldn't help but grin, thinking this town really did need me.

Party Planners, they were not.

I tried to go around, but both ends were blocked. Well, hell. I slid beneath the table and scrambled to my feet, bumping the edge with my backside. "Chaz, wait." I let out a little yelp as one table leg collapsed, and food tumbled over the side.

"And let you humiliate me again? Not a chance." He kept walking, not once turning around, and not coming to my rescue.

"But I need to talk to you." I did my best to save as many dishes as I could, along with several citizens, but ended up wearing most of the corn and mashed potatoes.

"Nothing more to say."

"The Christian thing to do would be to hear her out, son," Father O'Dority said, and Sister Mary Agnes nodded.

"She said it all a couple weeks ago, Father."

I let out a whistle, and Chaz shot a glance in my direction, puckering his brows as though I'd lost my mind. He had no idea the lengths I would go to fight for him, but he was about to find out. He shook his head and turned around only to find all seven of Harmony's brothers blocking his way.

"You've got to be kidding me." Chaz headed around them.

I gave up on saving the food and charged after him. Never try to run with Double Darlings. I slapped a hand over my chest and kept going, slipping and sliding all the way. "Block the door, ladies."

My girls shoved a table in front of the doors, then sat on top, grinning wide.

"What are we, back in high school?" Chaz asked.

"You wish." Harmony snorted.

"And we'd be sitting in a pyramid, not on a table, doll," Tiffany added.

"With you fetching our water." Morticia wrinkled her nose. "Sorry, couldn't resist, Doc."

"Yeah, well, this isn't the good ole days, ladies." Chaz stood with hands on hips, waiting for them to move.

They just grinned wider, not about to budge anytime soon.

He threw his hands up and headed to the side door.

Gerty Rogers swooned. "Oh, dear me."

Gabby Rogers dropped her hanky. "Oh, dear me, indeed."

Truman started to lean down, but Gabby managed to swat his hand in between moans.

Good grief, couldn't they come up with something better than that? I cut across the room, dodging the Caputos and the Morgans.

"Ladies." Chaz steadied Gerty with one hand, scooped up the hanky and handed it to Gabby with the other, patted Truman's shoulder, then kept walking.

Well, that slowed him down all of five seconds.

But five seconds was all I needed.

"Clear the way," Mrs. Bee bellowed. "That girl's on a mission."

Principal Brimstone and Mrs. Hurley shoved the chairs out of my way. Chaz had almost reached the door, when I dived and caught him around the ankles, tackling him until he fell to the floor. Cheers erupted behind me, and I thanked my lucky stars — the ones swimming in front of my eyes— he hadn't played football.

"Are you crazy?" Chaz wheezed, trying to catch his breath.

"About you." I took advantage of the situation, scrambling on top of him and pinning him to the floor, panting the entire time. "Harmony." I jerked my head to the corner of the room.

"Yo, Pickles," she hollered, "Do your thing."

"Oh, right." Officer Pickles jogged over and slapped the cuffs on us, securing our wrists together.

"What the hell are you doing, Pickles? I haven't done anything wrong."

"That's a matter of opinion." I stared down into Chaz's angry eyes. "You're breaking my heart."

"Sounds like a crime to me," Officer Pickles chimed in.

"I'm breaking *your* heart? That's a good one. Get me out of these damn things, Pickles."

"No can do." He glanced around at the eavesdropping

crowd, and then leaned forward and whispered, "She got me a date with Lolita."

"Just wait until your next physical. It won't be pretty," Chaz ground out.

I was a little worried when Officer Pickles pondered the threat, but then he shook his head. "Sorry man, a date with Lolita trumps that."

"What has gotten into you?" Chaz glared at me.

"Five minutes. That's all I want is for you to listen to me for five minutes." I stared down into his eyes, trying to convey all I felt for him with a single look.

The room had grown quiet as a morgue, and it felt as though we were the only people there, even though I knew the entire town was tuned into our every word. But it was important for me to bare my soul in front of them since I'd shot him down publicly.

They'd make up their own version anyway.

He sighed, and the angry lines surrounding his mouth relaxed as he sat up and helped me to do the same. He faced me and said with a tone that broke my heart, "You made me look like a fool, Zoe."

"I think we're even," I said softly, glancing down at my potato and corn covered blouse, then my eyes overflowed with tears. "I'm so sorry, Chaz. I never meant to hurt you. I was terrified, and not just of the town's opinion, but of moving on. You have no idea how scary that is." I sucked in a breath and continued, "I knew you cared about me, but love? The last thing I expected was for you to ask me to marry you. That's huge, and I freaked out."

"You can say that again." He grunted, and tenderness filled his eyes, proving what an exceptional human being he really was. Always thinking of my feelings before his. He lifted his free hand and cupped my cheek, wiping away my tears with his thumb. "That's not fair," he whispered. "You know it kills me to see you cry."

"I can't help it." I cried harder. "I-I love you."

He searched my eyes with that intense swirly gaze I'd come to adore, then he said in that whiskey-smooth voice that melted me, "Say it again."

"I said I love you... so damn much."

He cupped the back of my head and pulled my lips to his, kissing me long and hard.

The room broke into cheers, and I laughed against his mouth. Then I pulled away. "Wait. I'm not done."

"There's more?" He smiled. "I don't know if I can take more."

"Yes," I said.

"Yes what?" he asked.

"Yes, I will marry you."

"How do you know the offer still stands?" He raised his brows.

"Oh, well, I just assumed." I started to get up, but he held me in place.

"The offer does still stand, only I have conditions now." A slow smile spread across his face, and his eyes crinkled at the corners.

"And they are?" I bit my bottom lip, thinking turnabout was fair play.

"You keep your own name."

"You read my mind."

"And your business."

I smiled. "I planned to. Anything else?"

"Just one."

"What?"

"This is an equal partnership. We take care of each other."

I started crying all over again, never having felt more seen or heard in my life. "I can live with that."

"Good, because I can't live without you, Zoe Robinson. I love you so damn much it hurts."

"I love you, too, Doc. And don't worry. I've got a cure for what ails you. What do you say we get out of here, and I show you?"

"What about these?" He jiggled the handcuffs.

"They're part of the cure," I whispered for his ears only.

"I can definitely live with that."

"Good, because I've got one final surprise you just have to see."

TWO HOURS LATER, after eating what was left of the food and allowing the town to turn Chaz's mangled birthday party into our engagement party, we were finally alone in my living room.

"You've really been a good sport about the mess I made of your birthday." I tossed my keys and my purse on the table by the door and then faced him.

"I have to admit," he started walking slowly toward me, "I never imagined this morning I'd be here right now," he tucked a lock of my hair behind my ear, "with you," he cupped my cheek, "in your living room," he slid his palm over my collarbone, "getting ready to—"

I caught his hand before he could cup my breast. "Sit."

"Huh?" He looked adorable wearing that confused expression.

"Getting ready to sit." I giggled and pushed him back a step.

"Um, not exactly what I had in mind, but all right." He walked backward until he bumped into my couch, and then he sat, lifting a foot and placing it on his opposite knee. "I'm sitting, now what?"

"Now," I unbuttoned the top button of my blouse and took a step back toward the kitchen, "you wait," I unbuttoned the next button and took another step back, "while I," I unbuttoned a third button and stepped yet again until my back bumped against the kitchen door, "prepare your dessert."

Chaz's eyes had glazed over, and his chest rose and fell in a jerky rhythm. "I'm not hungry." He started to rise.

I held out a hand in a stop motion. "Sit." I licked my lips. "You'll be hungry for this, trust me."

His expression looked pained as he adjusted his pants. "Hurry."

"Done." I disappeared into the kitchen, a bundle of nerves, yet brimming with excitement. This was all part of the plan, providing I got Chaz to come around. My girls would keep the kids overnight, and I would ask Chaz to sleep over for the first time ever. I wanted to wake up in his arms from this day forward for the rest of my life.

This was big for us.

I slipped out of my clothes, hiding them in a cupboard, and then stepped inside the enormous cake I'd baked just for him. Big enough to hide in. Our fling might be over, but I'd only begun to play out my fantasies, and I wanted the first one as an engaged couple to be special. I pulled the top down and called out, "You can come in now."

I heard him walk through the door, then silence. "What the heck? Zoe? Honey, where are you?"

I popped up out of the cake in the full light of day in my birthday suit, not giving a damn that my breasts hung a bit low, and my stomach was a bit marked, and my thighs were a bit dimpled. I loved Chaz with every ounce of my being, and I couldn't think of a better way to show him that.

His lips parted as his eyes drank in the sight of me, lingering in all the right places. "Zoe," he breathed my name on a sigh. "You're so damn beautiful to me. You didn't have to do this, you know."

"I wanted to, and I know you think I'm beautiful," I said, and I actually meant it. "I can see it in your eyes and feel it in the way you touch me. You make me feel comfortable in my own skin, and that's priceless for a woman my age. For a woman *any* age."

"You look amazing, period." He reached out a hand. "Come here, sweetheart. I'm dying to touch you."

I tried to step over the cake but realized I made it too big when I slipped and rolled down the side. Chuckling, he leaned forward and helped me to my feet. I giggled, but not for long as he bent forward and licked the frosting off my nipple.

"Oh, my God, it's been way too long." My breathing picked up.

"My thoughts exactly." He scooped me in his arms.

"But your shirt." I wrapped my arms around his neck to hold on, slipping and sliding all over him.

"I prefer frosting to potatoes and corn. Especially *your* frosting."

He climbed the stairs and pressed his mouth to my lips, swirling his tongue around mine with each step. By the time we reached the top of the stairs, we were both panting. He laid me down on my bed but didn't take his eyes off me as he stripped off his clothes. He might make me feel beautiful, but he truly was beautiful. I held out my hand to him, and he covered my body with his own. For a moment, we just held each other, reveling in the fact that we were together. No more affair, no more secrecy, just us.

Out in the open in all our glory.

Then I felt something stir against my leg. My own personal

Snaky. Never thought in a million years I'd be fond of that name. I reached down and stroked him with my hand, then rolled him to his back and slid down, taking the length of him in my mouth.

"Oh, God, baby," he groaned and pulled me up high enough to slip inside of me. "I'm gonna lose it."

"That's okay." I caressed his cheek. "We've got all night."

His gaze locked on mine. "You mean...?"

"That's right. I want to wake up with you in my arms and never let you go."

His eyes filled with love, and he reached up to cradle the back of my head. "I love you, Zoe Robinson."

"I love you, too, Chaz Anderson."

He pulled me down and kissed me, then I sat up and began to move on top of him, and he held my hips, guiding me to a faster pace. I picked up the tempo, and he reached up to caress my breasts and toy with my nipples, bringing me to a fevered pitch.

It was incredible, he was incredible, and somehow, I knew it would always be this way. To think I had almost missed out on a second chance at love was even scarier than the thought of losing him. I arched my spine and tossed back my head, screaming his name on my release, and then felt him join me seconds later.

Collapsing on his chest, I lay spent in his arms. Chaz stroked my back as I rested my cheek on his shoulder. I turned my face into the crook of his neck and breathed in the unique scent that was Chaz alone, reveling that he was all mine.

Until he spoke.

"I changed my mind."

I blinked. "About what?"

"About marrying you."

I could hear a stifled chuckle in his voice, but still, I lifted my head to look him in the eye. "You'd better be kidding."

"Oh, I'm dead serious." He tried to look stern, but his eyes were smiling.

"Okay, I'm listening."

"I have one more condition before I'll marry you."

I swatted him. "You are very bad."

"And you are very good." He kissed me hard on the lips. "But that's beside the point. Do you agree to the condition or not?"

"Fine. What's the condition?"

"That we sell this place and move into mine. The damn thing suits you anyway."

I thought about that and realized he had a point. If we were truly going to start fresh, we needed to live in a place without any painful memories. "I can live with that," I echoed from earlier, my smile coming slow and sweet.

His smile matched mine, and I knew without a doubt that everything was going to be okay, especially when he said words that were music to my ears. "Good, because your bed is too damn small, and mine is big enough for both of us to sleep in the middle."

Acknowledgments

As always, thank you to my hubby, Brian. And my steady crew: Brandon, Josh, Matt and Emily. Another one bites the dust.

Thank you Christine Witthohn of Book Cents Literary Agency—you agent extraordinaire, you! Once again, you stand by my side! I'm grateful for everything you do. And Kelly Ferrara is a cover genius!

Thank you to my special peeps, Barbie Jo Mahoney and Danielle LaBue. My BFF's!

Thanks to my Book Cents peeps who were fresh eyes...I owe you one.

And thank you always to my extended family, the Harmons, the Russos and the Townsends. I'm a lucky woman.

Books By Kari Lee Townsend

KALLI BALLAS MYSTERY
Mind Over Murder

Two Cents of Doom

A Touch of Malice

An Inkling of Evil

Mayhem on the Mind

CECE MONROE MYSTERY
Harmful Habits

SUNNY MEADOWS MYSTERY
Tempest in the Tea Leaves

Corpse in the Crystal Ball

Trouble in the Tarot

Shenanigans in the Shadows

Perish in the Palm

Hazard in the Horoscope

Chaos and Cold Feet

Murder in the Meditation

Road Trip to Ruin

DIGITAL DIVA
Talk to the Hand

Rise of the Phenoteens

Books By Kari Lee Harmon

COLDWATER COVE

Dark Seas

Frozen Waters

Dangerous Thaw

Deadly Frost

STANDALONE NOVELS

Valley of Secrets

Until Tomorrow

Project Produce

Love Lessons

LAKEHOUSE TREASURES NOVELLAS

James

Amber

Meghan

Brook

MERRY SCROOG-MAS NOVELLAS

Naughty or Nice

Sleigh Bells Ring

Jingle all the Way

TRIPLE R RANCH SHORT STORIES

Destiny Wears Spurs

Spurred by Fate

Portrait of a Woman

Resilient

About the Author

Kari Lee Townsend is a National Bestselling Author of mysteries & a tween superhero series. She also writes romance and women's fiction as Kari Lee Harmon. With a background in English education, she's now a full-time writer, wife to her own superhero, mom of 3 sons, 1 darling diva, 1 daughter-in-law & 2 lovable fur babies. These days you'll find her walking her dogs or hard at work on her next story, living a blessed life.